Libraries and Information

2 7 NOV 2018

- 9 JAN 2021

10/18

This book should be returned by the last date stamped above.
You may renew the loan personally, by post or telephone for a
further period if the book is not required by another reader.

www.wakefield.gov.uk

wakefieldcouncil
working for you

D1425162

4000000140361 9

1125R1 Designed and Produced by Wakefield Council, Communications 04/14 ♻recycle

Also by Beth Cornelison

Discover more at millsandboon.co.uk

RANCHER'S HIGH-STAKES RESCUE

BETH CORNELISON

MILLS & BOON

First Published in Great Britain 2018
by Mills & Boon, an imprint of HarperCollins*Publishers*
1 London Bridge Street, London, SE1 9GF

Rancher's High-Stakes Rescue © 2018 Beth Cornelison

ISBN: 978-0-263-26605-4

1118

MIX
Paper from
responsible sources
FSC™ C007454

This book is produced from independently certified FSC™ paper to ensure responsible forest management.

For more information visit: www.harpercollins.co.uk/green

Printed and bound in Spain
by CPI, Barcelona

To Paul

Prologue

Eight-year-old Kate Carrington climbed the silo ladder, one rusty rung at a time, while her mother's voice shouted in her head, *Stay away from the old silo, Katie. It's dangerous!*

But Mama was a worrywart. That's what Daddy called her, and Kate tended to agree.

If she were a boy, you'd call her athletic and adventurous. Don't be overprotective just because she's a girl, her daddy would say.

The rusty ladder creaked and wobbled as she climbed, and Kate paused. Looked down. She was pretty high. She cast her gaze around her family's sundrenched Missouri farm. The corn was waist high and bright green. The sky was clear blue, and the scent of tilled earth was heavy in the air after Daddy had plowed the west field, prepping it for a new planting.

This kind of day filled her with the sort of excitement and curiosity to do and see and explore that Mama called recklessness.

She tried to be good for Mama's sake. She didn't want Mama to worry, but Kate figured she knew her limits. And today, Mama wasn't home. She and Daddy had gone to chaperone a 4-H conference all weekend with Henry and his class. Grandma, who was her baby-sitter for the weekend, would never know she'd climbed up here.

And she wouldn't be climbing the old silo if her brother's new remote-controlled airplane, the one he'd just gotten for his birthday, hadn't landed smack on top of the silo roof and gotten stuck upside down. Kate wasn't supposed to be playing with it. If she lost it, she'd be in *so much* trouble! So she had to at least try to get it.

The ladder up the outside of the silo rattled again and swayed. She hesitated, wiping her sweaty hand on the seat of her shorts. Just a little farther…

When she finally pulled herself high enough to see the roof of the silo, she exhaled a sigh of relief. The plane was still in one piece. And it wasn't that far in from the ladder. She could easily crawl out to get it.

She swung her legs over the top bar of the ladder and began scooting slowly up the rough slope of the sagging silo roof. She heard a *snap*, and her heart thumped harder. She stretched to reach the plane, but it was still just beyond her grasp. Swallowing hard, she edged farther along the rotted roof, inching her hand closer, closer…

In an instant, the roof beneath her gave way with a loud *crack*. Her stomach swooped as she plummeted down. The fall felt endless and lightning fast at the same time. Terrifying.

And then she hit the bottom. The abrupt stop rattled through her body with a tooth-jarring jolt. Pain worse than anything she'd ever known streaked up her leg. Her head smacked against something hard, and when she tried to scream, she couldn't catch her breath.

Then everything went silent. Black.

Chapter 1

Twenty years later

The Colorado terrain was breathtaking, Kate thought, as she peered out the backseat window. The tiny car belonged to the Uber driver who had picked up her and her coworker, Dawn, at the Denver airport. The owners of McCall Adventure Ranch had been scheduled to give them a ride to the ranch, but she and Dawn had managed to get an earlier flight out of Dallas and hadn't remembered to notify the ranch staff until they were about to land.

"Here's the turn," Dawn said, leaning forward to direct the driver with a pointing finger as well as her verbal cue.

The driver eyed her via the rearview mirror, his look clearly disgruntled.

"Thanks," he replied dryly and reached up to shut off the turn-by-turn directions on his cell phone in the dashboard mount.

Dawn took the hint and sat back again with a sheepish "Oh. Sorry."

Kate hid a grin behind her hand, pretending to scratch her cheek. She was well familiar with Dawn's bossiness but knew her coworker didn't mean to be controlling. Dawn simply had a high-energy, highly organized, highly efficient type A personality, and she let it get the best of her sometimes. Dawn got results, because she didn't take no for an answer. She did her research, knew her business and had a plan for everything.

If you hesitated or wishy-washed around her, you were likely to get swept along by her tidal wave of persuasion and direction. Case in point—Kate's presence on this trip.

When Dawn had brought the public relations firm's new client campaign to her and told her about the trip to gather firsthand knowledge and have in-depth, in-person strategy meetings with the ranch owners, Kate had balked.

"So they want us to go on one of these adventure excursions?" she'd asked, the contents of her stomach curdling.

Dawn's eyes had been bright with excitement and enthusiasm. "Yes! No charge. Isn't it great?"

"Um…"

"The trip includes rappelling, white-water rafting, zip-lining, camping, a hands-on ranch experience— meaning they'll show us roping and riding—and if we want, they'll even take us BASE jumping!" Dawn had laughed and smacked the palm of her hand on the desk. "How cool is that?"

Cool hadn't been the word that came to Kate's mind. *Terrifying* was more like it.

"Um. W-wow," she'd stuttered as her hands began to shake.

"We leave in two weeks. It's gonna be awesome!" Dawn had gushed.

And no excuse or expressed reluctance had convinced Dawn to find another staff member to go in Kate's place.

"No way! I want *you*. Don't be a chicken. This trip is the perfect way to shake up your staid life and get your adrenaline pumping!" Then Dawn had made Bambi eyes at her, adding, "You're my friend. I want to experience this with *you*, not Frank or Hattie. We'll have a blast."

Gauntlet thrown down. Friend card played. Pleading look employed. Yes, Dawn was good at getting her way.

So here Kate was, in the back of a tiny Uber, her heart in her throat as they bounced down the rutted drive to a beautiful Colorado ranch. She took a deep breath and squeezed the straps of the purse she held in her lap as if they were a lifeline. Maybe she could wrangle her way out of the more dangerous activities. Even as the anxious thought crossed her mind, a niggle of something long dormant kicked in her soul.

Ever since the incident at the silo when she was eight years old, she'd waged this internal battle. Her innate curiosity and longing for adventure got shouted down by the pervasive terror, the lingering memory of two gut-wrenching, pain-filled, nightmare-inducing days at the bottom of the abandoned silo.

As they pulled to a stop in front of the building with the sign that read Check In Here, the scents of manure and fresh hay greeted her. And made a cold sweat pop out on her upper lip that had nothing to do with the warm May weather. She hadn't lived on her family's Missouri farm for ten years, but just a whiff of the smells inherent to agribusiness stirred memories both bitter and sweet.

While Dawn spoke to the Uber driver, Kate climbed out and stretched her back. She could only partly blame her tight muscles on the narrow airplane seat and hours of sitting. Her heart beat an apprehensive tattoo as she took in the rural setting and filled her lungs with the fecund, late spring air.

"Hello there!" a male voice called, and she pivoted to face the tall, broad-shouldered rancher striding toward them with a sexy grin. "Welcome to the Double M! Can I help you with your bags?"

"Sure." She smiled at the cowboy, whose black hair was neatly trimmed and whose bright blue eyes stood out against his tanned complexion and dark eyebrows. "We're checking in. For the adventure excursion."

He paused, looking confused. "Wait. Are you Dawn Fetzer?"

Dawn strode over to him with her hand out. "I'm Dawn. This is my colleague, Kate Carrington."

He stuck out his hand to Dawn. "I'm Zane. We've talked several times."

"Of course. Nice to meet you in person."

He shook Kate's hand as well before turning a look of dismay to Dawn. "Did I miss a message about a change in your flight schedule? I was going to pick you up."

He hurried to the trunk of the small coupe, where the Uber driver was unloading their suitcases. Hoisting one suitcase in each hand, he moved the bags out of the driveway while Dawn explained about the opportunity to take the earlier flight.

"We had to hurry to board, and I completely forgot to call you before we turned our phones off for the flight. I'm sorry!"

Zane waved off her apology. "Forget it. Just glad to have you here safely. Let me show you to your rooms." He pulled out a small two-way radio receiver and held it to his mouth. "Hey, I need you out front. The reps from the PR firm are here."

A voice on the radio answered, "Already? They're early!"

Zane flashed an embarrassed grin to them. "Yeah, I know. Get out here." Then to Kate and Dawn, "This way, ladies."

He led them across the hard-packed dirt yard toward a freshly painted clapboard building with a wooden sign over the front door that read Guest House.

As they followed their host, Dawn leaned close to Kate and whispered, "This trip just gets better and better. High-adrenaline adventures *and* a hot cowboy as our host."

Kate grinned and elbowed Dawn in the ribs. "Flirt."

Dawn waggled her eyebrows. "You know I'm faithful to Dean. But that doesn't mean you can't have a nice fling."

Kate's pulse tripped. "What?"

Dawn sent her a sly grin. "Look at him, Kate. Don't tell me you don't want a little bit of that cowboy action."

Kate shifted her gaze to the admirable posterior encased in blue jeans and square jaw of their swoonworthy host. "I admit he's good-looking—"

"Mmm-hmm." Dawn's hum of agreement held a lascivious overtone.

"—but I'm not a fling kinda girl, vacation or otherwise." Two mistakes of that nature in three years cured her of that bad habit. She had a talent, it seemed, for allowing herself to get hurt in more ways than just physically.

"This used to be the bunkhouse for our hands when the ranching operation was bigger," Zane said. He set their suitcases down and swept a hand toward the front room. The living room had been decorated with shabby-chic ranch decor and homey furniture in warm shades of beige and chocolate with brightly colored accent pillows from red to rust. "This is a community area for relaxing. The TV remote is on the coffee table just there." He pointed it out then, rubbed his hands together and continued, "No room assignments. Just pick whichever one you choose. We do have two other small parties coming later in the day who'll be in the last two rooms. Dinner will be—"

His spiel was interrupted as another cowboy burst through the door they'd just entered, lugging the last of their bags. "Hi, ladies! Welcome," he said, sounding winded.

Kate caught the frown Zane directed at the other man, and she turned toward the new arrival. She eyed the cowboy in surprise, understanding Zane's displeasure. The out-of-breath cowboy wore dusty jeans and a stained white T-shirt, and his boots had definitely seen better days. He removed his hat to rake his fingers through shaggy black hair that grew past his ear-lobes with wisps that drooped messily over his eyes. He was the opposite of neat and trimmed Zane in so many ways…and yet he was a carbon copy. Same startlingly blue eyes, same ruggedly cut jawline—though this cowboy's chin was dusted with a couple days' worth of stubble—and the same broad-shouldered, muscular-legged physique.

Kate's mouth dried as she studied him, unsure why his disheveled appearance unsettled her.

Zane cleared his throat. "Ms. Fetzer, Ms. Carrington, this is my brother, Josh."

Dawn stepped closer to Josh with her hand out. "Nice to meet you, Josh. Call me Dawn."

Josh flashed a lopsided grin and held both hands up out of Dawn's reach. "I'm gonna pass on the handshake for now. When you arrived, I was in the stable with one of our first-calf heifers, overseeing the latest birth for our herd. I've mostly washed up, but I'm still kinda grimy."

"Aww," Dawn cooed. "A baby?"

"Yes, ma'am. We're a working ranch, and replenishing the herd is our livelihood." Josh spared Kate a glance, and his boyish grin slipped a little before returning to full wattage. Holding her gaze, he added, "If you want to meet the new calf, I'd be happy to take you to see him once you get settled."

Kate swallowed the flutter of disquiet that she could feel pulsing in the vein in her neck. "That sounds great."

Dawn wagged a finger between Zane and Josh. "You two are…identical twins?"

Zane nodded. "We are. And we have a sister, who rounds out the set. Triplets."

Kate blinked and goggled at Zane. "Triplets! Wow. Does your sister live here, too? Will we meet her?"

"She does now. Just moved back from Boston. You'll meet her at the welcome dinner tonight. Which, I was saying when Josh stormed in, is at six p.m. Out in the side yard." Zane directed them with a finger pointing out the window. "That way. Can't miss it." He clapped his hands together. "Well, we'll get out of your hair, let you unpack. The refrigerator has soft drinks and bottled water. Help yourself. Can we do anything else to get you settled before we scoot outta here?"

"I'm good, thanks," Kate told Zane, and when she glanced back at Josh, his piercing gaze was still riveted on her, the playful twitch of a grin tugging the corner of his mouth.

Her heart bumped, and her breath snagged in her throat. His stare was unnerving, both because of the intensity of his sky blue eyes and because of the mysterious smile he gave her. As if he knew a secret about her. As if he were undressing her with his eyes. As if he could read her fears and reluctance about being there and was privately mocking her.

She calmed her edginess with a deep inhale and slow exhale, the way her therapist had taught her after the trauma of being trapped in the silo. *Center yourself by focusing on something near you, something real, something safe.*

Kate tore her gaze away from Josh's and concentrated on a whimsical rooster figurine above the kitchenette cabinets until the uneasy feeling passed. She could hear Dawn telling the brothers goodbye and thank you. Heard the screened door slap closed followed by the squeak of hinges as the main door closed.

"Wow," Dawn said, returning to the living room area of the guesthouse. "Twice as nice! Two for the price of one…" She gave Kate a play-punch in the shoulder as she strolled past on her way to check out the bedrooms. "I do believe we need to get you into some double trouble."

With a grunt of disagreement, Kate followed her friend toward the bedrooms. The last thing she wanted from this trip was trouble. Double or otherwise.

Josh McCall scrubbed his hands and fingernails with the small brush at the stable's wash station, while the hot water sent billowing steam up in his face. His motions were mechanical, habit, which was good, because his thoughts were miles away. Or rather, a few dozen feet away in the guesthouse.

He was not sure what he'd expected from the two representatives from the Dallas PR firm Zane was working with, but the wheat-blonde beauty, even now unpacking in the old bunkhouse, had not been what he'd pictured. Kate Carrington, Zane had said her name was. Kate, with her heart-shaped face, full lips and nervous smile had left him awestruck. He wasn't as sappy as to believe in love at first sight, but lust at first sight, or intrigue, or captivation—whatever you wanted to call it—he was pretty sure had just happened. His body was thrumming, and his brain was clicking, anxious for the chance to talk with her again, get to know her. And yes, possibly sample those pink lips that had trembled a little when she'd smiled at their introduction.

He'd stared. He knew he had, and maybe his rapt

attention had unsettled her. Maybe she wasn't used to guys openly, unabashedly admiring her. Maybe—his heart stuttered—crap, was she married? He hadn't thought to look for a ring. Gorgeous as she was, beguiled as he was, he would put his attraction on ice before he messed with a married woman.

"I think you missed a spot," Dave Giblan, one of the Double M's ranch hands, said as he sidled up beside him to wash his hands.

"Huh?"

Dave chuckled. "Geez, where's your head? You've been scrubbing away over here for like ten minutes. Your skin's gonna be raw."

"Oh." Josh passed the scrubbing brush to Dave and stepped aside. "Just trying to be thorough."

Dave grunted and gave his boss a skeptical side-eye. "Heard the first guests arrived. You meet them?"

"Yeah," Josh said, drying his hands on a clean towel from the shelf above the industrial-sized sink. "Couple of ladies from the PR place that's handling our advertising and marketing." He put the towel on a hook near the sink where Dave could use it next and hitched his head toward the back stall. "How's mama doing?"

Dave nodded. "Great. She's tired, but she's taking care of her baby like she's supposed to. Calf weighed in right at seventy pounds. Vet says he looks good."

"Excellent." He slapped Dave on the shoulder. "I'll leave them in your capable hands. Let me know if anything changes with mama's or the little guy's conditions."

Dave shut off the water. "Will do, man." Dave hesitated, then asked, "Say…what's this adventure tour biz mean for me?"

Josh gave him a puzzled look. "For you?"

The hand jerked a nod. "I'm already busier than a one-legged man in a butt-kicking contest since Karl left. And now you, Brady and Zane have your hands full with the adventure tours. Are there plans to hire a new hand? Get me some help?"

Josh grimaced and ran a hand through his shaggy hair. "Not that I know of. Sorry. We don't plan to leave you hangin'. Brady'll only be involved in the new business in small ways, and Zane and I'll do our best to give you extra help when we're around."

Dave looked skeptical, but said nothing more about it.

Josh left the stable, pondering the truth that Dave had raised. The ranch did need more hands. But where would they find the money to hire more help? As he crossed the ranch yard, he heard the familiar squeak of the guesthouse's screen door hinges. He glanced over to find Ms. Fetzer hurrying over to him.

Changing direction, he moved to intercept the woman, whose red-brown hair had been pulled into a single braid at her nape and whose ample curves jiggled as she trotted toward him.

"Hi. Josh, is it?" she said cheerfully, her dark brown eyes sparkling with enthusiasm.

"Yes, ma'am. What can I do for you?"

"Well, you can call me Dawn instead of ma'am for starters. We are going to be working together, after all."

Josh grinned and poked his hands in his front pockets. And, yes, they were a little raw from his distracted and extended scrubbing. "Dawn, then."

She toyed with her braid—auburn, that's the name of the color he'd heard Piper use for that shade of brownish-red hair—and she gave him a coy smile. "I'm really looking forward to trying all the adventures. Especially the rafting. That looks like so much fun!"

"It's a blast," he returned, nodding and giving her a schooled smile.

The guesthouse screened door screeched again, and when he glanced toward the small porch, his blood surged and heated. His smile grew as Kate walked toward them. She had a graceful stride, but even her poise didn't mask the sexy sway of her hips. When she met his gaze, her cheek dimpled with a quick grin before her attention shifted to her friend. "Dean just called you. I answered it and told him I'd get you, but he said he was just checking that we arrived okay."

Dawn pressed a hand to her full bosom. "What a sweetie. Did he want me to call back?"

Kate shrugged. "When you get a minute. The connection wasn't good, so…"

"Yeah. Cell reception out here stinks. The landline in the guesthouse might be the better option for phone calls." Josh got his first up-close look at Kate's mossy green eyes, and something deep inside him kicked.

She tucked her blond hair behind her ear and moistened her lips with a quick swipe of her tongue. Josh's mouth watered, and he clenched his hand inside his pocket.

Damn but he wanted to kiss those pink lips!

Instead, he motioned toward her, saying, "You'll want to keep some lip balm close by. The air here is pretty dry, and it can be brutal to lips."

She seemed a little startled by his non sequitur, and a wrinkle of confusion creased the bridge of her nose briefly before she nodded. "Okay. I will. Thanks."

Her gaze went to his mouth before darting away.

"And sunscreen, especially when we're on the adventure outing. It might only be May, but skin as fair as yours—" he caught himself and included Dawn with his gaze "—and yours, will burn easily, even this time of year." He touched the brim of his black felt Tony Lama hat, adding, "A good wide-brimmed hat helps, too." He winked at them. "And you thought we just wore these doozies because they look good."

Both of the women laughed, and Dawn swatted his arm, clearly flirting. "That they do, cowboy!"

He stepped back from Dawn's hand and doffed his hat as he eased away. "Until later, ladies. Duty calls."

As he shuffled into the mudroom of the main house, he shook his head and chuckled. "Ironic."

"What's ironic?" his sister, Piper, said from a stool at the kitchen counter.

After shucking off his work boots, he strolled into the kitchen and snitched one of the potato chips on Piper's plate. She batted at his hand.

"Hey, mooch, get your own!"

"Why? Yours are right here." Man, he loved to tease her. Having her back at the ranch after seven years felt good. The McCall family was complete again. Having her part of this new business venture with Zane felt ordained.

"What's ironic?" she repeated, sliding her plate out of his reach.

"Oh, the two women who came this afternoon from the PR firm. I was just talking to them outside and... well, one of them is not so subtle about her interest in me..."

Piper snorted. "Vain much, Josh?"

"Hey, I know flirting when I see it." He walked around her and took another potato chip. "But the other lady, the one I actually think is pretty hot, seems…I dunno…kinda skittish."

Piper pivoted on the stool to face him, folding her arms over her chest. "Back up, Doofus. You find her *hot*?"

"Damn right. She's gorgeous."

Piper arched a dark eyebrow at him. "This is a travel adventures business we're trying to launch, bucko, not a dating service. The customers are off-limits."

He paused with a potato chip halfway to his mouth. "Says who?"

"Says…everyone. Mixing business and pleasure is bad form."

He gave her a withering scowl as he crunched the chip. "I disagree. If both parties are willing, why can't I have a little fun on the side…if you know what I mean." He gave her a wink.

Piper chuckled and shook her head. "Josh, even Zeke knows what you mean," she said, referring to the family's part–Maine coon cat, who was circling Josh's legs, meowing for attention. "You're about as subtle as a bat to the head."

Josh stooped to lift the long-haired cat into his arms. Zeke immediately draped himself over Josh's shoulder and commenced purring loudly. "You're on my side, right, buddy? You think I should be able to romance the customers if they're open to it, right?"

Piper grinned. "He's been neutered. He doesn't know what you're talking about."

Josh winced in sympathy for the feline, then gave

his sister a wry snort. "His being neutered is not the reason he doesn't know what I'm saying."

"Case remains, you cannot mess around with the customers." She stood and gave Zeke a scratch on the head, which the fur ball leaned into with relish. "It's bound to end badly, and we cannot afford to screw anything up with the business."

Josh shoved the cat into her arms, then took the last potato chip off her plate. "Maybe we'll put it to a vote of all the partners."

"Maybe we will," she returned. "But in the meantime, we have a welcome dinner to put on and more guests arriving in another hour." She looked him up and down. "And you smell like crap."

"Because I was helping deliver a calf an hour ago."

Piper perked up. "Really?" She set Zeke on the ground and dusted fur from her shirt. "Why didn't anyone tell me? I would have helped! I love births!"

"Plenty more to come, sister dear." He took his leave. "I'll be in the shower if anyone comes looking for me."

"Are you looking for anyone in particular?" Dawn asked Kate that night as they strolled into the small cluster of people gathered on the ranch yard around a festively decorated buffet table and smoking grill.

"Uh, no. Why?" Kate tucked a loose wisp of her hair behind her ear and felt a telltale prickle in her neck as she flushed with embarrassment. She hadn't realized she'd been so obvious, craning her neck as she scanned the faces in the crowd for one in particular.

Dawn bumped Kate's hip with hers and cackled. "You are the worst liar!"

Kate bumped her back. "Shut it."

"You know you don't need to look for him. I guarantee Josh'll find you before this shindig gets started good." Dawn straightened the neon multicolored scarf she had draped around her neck to accent her bright green blouse. "You need only sit back and wait."

Kate questioned her friend with a furrowed-brow glance.

"Oh, come on, Katie! You did see the little heat waves rising off him when he looked at you this afternoon?"

Kate pulled a face and dismissed her friend with a buzz of her lips.

Dawn stopped walking and faced Kate fully, taking her by the arm. "No, seriously. His tongue was dragging the ground. Eyes popping out of his head. You didn't catch all that?"

Kate laughed and brushed past Dawn. "You make him sound like one of those cartoon characters when they see the femme fatale."

"Uh...bingo!" Dawn took a few quick steps to catch up with her. "He was seriously interested, sister, and you'd be crazy not to act on it." Dawn tipped her head and narrowed her eyes. "Unless you have some problem with hunky dark-haired cowboys with eyes straight out of heaven. Or is his more clean-cut brother the one you're considering?"

"Would you stop?" Kate said with a chuckle. "I'm not considering either. I'm here on business, not pleasure."

"So?" Dawn persisted. "You could have both."

"I was just telling my sister the same thing," said a deep voice behind them.

Kate whirled around with a gasp. "Josh. Hi."

The subject of their discussion gave her a devastatingly handsome grin and tipped his hat.

Dawn didn't try to hide her smug grin as she muttered in a quiet singsong, "Told you…"

Josh had changed into clean jeans and a light blue polo-style shirt that set off his straight-outta-heaven eyes and hugged his muscled torso. His raven hair was still damp from his shower and combed back behind his ears, where it then curled slightly at his nape. And he smelled divine. Something woodsy and fresh, without the cloying and pretentious scents of the colognes the men in her Dallas office wore.

"Did you ladies get settled in okay?" He slid his fingers in the front pockets of his jeans and divided a look between them.

"Yeah. Just fine," Kate said and clutched the thin straps of her purse so that she didn't fidget. Good grief. She felt like some junior high girl with a crush on the school's quarterback. "I love the way you've decorated the guest rooms." *Doh! Could you sound more banal?*

"Thanks, but I had nothing to do with that. My mom and sister were the bosses of that part of the renovation." His smile dimpled his cheek, and she felt her stomach swoop and her knees soften.

"Well, they have good taste. They split the difference between masculine and feminine decor perfectly." She sensed more than saw Dawn easing backward, leaving her alone with Josh. She snuck a hand out and grabbed her friend's arm before she could duck completely away.

"We have time before dinner is served if you'd like

to go see the new calf now." He waved his thumb toward the stables.

Kate couldn't help but smile. She may have some bad memories of her parents' farm, but she missed the animals. "I'd love that."

Dawn lifted a foot to him, waggling her high-heeled sandal at him. "I'm not sure I'm in the right footwear. You two go ahead, and I'll see the baby tomorrow."

Kate tightened her grip on her coworker's arm, sending her a look that said, *Stop playing matchmaker!*

"Are you sure? We have boots you can borrow down by the stable," Josh said.

"Yes, Dawn," Kate said through her teeth, "you can borrow boots. Come with us."

Dawn pried Kate's fingers from her forearm and gave her a disgruntled look. "No thank you, Kate. You two go on. I'll just go get a drink and wait for you up here." With a wiggle of her fingers to wave goodbye, her traitorous friend backed away, wearing a victorious grin.

"All right then. Guess it's just us." Josh put a warm palm on her back to direct her toward the stable.

Her pulse jumped at his touch, and a tremor of acute awareness shimmied through her. She walked beside him, silently cursing Dawn and mentally fumbling for conversation that didn't sound as lame and juvenile as she felt. She was awestruck and tongue-tied like some smitten kitten, and she hated the sense of vulnerability and hesitation that held her. Why did he make her so nervous? While he didn't look a thing like Jason, her most recent mistake, her attraction to Josh was similar. Maybe that was why she was battling this odd mix of lust and wariness. Internal warning lights were flashing and sirens blaring. *Don't go down that path again! Danger ahead!*

"…are you from? Besides the Dallas firm, I mean," Josh was saying.

"Oh, um, I grew up in Missouri. On a farm. And then I went to school in Georgia and got my job in Dallas a couple years ago. How about you?" She kicked herself as soon as the question left her mouth. Idiot!

He chuckled. "Born and raised right here at the Double M."

"Of course. Stupid question."

"Naw, there are no stupid questions," he said with another of his lopsided, dimple-producing grins. She almost stumbled when she saw that dimple reappear.

"Maybe not. But mine comes close. Just…habit. You know, throw the same question or compliment back at someone to keep a conversation going. I…didn't think. I…"

Shut up. Shut up! You're babbling now.

She was going to kill Dawn. She wanted no part of a vacation tryst or her friend's misguided matchmaking, no matter how heartbreakingly handsome Josh was. *Heartbreaking* being the key word. She'd had her fill of short-term, lack-of-commitment, heart-wounding relationships.

"Well, truth be told, I actually spent the first three weeks of my life at the hospital in Denver. Zane, Piper and I were all less than four pounds when we were born."

She nodded. "You wouldn't know it by looking at you now," she said, then grimaced. "Not that you're fat… I, ugh!"

He laughed and patted his flat belly. "Well, thank

you. I've been eating my meat and vegetables for years to get this size."

She waved a hand, feeling her flush creep back up her neck and into her cheeks. "I'm rambling like a moron. Ignore me."

As they reached the entrance to the stable, he reached over and brushed a wisp of her hair back from her cheek. The scrape of his knuckle on her face sent delicious shivers through her and backed up her breath in her lungs. When her gaze darted up to his, she met the smile that shone from his eyes as brightly as from his lips. The piercing look he gave her made her feel desirable and feminine all the way to her core. "You're kinda hard to ignore. And I wouldn't want to try."

Oh, lordy. Her toes curled inside her slip-on shoes, and she wiped her palms on the skirt of her buttery-yellow sundress.

After a few seconds, staring back at him with her heart pounding in her ears, she managed to stutter, "Y-you said you had…boots I could borrow?"

"Absolutely." He stepped away and fetched a pair of rubber work boots. "You can probably just wear these over your other shoes if you want."

She nodded and slipped her feet into the man-size boots. She clumped along behind him as she followed him inside the stable. The oversize boots made her feel awkward and silly, yet a tingle still lingered on her cheek where he'd touched her.

"Back here." He led her to a stall at the back, away from the bulk of the bustle and activity, and opened the gate. "Come on in. It's okay." He stood aside and motioned her into the stall, where a brown-and-white cow stood over a small brown calf.

Warmth filled her chest, along with nostalgia. She'd seen numerous newborn animals through the years on her parents' farm, but the preciousness of new life never got old. "Oh, my goodness! She's precious!"

"He. It's a bull calf."

"Oh, he, then. He's adorable!" She cast a side glance to Josh, who was beaming with pride as if the baby were his.

"You can pat him if you want."

She gave the mama cow a dubious look. "Really? It won't upset mom?"

Josh grasped the straps of the mother's halter and tugged, urging the bovine to step away. Then, stooping, he lifted the calf and brought it closer to Kate.

She lifted a hand to the curling fur on the cow's head and melted inside. "Aren't you the cutest thing?"

"Yeah, I am," Josh said with an impish grin, "and the calf's kinda cute, too."

Kate snorted a chuckle. Then, when he laughed at her indelicate snort, she joined him in full-bellied gales. Even as she shared the moment of levity with him, she studied his handsome face, the spark of life in his startlingly blue eyes, and her heart flipped. She didn't need a crystal ball to know the combination of his charm, good looks and ability to put her at ease were a lethal combination versus her ability to resist him. Today was only her first day in Colorado, and she was already in deep trouble.

Chapter 2

When Josh and Kate returned to the welcome dinner, Dawn was seated at a long table with several people, including Josh's twin.

Zane smiled as they approached. "There you two are. We were about to send a search party. People here are hungry and ready to eat."

"I'm down with that." Josh motioned to an empty chair. "Kate, shall we?"

"Come meet everyone, Kate," Dawn called.

After she took her place, Josh helped her scoot her chair in, then sat across from her.

Josh motioned to the man to Zane's right as he started around the table with introductions. "This is my father, Michael. And my sister, Piper. And her fiancé, Brady Summers, who's another partner in McCall Adventures."

She smiled, giving a wave of greeting to them all, and shook Brady's hand when he offered his. Then Josh started down the other side of the table. "My mother, Melissa." He skipped Dawn, moved on to a little boy with rumpled brown hair and barbecue sauce on his chin. "And…that little squirt is my nephew, Beelzebub."

The boy frowned at him. "Connor!"

The adults laughed, and Josh held up a finger as if he'd just remembered. "Oh, that's right. Connor."

"Nice to meet you, Connor." Kate winked at the little boy, who gave a shy wave back.

"And…" Josh scanned the other tables and people milling about. "Over by the grill, flipping burgers, is our jack-of-all-trades and foreman, Roy Summers."

"He's my grampa," Connor added.

"So it really is all in the family," she said, making a mental inventory of relationships and faces.

Josh removed his hat and hung it on the back of his chair. "It is."

"I was just telling Zane about your ideas for the brochure," Dawn said, lifting a glass of a fruity drink, "how we want to be sure to capture pictures of all aspects of the ranch and the adventures while we're here."

"Oh, right." Kate nodded her agreement. "I brought a camera with me, professional-grade, to capture some shots. We'll need permission to use images of any people in the photos, though."

"We brought a waiver with us," Dawn explained.

"Of course. Sounds great." Zane passed a large plate of ribs, burgers and sliced beef down the table to Kate. "Dig in. This is all Double M beef. One hundred percent fresh, and the best Angus beef you'll ever eat."

Kate took the tray, but hesitated. Her stomach growled, affirming she was hungry. The last thing she'd eaten was the tiny packet of pretzels on the plane. But she thought of the sweet bull calf she'd just visited and balked. "I'm going to stick to the side dishes tonight, I think."

Josh sent her a concerned look and lifted a pitcher of tea, filling her glass when she nodded that she'd like some, then his own. "Are you a vegetarian? We didn't think to ask—"

"No," she said, passing the tray of meats to him. "Just…thinking about my new little friend and…" She flashed a sheepish grin. "I grew up on a farm. I know where meat comes from. I just can't go from fawning over the little baby to…eating his dad."

Josh grunted and helped himself to a few ribs and a burger. "Trust me, this is not that little guy's father. Papa is one of our best breeding bulls, and his life is safe as long as he keeps fathering prime offspring." He set down the platter. "But I get your point, and I promise the rest of the dinner Helen made is pretty spectacular, too. Try this." He handed her a pan of potato casserole. "She calls it potato supreme. I just call it delicious."

"Helen?" Kate took the pan, savoring the scents of cheese and onion that wafted from the dish.

"Our cook. She used to be full-time, when we had more hands. Now she just does lunch for the family and hands along with special events like tonight." Josh handed her another bowl, full of a mix of green vegetables.

"Can I have my pie now?" Connor said, drawing Kate's attention.

"Finish your meat first, buddy," said the guy introduced as Piper's fiancé. She dug through her memory for the name. B… B…

"Aw, Brady!" Connor whined, flopping back in his chair and folding his arms across his chest with a pout.

Brady! That was it!

When she studied the boy and Brady closer, she saw the resemblance between them. While Dawn continued chatting up the plans for the travel brochure with Zane and Piper, Kate leaned toward Josh, whispering, "Connor is your nephew, you said? But he called your foreman his grampa. So that means Brady is…?"

Josh gave her a crooked grin and whispered back. "It's complicated."

She arched an eyebrow, intrigued.

"Well, not that complicated, but…" He rubbed a hand over his lips. "I'll fill you in later."

She leaned back in her seat, regarding Josh with a puzzled gaze. When she glanced toward the boy's chair, she found it empty.

"Tell me about the calf, Kate," Dawn said, drawing her attention. "We should definitely include pictures of the new baby in the brochure. What a precious way to bring home the point that this is a working family ranch."

"Oh, he's definitely precious," Kate agreed. She was musing over the point that the Double M was a family ranch, a point brought home as she glanced around the table at the three generations gathered for dinner. Well, two generations…the third generation was still missing.

Something under the table bumped her knee, and

she raised the edge of the plastic table cover to peek underneath.

Connor sat huddled at her feet and met her gaze. His eyes widened, and he placed a finger over his pursed lips in a shushing signal. She gave him a conspiratorial wink and returned her attention to the adult conversation.

"We can do a print run of one hundred thousand copies to start with," Dawn was saying, "and print more as—"

"A hundred *thousand*?" Piper repeated, clearly aghast. "Why so many? Won't that cost a fortune?"

"Well, we want a wide distribution of the materials," Kate said. "You'd be surprised how few one hundred thousand really is, and with printed materials, the more you do, the less they cost per piece."

"Where's Connor?" Piper cut in, her face reflecting her alarm that the boy wasn't at the table. "He was just here." She looked around, clearly dismayed.

Brady covered her hand with his and gave her a calming smile, hitching his head toward their feet. "I don't know," he said in a stage voice, "but since he left, I guess that means I get to eat his pie."

Under the table, Connor gasped, bumped Kate's knees again, and cried out, "No! Here I am! I want my pie!"

Piper's face reflected her relief, and a combination of amusement and irritation. "Connor, what are you doing under the table?"

While Brady and Piper leaned closer to talk in low voices to the boy, Zane waved a hand for Kate to continue. "Sorry. Life around here can be chaotic at times. You were saying?"

She shook her head. "Why don't we save the business talk for later and just enjoy this pretty evening, the great dinner and good company?"

"I'll drink to that," Josh said, raising his glass of iced tea.

The rest of the meal passed with pleasant conversation about the history of the four-generations-old ranch, Piper and Brady's upcoming nuptials, and Connor's excitement over his friend's dog having puppies. When they'd all finished eating, Zane, Piper and Josh excused themselves to mingle with the other guests who'd arrived just before dinner. Kate dawdled over the last of her slice of cherry pie and watched Josh greet one of two couples she'd met briefly when they arrived.

Dawn slid down to the chair next to Kate's and leaned close. "He's certainly charming and personable."

Kate frowned at Dawn. "Who?"

Dawn's returned look said, *Like you don't know.*

Kate rolled her eyes. "The whole family is quite nice. It will be a pleasure to work with them."

A peal of laughter drew her attention in time to see Josh lift Connor and drape the boy upside down over his shoulder. Connor laughed as Josh spun around, then planted the dizzy boy back on the ground.

"Yeah, see how funny it is when he throws up on you, Doofus!" Piper called to her brother.

After a few more minutes of racing around the yard with the boy, Josh jogged up, panting, with Connor on his heels. "Tag, man," he gasped, slapping Brady on the shoulder. "You're up. I'm dying here."

"Thanks for wearing him out," Brady said, pushing to his feet. "The kid is gonna sleep well tonight!"

"He's not the only one," Josh said, taking the chair Brady vacated.

"So the itinerary posted in the guesthouse says tomorrow we learn to saddle and ride horses and get a glimpse of other aspects of ranching life." Kate ran a finger down the side of her glass, wiping off the drips of condensation.

"Yep," Josh said. "Bright and early. We'll start with a hearty breakfast, then gather up in the corral behind the stable."

"I just remembered I never called Dean back," Dawn said. "Will you excuse me?" Dawn rose from the table, wearing a smirk.

But Kate was having none of Dawn's ploy. She already saw a battle with her attraction to him ahead and the day's travel was catching up to her. "I'm going to call it a night, as well. Thanks for everything."

Josh touched the brim of his hat and winked at her. "See you in the morning."

Kate took her trash to the waiting receptacle, then headed into the guesthouse. Dawn wasn't on the phone when she got there, lending more credence to her theory about her friend's continuing efforts to play matchmaker.

Dawn grunted and frowned at Kate from the kitchenette, where she was pouring herself a glass of wine. "Why are you in here instead of enjoying Josh's company?"

"Because, like I've said, this is a business trip. I'm not looking for a hookup."

Dawn set the wine bottle down and licked a drip of the merlot from her finger as she pinned a hard look on Kate. "Are you sure that's all it is? Is everything okay?"

Kate blinked, a bit startled by the question. "Of course. Why?"

Her colleague twisted her mouth and gave her a narrow-eyed scrutiny. "You just don't seem that excited to be here. You've acted rather reluctant since we landed this account and scheduled this trip. What's wrong? What am I missing?"

Kate waffled briefly between telling Dawn the whole truth and brushing off her reservations. "I'm just tired."

Dawn continued to stare at her.

"Really! This place is great. The people are super friendly, the scenery is awesome, and it's an exciting account to be working on. I just..." *Shoot.* Why did she add the unfinished addendum?

"If something about this account is bothering you, if you feel we need to go a different direction on some aspect of the campaign, you should tell me." Dawn strolled into the common area with her wine, obviously waiting for Kate's explanation.

"No, no. It's nothing about the account or our plans for the ad campaign. It's me."

Dawn raised her chin. "So there is something?"

Kate closed her eyes and let her shoulders droop. "Ugh. Okay, yes. I didn't want to say anything because it's my issue to work out. But..." She moistened her lips, then took Dawn's hand and led her to the couch. They sat facing each other, and Kate rubbed her hands on the skirt of her dress. "I'm chicken. All these 'adventures,'" she said, drawing air quotes with her fingers, "scare me."

Dawn's face split with a grin. "Seriously? That's all?"

Kate straightened her back. "All? Dawn, day after

tomorrow, we're supposed to leave on a camping trip filled with all kinds of dangerous and death-defying stunts. I can't do it! Just the thought of all those high places and steep drop-offs leaves me in a cold sweat." She raised her damp, trembling palms to show Dawn. "Look!"

Dawn laughed and grabbed Kate's hands, then clutched them against her chest. "Oh, Katie! You're supposed to be a little scared. That's part of the thrill, the adrenaline rush. Facing down that instinctive fear and conquering it is what makes these kinds of adventures so exciting!" She squeezed both of Kate's hands, smiling her enthusiasm.

Kate shook her head. "You don't get it. I used to be adventurous. As a kid, I did all kinds of stupid, daring, dangerous stuff."

"Well, there you go! You've got the adventurous spirit in you. Just dig it out and wear it pr—"

"No." Kate jerked her hands back and ran her fingers through her hair. Her gut quivered as memories of her days spent in the bottom of the silo, injured, scared, alone, reverberated through her mind's eye. "I lost that spirit a long time ago. I almost died once. I fell—" She swallowed hard. "I shouldn't have been climbing on that roof, but…" She paused and took a deep breath to calm the jangle of nerves.

Dawn's forehead was wrinkled with curiosity. "You almost died? When? What happened?"

Kate balled her hands into fists and told her co-worker the whole story in digest version. She finished by saying, "That's why this whole adventure trip scares me so much. I don't think I can do it. I still have nightmares about being in that silo, about falling, about being lost."

Dawn leaned back against the cushions of the couch and shook her head slowly. "Wow. That had to have sucked."

"To put it mildly."

"But…" Her friend arched one eyebrow, and her gaze glinted with challenge. "What better time to get past those fears, huh? Face 'em down. Conquer them!"

Kate was shaking her head before Dawn even finished.

"Come on, Kate! Zane and Josh know what they are doing. You heard them out there tonight." Dawn waved a hand toward the door. "They've been doing this stuff for years. They've taken every safety precaution, had the equipment inspected. It's all perfectly safe. Josh and Zane are pros at this, and they will not let you get hurt."

Kate worried her bottom lip with her teeth. She'd told herself all of the same things a dozen times, but nothing could calm the drumbeat of dread deep in her soul. Instead of arguing points that she had no good defense for, she aimed a finger at Dawn and said, "That's another thing."

Dawn blinked. "What is?"

"Stop pushing me at Josh and vice versa. I don't need a matchmaker."

Her friend's grin turned smug. "But he's so good-looking and so into you."

"I *know* he's good-looking. I'd have to be blind not to notice that. But I'm not in the market for a vacation romance."

"Oh, girl…why not? If I weren't with Dean—"

"Because I'm...*not*! I have my reasons!" she said in a tone sharper than she intended.

Dawn drew back slightly, and her face reflected a degree of hurt and remorse.

Lowering her voice, Kate continued, "I've been down that path before and it was a disaster I don't care to repeat. So...please drop it. No matchmaking."

The front door of the guesthouse opened, and two of the other guests strolled in, holding hands and smiling warmly at each other. Both couples joining them on the adventure trip, Paige and Jake McCall and Brianna and Hunter Mansfield, hailed from Louisiana. They'd been invited because Brianna was a friend of Piper's from college, and Jake McCall, a former navy SEAL, was Zane, Josh and Piper's cousin.

"Beautiful evening for a walk," Paige said. "The moon is almost full."

"Oh, how romantic," Dawn said.

"Exactly," Jake replied with a wanton wink. "Well, good night." He headed down the hall to their bedroom, towing his chuckling wife in his wake.

"That's what I want," Kate said, waving a hand toward the hall after the couple had closed their door.

"Sorry, he's taken. Quite happily from the looks of it." Dawn gave her a lopsided grin.

"I mean I want the happily-ever-after. I want to be taking romantic walks in the moonlight after years of marriage."

Dawn lifted a shoulder. "Nothing says you can't have that. But to find it, you have to be open to opportunities when they present themselves."

"But it doesn't mean I have to chase every wild goose that crosses my path." She scooted to the edge of the couch, ready to head off to bed. "Especially if I know that a particular goose doesn't offer any possibilities beyond a short vacation."

"Gander."

Kate gave Dawn a puzzled glance. "What?"

"A gander is a male goose. Josh would be a gander."

Kate grunted, then rose to her feet. "My point is the same. Good night."

"So…" Dawn said, following Kate down the hall, "no adventures and no fun on the path to Mr. Right?"

Kate stopped, bracing her hands on her hips as she faced Dawn. "That's painting it in rather bleak tones. Just because I've learned to be cautious doesn't mean I'm some kind of cowardly nun."

Dawn wrapped her arms around Kate in a hug. "I know you're not. That's why this trip is the perfect chance to seize some of that passion you have just under the surface and let it out. Carpe diem, my friend. Starting tomorrow, I'm going to help you face those fears and grab life by the horns." She kissed Kate's cheek and gave her a finger wave as she disappeared into her bedroom.

Kate stood in the hall, staring at Dawn's closed door for several seconds, speechless. She'd always known Dawn was pushy and direct. Assertiveness was helpful in business. But Kate didn't so much like being on the receiving end of her coworker's brass. Still… Dawn's characterization of her, and the suggestion she could be letting opportunity pass her by, rankled. Maybe the root of the disquiet in her gut was the restlessness she'd thrived on as a child battling to be expressed again. Could she do it? Could she embrace that side of her nature once again and finally silence the doubt demons that had plagued her for twenty years?

As she headed off to bed, her pulse scampering at the thought of facing her fears, the image that fixed itself in her mind's eye was not of the old silo, nor was it of a high bluff to be rappelled on a Colorado mountain. No, what she saw as she closed her eyes in search of sleep that night was a pair of sky blue eyes, a well-fitting pair of jeans and Josh's sultry grin.

Early the next morning, Kate was roused from a deep, contented sleep by the clang of a bell and a male voice shouting outside her window. "Breakfast time!"

"What the...?" she grumbled, groping for her phone on the nightstand.

The door to her room opened, and Dawn strolled in. She grabbed and shook Kate's toes through the covers. "Come on, sleepyhead. We're on ranch time now. The day starts early around here."

"What time is it?"

"Oh-dark-thirty." Dawn moved back to the door, turning on a lamp as she departed. "Get a wiggle on. We're here to get the full ranching experience, and that includes the morning chores."

Kate groaned and pulled the covers over her head.

"Oh, and don't bother showering yet. Zane recommends saving that until after the chores and breakfast. Meet me at breakfast in five." With that, Dawn closed the door, leaving Kate to struggle out of bed.

Seven minutes later, she staggered down the hall to find the dining table bustling as her fellow guests passed bowls of fluffy eggs, platters of bacon, pans of fried potatoes and pots of fresh coffee to each other.

"Saved you a seat," Dawn called, motioning to the empty chair next to her.

Kate moved stiffly to the chair and gaped at all the food. "Good grief. There's enough here to feed an army."

Beside her, Dawn poured coffee in the mug at Kate's plate. "The foreman, Mr. Summers, is supposed to be by in about twenty minutes to show us where we can help with the morning chores. Then we'll clean up a bit before we saddle up and ride out in the fields to check on the herd, ride the fence—"

"Ride the fence?" Brianna Mansfield paused as she added pepper to her plate of eggs.

"Miles and miles of fences are part of this and every ranch. They get worn out and damaged regularly. We'll be helping look for that damage and fix it." Dawn smiled at their fellow guest. "Pretty routine stuff, but a great way to see the land and practice our horsemanship before we hit the adventure trail tomorrow."

Brianna glanced at her husband. "When you said we were going to be helping with the ranch chores, you weren't kidding."

"It'll be fun. Just stick with me, kid. You'll do great." Hunter gave his wife a peck on the cheek.

When Roy Summers arrived, Dawn, Kate and the two couples followed the foreman out to the stable. "You'll each work one-on-one with one of the ranch staff, learning how to care for your assigned horse and prepping for the day ahead."

The group assembled in the main alley of the stable, where the ranch crew was waiting for them. Kate spotted Josh immediately, leaning casually against the gate of the first stall. Her stomach swooped when he met her gaze and sent her a wink and a lopsided grin.

The other guests were paired up with the hands, Piper McCall and Brady Summers. Then Roy turned to Kate and Dawn.

"You two will work with these bozos." He aimed a thumb over his shoulder to Zane and Josh. "That way you can discuss promotion biz while you learn the ranch."

Dawn jerked a nod and stepped over to slip her arm through Zane's. "Perfect."

Which left Kate paired with Josh. She gave Dawn a withering glance, and her friend mouthed back, "Carpe diem."

Josh sauntered over to her and waved a hand down the alley toward the back end of the stable. "After you."

Kate rubbed her palms on her jeans and fell in step behind Josh, trying not to notice how his T-shirt hugged his broad back and biceps. She'd rather hoped that in the light of a new day she'd discover she'd exaggerated in her mind how handsome he was, how good he smelled, how affecting his lopsided grin could be. But if anything, she'd minimized him in her mind as she tried to dissuade herself from the attraction she couldn't deny. Her pulse pounded out a staccato rhythm as she entered the stall with him, where a bay horse swished its black tail and nuzzled Josh with its white snout.

"Hey, girl," Josh cooed to the animal, stroking her neck and nose. "How are you? Good girl." The soothing, low rumble of his voice as he talked to the horse caused a fluttering in Kate's core. The purring, intimate quality of his voice conjured images of rumpled sheets and late night pillow talk. Sweet nothings. Sexy whispers.

She put a hand low on her belly as if she could quash the tingle of lust coalesced there.

"This is Lucy. Come say hello," Josh said, meeting Kate's gaze.

She stepped deeper into the stall and reached a hand out to pat the mare's neck. "Hello, Lucy. Nice to meet you."

Josh ducked out of the stable for a moment and came back with a few slices of apple in a zip-sealed baggie. He gave her one. "Put this on your open palm and let her eat it off your hand. She'll be your best friend forever after."

Kate fed the treat to Lucy and grinned as the mare's ears turned forward, showing her delight. "Good girl, Lucy."

"She loves apple slices, but don't give her too many." Josh took a bit with a harness from a hook on the wall. "They are like candy for a kid. Just treats. Too many mess with her diet."

"Right," she said, still stroking Lucy's nose. "I grew up on a farm. Remember?"

Josh paused from loosening the knot tied in the reins. "Oh, right. So you know horses? This lesson is moot?"

She raised a shoulder. "Refresh my memory. It has been quite a while since I saddled a horse."

"You got it." He handed her a currycomb. "Let's see how much you recall."

Zane walked up to the door of the stall. He smiled a greeting to Kate, but she sensed tension in him that tightened the edges of his mouth. "Josh, can I borrow you for a few minutes?"

"Um…" Josh glanced at her, and she gave a nod.

"I'm good. I'll be grooming her until you get back."

Josh touched the brim of his hat. "Good deal."

Kate began brushing Lucy with long strokes, slipping the mare another apple slice almost as soon as Josh was out of sight. "Yeah, I take care of you, and you take care of me. That's how it works. Right, girl? You're gonna be good to me?"

The horse nickered softly and nuzzled Kate's shoulder.

Outside, Kate could hear men's voices joining Josh's. Low at first, then growing louder and more angry. She stilled, then edged nearer the stall window, shamelessly eavesdropping. What was wrong? What could have made her dimpled cowboy so upset?

Chapter 3

Josh clenched his fists, seething. "I told you no good would come from doing business with that rat bastard."

They hadn't even officially opened McCall Adventure Ranch, and already the triplets' high school rival—and, unfortunately, their loan officer—had found a way to screw them. Josh wanted to punch something. Preferably someone—Gill Carver. Dave had returned from an errand in town, where he'd learned troubling news and shared it with their foreman, Roy Summers, then with Zane, Josh and Brady.

"Look," Zane said, his mouth set in a grim line, "I'm not happy about this either, but there's no law against Gill opening or investing in his own adventure ranch. It's called free enterprise, and competition is at the root of how the American economy works."

"Not in the mood for a civics lesson, bro." Josh snatched his hat off and thwacked it against his legs.

"Gill doesn't own a ranch, not since his father's went belly up, and he doesn't know jack about adrenaline sports. Who's running this new enterprise for him?" Brady asked.

"That's the real kicker," Roy said. "Dave said he's hired Townsen."

"Karl?" Josh gaped at their foreman.

"You know another Townsen?" Roy asked. "Dave said the Jacksons had defaulted on their loan, and Gill offered to assume the payments and pay the startup costs if they'd allow their ranch to be used as the home base for a new business idea he had."

"A business idea he *stole*!" Josh growled. "Along with stealing our employees!"

Zane shook his head. "He didn't steal Townsen. After we let him go, Karl was free to go where he wanted."

"I'm not surprised he took the opportunity to put the screws to us, considering how ticked he was over the theft accusations and his firing," Josh said, grinding his back teeth.

"So what do we do?" Brady asked, veins standing out on his neck.

"Nothing we can do," Zane said, far too calmly.

"Nothing?" Josh repeated, aghast. "You want us to roll over and play dead? Are you telling me this doesn't piss you off in the first degree?"

Zane faced his twin, his nose flaring and his jaw tight. "Of course I'm pissed. But we have guests in there." He aimed his thumb over his shoulder to the stable. "Guests whom it is more important than ever that we impress. And by *nothing*, I mean there's nothing we can do about Gill opening a competing business. What we *can* do is offer a better product. We out-perform him. We bring our A game and kick his sorry ass. Our success is all the vengeance we need."

Josh exchanged a glance with Brady, his lifelong friend, new business partner and future brother-in-law. If possible, Brady hated Gill more than the Mc-Call siblings did. Josh could see the roil of disgust in Brady's expression morph into sheer determination. Brady finally jerked a nod of agreement and raised a fist. "Yeah. Let's kick some ass."

Zane cracked a grim smile and bumped Brady's fist with his own.

Sucking in a cleansing breath, Josh joined the fist bumps. "Let's do it."

As he turned to go back in the stable to check on Kate, Josh felt a weight settle on him. His family had already needed the adventure ranch he and Zane had dreamed up to be a success to save them from financial ruin. Now they needed to succeed as a matter of pride. A feat made more difficult thanks to the competing efforts of Gill Carver, slime bag extraordinaire.

The triplets' history with Gill was as dicey as it was long. Gill had been a thorn in their side from the day in fourth grade when Zane had beaten Gill in the spelling bee, and Gill, ever the sore loser, had arranged a posse of his friends to waylay Zane on the playground. That was the first time of many that Gill learned that if he picked on one McCall triplet, he got all three and Brady to boot.

A bitter rivalry had been born and fed throughout high school. Salt had been added to the wounds when Gill's father fell on hard times, like many of the ranchers in the area. The bank had foreclosed on the

Carvers' holdings and at the foreclosure auction, the triplets' father had purchased not only a top breeding bull for the Double M, but had added a parcel of the Carvers' land that abutted the McCalls' property. Gill had turned his spite up to DEFCON 1, not just toward the McCalls and Brady, but most of the town. He'd made clear to the triplets that his career path, becoming a loan officer at the local bank, having the power to foreclose on homes, ranches and small businesses of the townspeople he'd grown up with, was part of his plan to seek revenge against the people of Boyd Valley.

Josh had just stepped back into the shaded stable alley when a figure moved out of one of the stalls and issued a quiet "Psst." He blinked, his eyes adjusting to the dimmer light, and Dawn Fetzer came into focus, waving him over to her.

He shook off his bad mood, knowing he couldn't let the dark cloud of bad news affect his dealings with their first customers. Pasting on a smile, he strode over to her and nodded a greeting. "What can I do for you, Dawn?"

"Listen," she started in a hushed tone and drew him into one of the empty stalls. "I need a favor."

"Okay…" he whispered back, matching her volume.

"Kate is—how should I put it?—trying to overcome some personal issues, some fears based on a childhood trauma."

Josh arched an eyebrow, intrigued. What sort of childhood trauma? This insight to the woman he found himself so powerfully drawn to fueled his curiosity about her.

"She's probably going to need a little cajoling and special encouragement to go the extra step on most of the adventures this week." Dawn bit her bottom lip and glanced guiltily out of the stall as if afraid her collusion with him would be discovered. "She'd kill me if she knew I was telling you this. She only told me because I asked her flat out why she was acting so freaked out on this trip."

"I see." Josh poked his fingers in his front pockets and rocked back on the heels of his boots. "So, what is it exactly you want me to do?"

"Well…" Dawn fidgeted with one of her hoop earrings. "If it isn't as obvious as I think it is…she's into you. You've definitely turned her head, and I think you can use that to our advantage."

"Um…" Josh shifted his weight, uneasy with the track of the conversation. While it pleased him to know his attraction to Kate was mutual, he was wholly uncomfortable with any ploy to trick her based on that attraction.

When he hesitated, Dawn rushed on to say, "Nothing untoward. But…I think she'd find it harder to tell you no. She's not going to participate in the riskier activities, I fear, without a great deal of motivation and encouragement all around."

"I'd be happy to encourage her and help ease her anxieties any way I can."

"Good!"

"I just…" He paused and glanced away for a moment, trying to put into words the tickle of uneasiness in his belly. "I don't like the idea of manipulating her or using her interest in me against her."

"It wouldn't be using it against her!" Dawn grabbed his wrist. "Helping her face her fears is in her best interests. Don't you think?"

"Well…" Knowing that Kate had a childhood trauma to blame for her fears made Dawn's suggestion feel even more intrusive. As much as he wanted to help Kate, he didn't want to use illicit tactics to sway her feelings. But to satisfy Dawn, he said, "I'll do what I can."

The first day on the ranch passed pleasantly, with horseback riding out into the pastures, roundup and knot-tying demonstrations, a roping contest (which Jake the former SEAL with his athletic talent predictably won), and another cookout with bountiful food and good company. That evening each guest prepared a backpack with spare clothes for the three-day camping and hiking excursion, and the ranch staff added basic camping, hiking and safety supplies to each pack and saw to it that the packs were delivered to the base camp for the next night.

Despite the fun first day, Kate knew the challenges that lay ahead, and she had a kink of apprehension in her gut as she piled into bed that evening. She stared at the ceiling much of the night, then had no appetite for the pancake and sausage breakfast the others feasted on before dawn the next morning. Her coffee gnawed her stomach as she faked enthusiasm at the breakfast table with the couples who'd be traveling with them.

At the appointed time, Brady met their party at the door of the guesthouse. He showed them to the SUV that would drive them to the starting point of the horseback ride into the mountainous terrain where the adventures would begin. Zane and Roy had transported the horses by trailer to the start point a half hour earlier.

The married couples, Piper and Dawn loaded into

the SUV first, leaving Kate to squeeze into the middle seat between Jake and Josh.

From the front seat, Dawn sent a sly grin to Kate over her shoulder, chirping, "Look at you, Katie! In the middle of a hunk sandwich."

Kate returned a raised-eyebrow glare that told her friend she knew exactly what Dawn was up to. Then, throughout the two-hour ride, as they wound along twisting back roads, Kate tried not to think about Josh's muscled thigh brushing hers or his sexy, freshly showered scent filling her nose. Forget the fact that the equally handsome Jake was squashed against her other side. Her brain only registered her cowboy host. She could feel Josh's chest vibrate each time he laughed, thanks to her side being snuggled against him. He'd stretched his arm along the back of the seat behind her shoulders, and his body heat enveloped her like a hug.

When they reached the starting point for their horse-back ride farther into the mountains, she'd never been so glad, and simultaneously disappointed, to arrive at a destination. And though the sexual tension coiled inside her loosened its grip, a different pressure built in her chest as they mounted up for the ride. The excursion would take place on property left to the McCalls by their grandfather and a string of ancestors before him. Piper kissed her fiancé and waved goodbye to the group as she left to drive the SUV back to the ranch.

"Move 'em out!" Zane called to the group.

"Next stop, the zip line!" Josh added.

The rest of the group whooped, but Kate's heart swooped. She tried to brace herself for the slide down a cable, strung over a deep valley, with only a few straps and carabiner clips for support.

They rode higher and higher into the rugged terrain, chatting and tossing bantering jokes up and down the line of horses. Zane took the lead with Roy and Brady bringing up the rear. Josh took his position between Dawn's horse and Kate's and pointed out interesting views for Kate to snap photos of as they made their way along the horse trail.

Kate cast an encompassing glance across the scenic view. The towering peaks, beautiful trees, rocks and wildflowers were awe-inspiring. Until she saw the steel cable stretching across the ravine. Her stomach clenched as she looked down, deep into the crevasse that lay below. The drop-off was sheer rock, straight down. The gulf that the cable spanned was hundreds of feet wide and almost as far to the bottom.

She gripped her reins tightly, searching her brain for a way to get out of the feat while still saving face with her client…and without having a complete, humiliating breakdown. Her heart thundered in her chest, and the rush of adrenaline and dread left her shaking to her core.

"All right, ladies and gentlemen," Zane called to the group, "we are at our first challenge."

Another hoot of excitement rose from the other guests, Dawn's cheer loudest of all.

"Remember to dismount your horse to the left and hand off your reins to Roy or Brady. They'll be leading your horses back to the trailer."

"We won't be on our horses anymore?" Brianna asked, sounding disappointed.

"We will. But the horses can't use the zip line to get across the gorge like we can," Zane explained, and the group chuckled. "They'll meet us tomorrow at the trailhead to ride up to the launch point for our white-water excursion."

Around her, her fellow adventurers were dismounting and chatting excitedly with each other. Kate's mouth dried, and her legs trembled as she stood in her stirrups to swing down from Lucy's back. Just as she felt her knees buckle, sure she was going to flop onto her backside in an ignominious tumble, strong hands spanned her waist, lifting her securely to the ground.

Startled by the unexpected help, she spun around to find her nose inches from Josh's chest.

"Uh, thanks," she muttered, tipping her head back to meet his gaze. The sun shone brightly just behind his head, and she had to squint against the blinding light. Then he took a small step to the side, giving her breathing room, and his wide-brimmed hat blocked the sun.

"No problem." The smile he flashed her and the sparkle in his breathtaking blue eyes were every bit as luminous as the sunshine. Her already unsteady legs wobbled again, and she grabbed the strap of Lucy's saddle to steady herself.

"I'll take those." He reached for the reins she'd left dangling from the horn of her saddle, and his arm grazed her ear as he stretched past her. "If you'll wait over there with Zane, we're about to go through the zip-line procedure and safety rules."

She drew a shuddering breath and released the death grip she had on Lucy's straps. "Right." As she turned to join the rest of the group gathering around Zane, Josh wrapped his hand around her forearm, stopping her.

"Are you okay?" he asked.

She worked to give him a confident smile. "Sure. Just…a little nervous."

He tightened his grip and held her gaze with a piercing stare. "It's perfectly safe. I promise. You've got this."

His words, the gentleness of his tone and reassurance behind his smile flowed through her like a balm. She inhaled a steadier breath, and twitching the corner of her mouth in a quick grin, she nodded to him. "Thanks. I'm going to hold you to that promise." She fumbled for her camera, which hung by a strap around her neck. "I'll join the others in a second. I just want to snap a few pictures of the zip line for the brochure first."

"Good deal."

Josh led Lucy and another horse away and passed the reins to Roy. The two men exchanged a few words, Roy giving Josh a serious look. She heard the foreman say, "Be careful," before Josh chuckled a response and walked away.

Kate eased to the edge of the steep drop-off and peered down into the forested and sheer rock ravine below. A chill rippled through her, and she purposefully shoved down the clamoring nerves and raised her camera to click off a few shots. Turning toward the group, she took a picture of Zane helping Brianna don a harness and one of Hunter snapping on a helmet. Turning, she took a picture of Roy with the horses. She caught Josh laughing over something with Jake with the zip-line platform and spectacular view behind him. She shielded her eyes from the sun so she could see the small screen on her camera. The shot of Josh and Jake was a winner. Definitely good for the brochure.

"Look at this one," she told Dawn, angling her cam-

era to show her coworker the shot. "Perfect for the brochure, don't you think?"

Dawn squinted at the screen. "Oh, most excellent! Good job! Now…" Her friend caught her arm
and dragged her over to the harnesses and carabiners
piled in front of Zane. "No more stalling. Buckle up!"

Zane had one of the harnesses in his hand and
shouted to the group. "Okay, listen up! You'll each
get one of these nifty getups, which I will now demonstrate how to hook on."

Josh joined his brother, demonstrating the technique
by stepping into the harness, clasping hooks, tightening straps and choosing a well-fitting helmet. She
tried to listen, but an odd buzzing filled her ears, and
her thoughts kept straying back to the old silo in Missouri. The loud cracking sound just before she plummeted. The pain that streaked through her on impact
and plagued her for days as she awaited rescue. Her
breathing grew ragged and shallow. How could she
possibly do this? She cast a side glance to the deep ravine, and the earth seemed to spin.

"Josh will now demonstrate, and he will be waiting
at the other end of the line to help you unhook your
gear after your ride. Any questions?" Zane called.

"You sure that little wire up there will hold?" Hunter
shouted, grinning.

A nervous laugh rumbled around her, telling her she
wasn't the only one with jitters.

"It's solid steel cable. Professionally installed and
tested several times. It'll hold," Josh returned. "See
you on the other side!"

She rubbed the sudden chill bumps on her arms as
she watched Josh hook onto the pulley system with the

grooved wheel that would carry him down the sloped cable. He moved to the edge of the platform to launch his descent and found her gaze. He sent her a cocky grin and a wink, then pushed off. Kate held her breath as he whizzed away, and Dawn squealed her delight.

"All right. Who wants to be first?" Zane asked, scanning the group.

"Kate does!" Dawn shouted.

Josh savored the dramatic view of the ravine, relished the warm air whipping through his hair and inhaled the clean air. He loved the adrenaline rush, loved these mountains, loved that he could turn his passion into a profitable business to help his family. Finally he felt like he was an integral part of the Double M, someone more than the reckless and irresponsible brother. He could finally—

An odd jerk and sudden drop yanked him from his musing. He continued his descent but…something was different. Something was *wrong*.

The cable shuddered again, and a growing sense of foreboding swelled in Josh's gut. He could see the landing platform ahead and prepared to stop. Another strange jerk slowed his progress, and he could see the slack in the line overhead. What the—?

The first fingers of real trepidation clawed at him. They'd tested the zip line many times, had it inspected, cleared by all the proper authorities. But he didn't need a professional to tell him something was off.

He slid closer to the landing platform, perched a good fifty feet above the ground, but the final few yards of the ride were even more jerky and unstable than before. When his feet touched the landing, and he knew he was safely across, he exhaled a breath he hadn't known he was holding.

Relief washed through him, but on the heels of that released tension came another hit. As he unhooked himself from the pulley system, he discovered the source of his bumpy ride.

A chill washed through him, along with panic.

The tree trunk had been cut, both above and below the metal plate where the bolts holding the main pulley for the cable system were attached. Saw dust littered the platform, and the steel bands that should have been providing additional support for the main cable had been cut away. Deep wedges had been removed surrounding the bolted metal plate such that the wood was splintering as the weight of the cable pulled at the weakened trunk. The gouged section of the trunk, and therefore the steel transverse cable, was in serious danger of failing.

With his heartbeat roaring in his ears, Josh abandoned his attempts to unfasten his harness and scrambled for the two-way radio. He had to warn Zane before anyone else tried to cross—and died.

"Come on, Kate," Dawn said. "You go first!"

Kate snapped her head toward her coworker so fast she could have given herself whiplash. "What? No!"

Dawn leaned closer, whispering, "The longer you stand here and watch, the more nervous you'll get. Just bite the bullet and jump in."

"I don't know. I—"

"Kate! Kate! Kate!" Dawn started chanting.

"No!" Kate tried to back away from the platform but bumped into Jake's wide chest.

"Kate! Kate! Kate!" the others in the group joined in the chant.

Dawn seized Kate's arm and tugged her forward. "You can do this! It'll be fun!"

Kate didn't reply. She had to concentrate on breathing, on swallowing the surge of bile that rushed up in her throat. Brady held out the tangle of straps and clasps, and with Dawn's help, she found the contraption being slid over her head, buckled across her chest and secured between her legs.

She had to do this, she realized. To back out now would mean more than humiliating herself in front of the PR firm's client. If she refused, she would be letting her fear win. She might as well still be trapped in the bottom of that silo. Dawn was right. She needed to face her fears. She just wished she could take baby steps, could wade into the kiddie pool before jumping in the deep end from the high dive.

Brady adjusted the last of her straps and positioned her hands. "Hold on here. When you get to the platform, keep your feet up, and be prepared to catch your balance. Josh will be waiting to help you." He patted the top of her helmet. "Ready?"

She squeezed her eyes closed, and her stomach flip-flopped. She wasn't sure she'd ever be ready.

"Okay," she rasped.

"Kate's ready to go at your signal," Brady called to Zane.

"Ready here. Waiting on your 'go,' Josh," Zane said into his two-way radio.

The group continued chanting. "Kate! Kate!"

Dawn sidled closer to Kate and squeezed her shoulder. "You got this!"

Zane was plugging one ear and holding the two-way radio close to his other. "Did you say 'no' or 'go'?"

Dawn's face brightened. "Josh says go!"

Brady nodded and gave Kate a gentle push. The straps tugged as they grabbed to support her weight. Her feet dangled free as she began her descent, and she heard a muted cheer behind her.

Then, as she gathered a little speed, Josh's faint static-laced response from the radio. "Zane, no! Hold up!"

"Zane? Did you hear me?" Josh said, his heart thundering and his gut twisted in knots of dread.

"Too late, man. Kate just launched. What's up?" Zane answered through the radio.

Josh bit out a curse. Already the cables were jiggling and rattling as Kate made her way down the zip line. "Hold everyone else! We have a problem down here!"

He tossed the radio down, ignoring Zane's demands for further explanation. He needed to give his attention now to Kate and the very real danger she was in. He spared a moment to study the tree trunk where the terminus equipment was attached. He saw no way to shore up the trunk, no way to stop the inevitable collapse of the line. The gouged section of trunk would continue to give way as more of the tree cracked, shifting more tension to smaller amounts of wood, until at last it broke free completely. Even now, the wood slowly splintered, each time making the line jerk. But how long would the last part of the trunk hold before the entire cable fell?

Nausea swirled in his gut. He had no way of preventing disaster if Kate didn't reach the platform before the cracking trunk gave way. Leather gloves or not, one man couldn't possibly hold the half-ton cable, the passenger's weight and the other steel parts of the zip-line equipment.

His heart thrashed against his ribs. He had to do *something*. And fast.

His line was still attached to the main zip cable. *Think, McCall. Think!*

Even if he couldn't hold the line, maybe he could redirect it. If the steel plate that the cable was attached to were to snag on something that would hold it, even temporarily...

Unhooking his harness, Josh cast a frantic glance around for something, *anything* he could attach his line to. His riser was only long enough to reach a nearby tree branch. It wasn't much, but it would have to do. Looping the cord around the low branch, he wrapped it twice and tucked it through the end, then quickly hooked the end to an opening in the turnbuckle on the main cable.

Muttering a prayer under his breath, he turned his attention to the woman whose life hung in the balance.

The ride down the cable was faster than she'd expected. And jerkier. Kate had thought the descent would be a smooth, brisk glide, but in reality she sped along at a breakneck pace, her stomach swooping as if she were on a roller coaster. And the bumps and twitches in the line were jarring to her. Every buck and sway sent fresh waves of anxiety through her. Kate determinedly kept her eyes ahead and refused to look down. Remembering the snatches of instruction Zane had given moments ago, she applied her hand brake, hoping to ease the bumps and slow her decent.

She could see the platform ahead, getting closer, and she focused on reaching the deck where Josh stood. If she could just reach that landing platform…

He shouted something to her, and even from her distance she could tell something had him upset. Was she coming in too fast? She braked again, and he shook his head.

"Don't brake! Faster!"

Faster? She scoffed mentally. She was already going far faster than she wanted. Yet his obvious distress buzzed through her like a thousand stinging bees. If Josh was worried—

The line jerked hard again, and she heard him curse.

No! No, no, no! Please God, no! she thought, squeezing her eyes closed, her denials as much prayer as panic.

The line jolted again…and sagged, slowing her approach markedly. Startled, she opened her eyes. She was mere feet from the platform. Josh had his hand extended toward her.

"Kate! Grab my hand!"

She hesitated, confused, for a fraction of a second before releasing her grip on the straps of her harness. Almost as soon as she let go, stretching her arm toward Josh, mere feet from the landing deck, the cord gave another tremendous jerk—and she dropped straight down.

Chapter 4

It happened in an instant, yet Josh saw it all in slow motion. The last of the splintering wood holding the main cable gave way, seconds before Kate would have been safely to the platform.

The released tension caused the cable to whip about as it sailed past him. The loose end with all the hardware of the terminus struck his shoulder with an excruciating blow that knocked him off his feet.

He heard the snap of breaking limbs and crack of splintering wood. Josh whipped his attention to the branch where he'd tied off his cord. The strap had jerked tight, stripping the smaller limbs and bark as the cord was dragged along the branch. The cord caught at an upturn in the branch. Thank God! But the weight of the steel cable and the woman still dangling from the line was bending the branch. The limb wouldn't hold long.

Kate!

Rolling to his stomach, he looked over the edge of the landing deck. Kate hung about twenty-five feet below him, near the upper branches of another tree that grew out from the side of the ravine. She was silent, unmoving. Josh's chest clenched.

"Kate!"

She stirred, glancing around, clearly in shock.

"Kate!"

Her head tipped back, and her terror-filled gaze clashed with his.

What should he tell her? What should he do? He forced his own panic aside, knowing he had seconds to act. What he did in the next few precious moments meant life or death for Kate.

First and foremost, she had to get to the nearest tree and get unhooked from the main cable. When the branch impeding the cable broke, the main line would fall into the ravine. If Kate was still hooked on, she'd be dragged along for the fall. "Unhook your line!"

"Wh-what?"

"Your harness line!" He tapped his chest, indicating where the main riser attached to the harness. "Unhook your line! Hurry!"

Even from his distance he could see how badly her hands were shaking. He realized her weight would be pulling down on the large carabiner, making it virtually impossible for her to unhook herself.

"Damn it!" he barked.

Cut the straps, a voice in his head said. He patted his pocket and found the hard lump that said his buck knife was there. "I'm coming! Stay still!"

Josh shot a look around at the trees below him,

quickly sizing up his best route down. The first drop would be the biggest, and if he didn't aim well and land on the right spot, he'd join Kate in plummeting to the bottom of the ravine.

He spent no time pondering that disaster. If he weighed the risk, he'd give himself time to second-guess, and Kate didn't have time. Instead, he set his sights and leaped.

Small limbs slapped at him and scratched his arms and face as he crashed through to the largest branch of the tree just above Kate. His legs buckled as he landed. Josh seized handfuls of leaves and twigs, trying to catch himself as he tottered and fell hard on his ass. Shifting his weight, he wrapped his arms around the branch just before he would have slid off. He didn't even stop long enough to catch his breath before he launched himself again, aiming for the perpendicular trunk of the tree nearest to Kate.

He jumped, and…his feet missed the trunk.

Instinctively, he grabbed for the tree as he went down, and his torso landed across it with a jarring thud. Pain radiated through his body, and he struggled to catch his breath.

Above him he heard another crack of wood. He raised his gaze to find Kate, gauge his next move. She was still fumbling with the straps.

"I'm coming!" He shimmied out on the trunk, his eyes on the panicked woman.

She stretched a shaky arm out to him. "Help me!"

"Grab my hand!" He reached as far as he could. Their fingers touched, and she whimpered when they couldn't clasp hands. "Hang on!" He pulled his arm back to scoot farther out on the trunk until he reached a branch growing upward at a right angle from the trunk. The tree dipped with his weight, but he ignored the groan of the bending tree and clutched the branch to stabilize his position. "Here!"

This time when he reached for her, she was able to curl enough of her fingers around his for him to pull her toward him. With her other hand, she seized his wrist with a cry of relief.

But she wasn't out of danger yet. And neither was he. The branch above them would snap any second. When it fell, the weight of the cable would pull her down. And him with her if she was clinging to him.

"Hold my waist. I need my arms free to cut you loose." He fumbled in his pocket for his buck knife and flicked it open.

She stared at him in wide-eyed dismay. "Cut me loose?"

"Hurry! Before the line falls!"

He saw the moment the danger registered fully in her expression, and she scrambled to suit actions to his order. She swung a leg up and over the horizontal trunk, pulling herself until she could straddle the trunk and hold his torso, her cheek against his leg.

He began sawing on the main cord, making steady progress until...

Another loud crack. The cable dipped farther, tugging at her.

Kate gasped, clutching at him. "Oh, God, no!"

He sawed harder. Faster. Numb to everything but the fraying cord beneath the blade.

One last pop of breaking wood above them. And the steel cable fell.

Kate's harness line stretched taut as the cable jerked

at it for a split second. She screamed. And his blade severed the last fibers of the cord.

Freed from the restraining weight, Kate lunged forward, holding him tighter. Burying her face in his chest. Hyperventilating.

"I've got you!" he said, circling her with his arms, the vertical branch between them as they embraced. Sweet relief flowed through him.

She continued shaking, her breathing shallow, frightened pants.

"Kate, you're okay. Take slow breaths, or you're going to pass out." He secured his hold on her with one arm, while closing his knife with the other hand and shoving it back in his pocket. He still had to get them safely up to the platform, and she seemed ready to fall apart.

"I need you to take a deep breath and listen to me. We're going to climb back up to the landing deck now, but I need your help."

She raised her head and met his eyes. The stark fear in her beautiful green eyes twisted in his gut. She'd trusted him when she came on this trip, when she'd allowed herself to be strapped onto the zip line. And he'd failed her. Her fear was his fault. Her peril was his fault. She was his responsibility, and he owed her.

His mouth dried, and guilt pounded through him. "I will get you home, safe and in one piece. I promise."

A tear broke free from her eyelashes, landing a sucker punch in his already sore ribs. She gave him a weak nod, and angled her head to look below them at the fallen cable. With a gasp, she scrunched her eyes closed and squeezed him harder.

"Yeah, don't look down." He rubbed her back, hoping to calm her. "Listen, Kate, you're gonna have to let go of me, so we can climb back up." When she squeaked her dismay, he added, "I'll help you. You can do it."

"Oh, my God," she muttered to herself. "Why? Why is this happening again?"

Again? He puzzled over her comment, but now was not the time to question her about it.

"Okay, here's the plan." He explained to her how he would help her ease around the vertical branch, then shimmy on her belly along the trunk until they reached a spot where some intersecting limbs from other trees provided a ladder of sorts to climb toward the platform.

He brushed hair back from her face and held her gaze. Her skin was silky and damp with her tears, and he wished he had time to simply caress her face with gentle strokes and revel in its softness. But he had to stay focused. Now was the time to step up, be there for her, get them out of this mess.

"Kate, do you understand? I'll be right in front of you, and I'll help pull you up the big gaps. Okay?"

She swallowed hard and nodded.

Over the next several agonizing minutes, they inched back toward the landing platform. Perched as they were over the deepest part of the ravine, he knew any loss of balance, any misstep would be deadly. When they reached the end of the tree trunk, he climbed to the next available branch, testing its strength before allowing his full weight to settle on it. He leaned back down, extending a hand to Kate and instructing her where to place her feet as he pulled her up.

Branch to branch they climbed, many gaps requiring that he jump to catch the next limb or boost Kate from below. When they'd scaled the last distance and he'd helped her crawl onto the platform, she collapsed against him, trembling and crying.

They were safe at last, and the release of sheer terror he'd known in the last thirty minutes made Josh want to cry, as well. Remorse and guilt curled in his gut. The fragile woman in his arms had placed her faith—her life—in his hands, based on a promise that he'd keep her safe—but he hadn't. Her tears humbled and castigated him.

Her fingers curled into his back as she clung to him, sobbing. He rocked his body, trying to soothe her, stroking her hair, her back. He absorbed the tremors that shook her, then realized not all of the shaking he felt was hers. His own body was wracked with shudders as he came down from the adrenaline and panic-packed stress.

"We're safe now. It's over. I've got you." He muttered the reassurances to her, confirming for himself as much as for her that the danger had passed. He worked to collect his thoughts and regain his focus. He had a job to do. A job made all the more important now that the dynamics had changed so drastically.

Only after allowing his heart rate and breathing to slow to a more normal pace did he hear the crackle and shouting from the radio he'd tossed aside.

"Josh, answer me! Damn it, if you're there, say something!" Zane said, and Josh heard—could *feel*—layers of emotion in his twin's plea. "Josh? Josh!"

He took one more moment to attend Kate's needs. He eased her back and began a cursory examination of her arms and legs. "Are you hurt anywhere?"

They were both covered in scratches and scrapes.

His shoulder throbbed where the cable had smacked him, and his midsection where he'd crashed onto the tree trunk hurt like the dickens now that the dulling effect of adrenaline had ebbed.

Kate raked her own gaze over her body, as if assessing for the first time, then shook her head. "I d-don't think so."

She had a small cut on her temple, which he'd tend to as soon as he could get into the first aid kit at the campsite. They'd both have plenty of bruises showing by nightfall. But they were both alive and had no broken bones, no serious injuries. It was nothing short of a miracle.

"Thank God," he whispered.

In the background of Zane's repeated calls to him, he could hear a woman crying, wailing in fear. The rest of the group had to know by now that the cable had fallen. His lack of response to Zane's calls would be heightening their fears that the worst had happened.

He framed Kate's face, thumbing dry her cheeks. "Hey, I need to let the others know we're safe. You okay for a moment?"

She still trembled and hiccuped as she wept, but she let him pull free and gave a tiny nod as he pushed to his feet. His knees buckled slightly as he rose, the last vestiges of adrenaline making themselves known. He scooped up the radio and pressed the talk button. "Zane, I'm here. We're both okay. A bit beaten up and pretty rattled but…alive."

A brief silence followed in which he could sense his twin heaving a huge sigh of relief. Finally, Zane replied, "Holy hell, man! We've been going crazy over here! What happened?"

"The cable collapsed." A fresh shudder rolled through him as he voiced the horror.

"Ya think?" Zane barked, his tone sharp, but Josh knew the edge was due to fear and frustration and not anger. "But…Kate made it across?"

"Sort of. We had some dicey moments, but I cut her line before the cable dropped." *Barely.* He didn't even want to think about how close they'd come to disaster. "We had to climb some to get back to the platform but…we're here now. Shaken, but alive."

Another silence as Zane absorbed the information. Then, "How? Why? What the hell happened?"

Josh raised his gaze to the wedge cut out of the tree and the sawdust on the deck, and knots of disbelief and horror tightened in his chest. He said simply, "Sabotage."

He and his family were all too familiar of late with the word and all its implications.

Zane bit out a heated curse in response.

Josh sank back down on the deck and leaned his back against the tree trunk. He reviewed this vandalism in light of the other damage done in recent months to the family's ranch. "So…now what?"

He heard Zane huff a deep breath. "Give me a minute. I gotta think."

Clearly the rest of the group wasn't getting across the ravine today. They'd have to ride the horses back the way they'd come up and drive around the long way to get to the camp. Assuming they hadn't just lost everyone's business. Assuming there was any business left to save. Assuming the saboteur hadn't just wrecked everything they'd worked for and dreamed of for the last year.

"Get pictures," Zane said, and Josh frowned.

"Yeah, because I really want to commemorate this day," he said, his tone dripping sarcasm.

"For the insurance company," Zane clarified. "And the police. Although I guess the cops'll want to take their own." Leave it to his practical, responsible twin to think of a detail like that.

"Right. Will do." Josh raked fingers through his hair, surprised to find his hand still shaking a bit. "I guess Kate and I will wait here at the camp for you and the group to meet us…what? Tomorrow morning?"

Zane scoffed. "Are you serious? You think we're still gonna make the trip after this? Brianna and Hunter are already planning to go home. I've promised them a refund."

"So, that's it? You're just *quitting*? Giving up?" Josh asked, aghast at his brother's attitude and a bit stunned at himself for wanting to continue.

"We almost had a woman die on our watch, man," Zane said in a quiet, severe tone.

Josh glanced back at Kate, then carried the radio farther from her, turned down the volume and replied in a hushed tone, "I'm well aware of that, Zane. I lived it. I'm the one who put my ass on the line climbing out to rescue her when the cable fell."

"Yet you want to keep going? Are you *insane*?"

Josh scrubbed a hand over his face, weighing his answer. Maybe he was crazy, but the thought of calling off the trip now left a dark void inside him that stole his breath. "Look, we're all upset right now. Let's not make any snap decisions." He filled his lungs and released the air slowly. "Let me get Kate down to the camp, give us all time to regroup and assess. You deal with stuff at your end, and I'll talk with you in a couple hours."

Zane didn't answer at first. Finally he muttered a terse "Fine."

The one word was filled with a regret and discouragement that echoed in Josh's soul. But quitting filled his soul with a sticky blackness. He felt mired in a grief and anxiety that sucked at him and pulled him deeper into a sense of helplessness that he hated. Only the idea of forging on, or turning this disaster around and finding a way to make the trip and call it a success, gave him any relief to the quicksand emotions pulling at him.

"It'll take a few hours to get everyone back down the mountain, the horses tended to, the insurance company called..." Zane sighed. "It'll be close to dark before we can get to you."

"So let us spend the night. We have food, tents and first aid supplies. We'll be fine."

Zane responded with a growl, then, "Hey... Dawn wants to talk to Kate. Is she there?"

Feeling as if he'd won a short reprieve, Josh dragged in another cleansing breath and stepped back over to Kate. "Yeah. Right here." He placed a hand on her shoulder, and she met his gaze with red-rimmed, still-unnerved eyes. "Dawn wants to talk to you."

"Kate? Kate? Are you all right?" Dawn said over the receiver as he handed the radio to Kate.

"I—I guess. I—"

"Oh, my God, Kate! When we saw the line fall, I freaked! I was so scared! I thought for sure you were dead."

Kate stared at the two-way, her face draining of what little color had returned.

Josh gritted his teeth. Dawn was *not* helping. He squelched the urge to snatch the radio back from Kate and tell Dawn as much.

Kate raised the walkie-talkie to her mouth again, adding, "Yeah. It was scary. B-but Josh saved me." His heart stilled as she raised grateful eyes to him and flashed a tremulous smile. "I'm not hurt. Nothing b-bad anyway. Just…very glad to b-be alive."

"Oh, honey, I know! I can't believe this happened to y—"

Kate found the volume dial and turned the sound of her friend's voice to zero, then set the radio on the platform next to her. She gave Josh a guilty glance, saying, "I'm just…not in the mood to talk. Sorry."

"Hey, don't apologize. I'm not much in the mood for talk right now either." He lifted the radio and clicked it off. He would check in with Zane later and make their plan for how to proceed.

Right now, he wanted to give Kate his full attention. He'd get her settled at the camp and bring her camera back up to snap photos of the damage to the zip line. A cocktail of fury and horror swirled like acid in his stomach. Whoever had been vandalizing the Double M over the past year, trying to hurt his family's business, had escalated. The saboteur had moved from poisoning a pond and burning crops to putting human lives at risk. Clenching his back teeth, Josh swore that if the cops wouldn't do their job finding the cretin, he would. And there'd be hell to pay.

"You ready to move out?"

Kate glanced up at Josh when he spoke, needing a

minute to replay his question in her head. Her thoughts were still miles away—namely, in a dank silo in Missouri, the memories as fresh as they were the day she'd been rescued.

"We should get on down to the campground. We've got things to do before it gets dark." He held his hand out to her, offering her help getting to her feet.

A sense of warmth and security slid through her as his large, calloused hand encompassed hers, his grip firm and strong. *He'd risked his life to save her.* The truth flitted through her mind, sending waves of adoration and gratitude rippling through her.

On the heels of that thought, a doubt demon nipped at her sense of relief. *But he put you in that position. His company was negligent.*

She scowled as he pulled her up on still-wobbly legs.

His head canted to the side as he studied her furrowed brow. "Kate? What is it? Why the frown? Are you injured?"

"Um…no. Just…too much in my head." She rubbed her temple as if she could block the disconcerting thoughts, and her fingers encountered a sticky substance. Lowering her hand, she saw the red stain, and her gut swooped. "Blood."

Josh nodded, his mouth in a grim line. "Yeah. You've got a cut." He touched the spot gently, and she noticed the sting for the first time. "Another reason to get down to the camp. I want to disinfect that. Maybe put a butterfly bandage on it."

She turned up her palms and raked a more careful gaze over the rest of her body. What else had she missed? Her hands and arms were scraped, but not too badly. The knee of her jeans was torn, and her body ached in general from the tension in her muscles.

But she was alive. In one piece.

Josh kept his hand wrapped around hers, then tugged lightly, directing her to the back of the landing deck. "This way. I've got you."

She allowed herself to lean into him, clinging to his hand, and followed him to the wooden stairs that descended to the ground. "Wh-when will they be here to pick us up?"

With one hand ensconced in Josh's grip and her other hand holding the railing, she made her way down the steps, eager to get back to the ranch and collapse with a couple of Tylenol and a large glass of wine. In fact, forget Dawn's challenge to face her fears. She was done. Ready to go home. Not just back to the ranch. Back to Dallas. To her condo. To her quiet life with her cat.

She'd built a simple, secure life for herself, and she was happy with it. Or…at least content.

At this moment, she could think of nothing she wanted more than her safe couch with Sadie purring beside her.

"Well…" The hesitation in Josh's voice caught her attention.

"Well, what?"

He cut a side glance to her as they reached the bottom of the stairs. "That hasn't been decided."

She gave her head a small shake. "What's to decide? They need to send someone to get us. The sooner, the better."

"Kate, I just thought that maybe…" His voice trailed off, and he glanced away.

"Josh?" She felt the slight tightening of his grip on her hand, and a frisson of concern slithered down her spine. "They are coming, right?"

He gave her an odd look that heightened her suspicions. "Right now, Zane is taking the rest of the group back to the ranch, and…he has to deal with the insurance company…in light of…" He hitched his head toward the landing platform, not verbalizing the disaster they'd just survived.

"But we're—"

"Safe," he quickly finished for her, "and we have ample supplies to camp here tonight as planned."

"Couldn't someone else come for us? The foreman or Brady or—" She narrowed her eyes when the muscle in his jaw flexed and his brow dented in consternation. "What?"

"I'm going to talk with Zane again in a little while, but…I'd like to tell Zane that we'll camp here tonight, then hike up to meet the rest of the group at the launch spot for the white-water rafting. We can still finish this trip."

Her insides knotted, and jerking free of his grip, she took a stumbling step back from him as if he'd punched her in the gut. "We're not calling off the rest of the trip? But—" Her breath caught, choking the rest of her sentence.

Josh met her gaze with a deep furrow in his brow. "Is that what you want? To quit?"

Quit. The word sawed in her gut. She hated to think of herself as a quitter, but…didn't the circumstances call for it? If they'd been talking about a PR project or a 10K race or a low-carb diet plan, quitting would have been out of the question. Kate finished what she started. But, holy crap, she'd almost died today! If that didn't give her an out, then what did?

"Kate," he said, his tone soothing and his gaze softening, "full disclosure… Dawn told me about your… concerns over the trip. Because of your past."

Her breath caught, and her heart thrashed with her outrage over Dawn's indiscretion. She lifted a fluttering hand to the hollow of her throat, where her anxious fingers groped for the necklace she usually wore. "She *told* you?"

"Nothing specific. Just that you had some childhood fears to overcome." He moved her hand from her throat and pressed it between both of his wide palms. "She wanted me to help you face your doubts and overcome your past. And you still can. I know that what happened earlier scared the hell outta you. But I swear I will keep you safe for the rest of this trip. Every strap and mounting will be double-checked, *triple*-checked. Every safety measure in place." He pressed one hand over his heart. "I promise."

"I, uh…" The heartfelt appeal in his eyes and warmth of his grip on her fingers muddled her thoughts. Why was she wavering? Squaring her shoulders, she refocused. "Every safety measure should have *already* been in place."

"They were." When she arched a skeptical eyebrow, he added, "Originally. We checked everything as recently as yesterday morning when we brought the supplies to the campsite. Someone managed to inflict the damage to the cable terminus after that."

Her heart jolted. "As in *sabotage*?" she asked, fresh horror washing through her.

"Yeah." His face darkened, and the pale blue of his

eyes clouded. "Our family's ranch has been attacked in past months, too. But here's my thinking… If we quit right now, the vandal wins. Just like when terrorists bomb airports or concert venues, trying to disrupt our way of life, frighten us away from traveling or enjoying our freedoms. If we hide in our houses behind locked doors, the terrorists win."

She drew a shaky breath and blew it out slowly. "But this is different." She glanced around, feeling vulnerable but nudged by the truth Josh had just laid out. She waved a hand, trying to put her reluctance into words. "This is—"

"Exactly the same. A bully is a bully, whether they attack a country or just one person. I can't let the saboteur win."

The pain in his expression chipped at her will to refuse him.

His hand squeezed hers, and his eyes pleaded. "If you'll stick it out with me, trust me to guide you through the other challenges, we can finish what we started. Finishing would be a moral victory. For both of us. Showing the vandal he hasn't scared us off, and giving you a chance to live down your past." He paused, his expression genuinely discouraged. "But if, at the end of the rafting, you still want to cash in your chips and go back to the ranch, we'll arrange a transport of some sort out for you."

"So I'm stuck here until the end of the rafting?"

He visibly winced at her use of the word *stuck*. He gnawed his bottom lip for a moment, then added, "Look, let's get settled in at the camp, get our fire started and that cut on your head tended to before the sun sets. We can reassess then."

She stared at him, still wondering how she ended up in the middle of nowhere, alone with this dream-worthy cowboy, and her prospects for rescue dependent on taking more nerve-shattering risks. But in the face of his impassioned argument, his appeal to a moral victory, he'd left her little choice. He'd challenged her in a way that spoke to a buried part of her soul that longed for adventure. He'd deftly enlisted her sense of honor and justice, tweaked her tenacity—powerful allies swaying her to his cause. And she knew without deliberating further that she would continue on the trip, that she would put her life in his hands. His strong, calloused, tremble-calming hands.

As if he sensed her wavering, he moved one hand to glide along her jaw, his finger sliding across her cheek to cup her face. His thumb gently stroked the tender skin beside her eye, and thrilling sensations spiraled through her. "Kate, give me another chance to get this right. I won't let you down. If you agree to stay, to make the trip with me, I *promise* you will not get hurt."

She knew he couldn't make any such promise. Accidents happened. To wit…her brush with death today. Her pulse tripped, and yet she heard herself saying, "O-k-kay."

A smile spread across his handsome face, and he drew her close to drop a light kiss on her temple. As he turned, motioning for her to follow him to the campsite, the pragmatic part of her brain, which had obviously short-circuited at his touch, reengaged. She'd agreed to stay? To continue on this nightmare that had already almost killed her? Was she *nuts*?

Why had she agreed to trust Josh? Did she really believe he could deliver her home safely? He'd appealed to her emotional side, but following her feelings had landed her in trouble in the past. She knew better than to be swayed by his swoon-worthy good looks, passion-based arguments and devastating grin. Not when logic said continuing would be dangerous…in more ways than one. Traveling alone with a handsome man who'd proven he could knock down her defenses, had insights to her fears and had rooted out what made her tick could only spell disaster for her heart.

Three hours later, having cleaned up a bit, gotten a sterile bandage for her cut forehead and roasted a light supper of hot dogs over their campfire, Kate was still fretting over the plan to keep going on the trip. She sat with her legs bent, her knees drawn up to her chest, and her chin resting on crossed arms as she stared into the dancing flames. She knew she could tell Josh she'd changed her mind, but did she really want to quit or was her terrifying experience today clouding her judgment? Her old ghosts had rallied and were taunting her. She really didn't want to make her choice based on her fear any more than she wanted to choose to stay because of an ill-advised fondness for Josh and his confusing influence over her.

Better safe than sorry, a doubt demon nudged. Safe…oh, how she longed to just stay safe, physically, emotionally. And yet—what kind of life was that?

I promise you will not get hurt. But did she trust Josh to keep that promise?

"Kate?" he said, cutting into her circular thoughts.

She blinked and focused on him, his face lit by the campfire. "Yes?"

Josh poked at the burning logs with the stick, moving a piece of wood into the glowing embers. "Can I ask you something…personal?"

She raised her chin from her crossed arms, a frisson of alarm and wariness sliding through her. She met his level gaze, his eyes so blue and piercing they seemed to glow in the dim firelight. "You can ask." She tugged up her mouth in a quick grin. "No promises I'll answer."

Lifting a shoulder, he said, "Fair enough." He turned his attention back to the fire and drew his eyebrows into a V. "Earlier today, when…everything happened…"

She gave a small grunt at his euphemism for the terrifying moments that even she hated to name, as if they still held the power to claim her life if she acknowledged them. His reasons for not wanting to name the incident specifically, she'd wager, were more rooted in guilt.

After another moment, where he seemed to be trying to find a tactful way to ask his personal question, he said, "You said, 'Why is this happening again?'"

Kate blinked her surprise, her gut swooping. "I did?"

"Yeah." He rolled his palm up in query. "What did you mean by that? Does it have anything to do with the fears Dawn mentioned?"

She exhaled slowly. Today of all days, after *everything* that had happened, she hated to give those ghosts any more face time. But since they were already out, haunting her, what could it hurt telling Josh about the event that had sent her life on a different trajectory?

"Had you zip-lined before?" he prodded when she remained silent for a moment too long. "Had other problems—"

"No, to zip-lining before." She shifted to sit cross-legged and hugged her elbows. Despite the fire's heat, a chill burrowed to her bones. "I fell into a grain silo when I was eight."

He narrowed his eyes slightly as he stared at her, as if processing what she'd said. "You fell? From where? How high up?"

"The roof. I'd climbed out on it, and…it caved in."

His eyes had rounded, and he gaped at her, slack-jawed.

She nodded, confirming his unspoken awe. "I was fearless as a kid. Adventurous. And I'd climbed the ladder on the side of one of our farm's abandoned silos to retrieve my brother's remote control plane. I'd taken it when I wasn't supposed to, and it was stuck on the roof of the silo." She paused for a moment. "I thought I could get it. But the roof was rusted, in bad shape, and I didn't get far before it gave way."

"Damn."

"Mmm-hmm."

His brow furrowed in thought before he said, "Clearly you lived to tell the tale." He waved a hand in her direction. "But how? You had to have been hurt."

She snorted a humorless laugh. "Oh, I was. Broken leg, concussion, many, *many* other bruises and internal contusions." She shuddered remembering the pain she'd been in. "But a small amount of corn had been left in the silo for some reason. It was mostly rotten, but there was enough cushion in the muck and leftover grain to pad my fall. That slop saved my life."

His countenance dark, Josh raked a hand over his mouth as he mulled her confession. "Geez, Kate."

"That's not the worst of it." She bit her bottom lip,

and her stomach rebelled as she thought about the days that followed her fall.

He'd abandoned the stick he'd been poking the fire with and swiveled to face her fully. "Not the worst? What could be worse?"

Zane leaned against the fence to the corral behind the stable and stared without really seeing anything at the almost full moon. Instead his mind's eye saw the months of careful planning, risky financial maneuvers and hundreds of hours in execution that hung in the balance thanks to the accident today. The accident that wasn't an accident, according to Josh.

The saboteur had struck again. Attacking his and his siblings' startup business. If he'd thought the vandal had his sights only on his parents' ranch, he knew better now. But why had McCall Adventures been targeted? And who could be so downright *evil* as to put human lives at risk this way?

The sound of voices and thud of boots on the hard-packed dirt of the ranch yard roused him from his deliberations. He cast a look over his shoulder, just as Roy and Dave approached, flanking him at the fence.

Roy clapped a hand on Zane's shoulder. "You doin' all right?"

"Honestly? No. Everything's a damn mess." He kicked the bottom rung of the fence and bit out a curse.

"So..." Dave said, his tone cautious, "does this mean the adventure ranch business is finished?"

Zane gave the hand a side glance. "Undecided. I hope not. I'm gonna fight like hell to salvage it."

"But for now?" Dave folded his arms on the top of the fence, his gaze still on his boss.

"We're shutting down for now. Have to."

"I'm sorry, man." Dave turned to peer through the darkness to the empty corral.

"Hell of a thing, Zane. At least no one was hurt," Roy added.

"Yeah," Zane muttered in a desolate tone.

"You ladies having a hen party out here?" Zane's father said, approaching from the house. The three men each greeted Michael, who sidled up to the fence next to Roy. "Something going on I should know about?"

"Just talking about the accident today and the future of the adventure biz," Roy said.

Zane sighed. He really didn't want to rehash or make small talk about the disaster. He had serious thinking to do. Planning. He knew the men meant well, but his nerves were still raw and he still had to deal with his rebellious brother. How could Josh even think of continuing the trip? They had to tread carefully in the next few weeks if they wanted to save the business.

"Well, if I know one thing, Zane," his father said, "it's that you can do anything you put your mind to. You always have. You'll make a success of this adventures company, because my children aren't quitters."

"What if quitting is the financially responsible thing to do?" he asked.

His father leaned one arm and a hip against the corral fence and eyed Zane. "There are always going to be tough calls to make when you own a business. But I have faith that when the time comes, you'll do the right thing."

Dave cleared his throat. "Well, good night, folks. Helen's waiting for me, and I'm already running late."

One by one, the men dispersed, leaving Zane alone again with the moon and his quiet turmoil.

"How did it get worse?" Josh asked.

Kate bit her bottom lip, her gut swirling at the memories of her fall into the silo and the aftermath. "I wasn't found for two days."

He cocked his head slightly, his expression incredulous. "Excuse me? Wha— Where were your parents? Why—"

"My parents were in Kansas City with my brother on a 4-H trip." She shivered, whether from the chilled air or the memory she couldn't say, and she rubbed her arms.

Josh turned, stretched toward his tent and plucked a blanket out. He scooted close enough to drape the cover around her shoulders.

Smiling her thanks, she pinched the blanket closed at her throat with one hand and continued her story. "My grandmother was babysitting for me, and it turns out she was more senile at the time than my parents knew. She didn't realize I was missing until the next morning. At that point, she went out and *looked for me*," she drew air quotes for him, "which involved calling for me and walking around the yard before going back in the house to wait for me. Around lunchtime that day, she called a few of my friends asking for me, and my friends' parents were the ones who finally became concerned enough to mount a more extensive search of our property."

"Did she call your parents to let them know what was happening? Why didn't they come home when—"

"She didn't call them. My neighbors did. More evidence of how screwed up her judgment and reasoning had become. She knew telling them I was missing would be an admission of her failing memory and incompetence. She was terrified they'd want to put her in a nursing home and had gotten good at covering her memory lapses and faking her ability to care for herself."

He scoffed and, shaking his head, made a sound of disgust. "You're her granddaughter. Wasn't she worried about you? How could she—"

"She didn't have a good grip on reality. She'd convinced herself I was just hiding somewhere and would be back soon. Eventually our neighbors forced her hand when it was obvious the police needed to be involved to find me."

Josh waved his hands, stopping her. "Back up. You said your friends' parents came over and helped search. Why didn't they find you then?"

She shrugged. "I don't know. I didn't hear them calling. Thanks to my concussion and the pain I was in, I was in and out of consciousness. They claim they looked at the silo, called for me and got no reply, but obviously they didn't climb up the ladder to look inside."

He leaned toward her, his expression saying her story had him flabbergasted. "So when were your parents finally called? When were the cops brought in?"

"My neighbors called the cops and my parents when they couldn't find me. The police took a statement from my grandmother, and eventually brought dogs out to search for me, but my scent was all over the farm and the dogs didn't know which trail to search."

"So you were in there for *two days*?"

She nodded. "Two days. I was in that silo with a broken leg, no food or bathroom, and mice for company for two days." Her voice cracked. "The nights were the worst. It was so dark in there. And smelly. All that rotten corn. It was horrible. I thought I was going to die."

"I bet you did. Damn, Kate! That's awful."

"I had nightmares about it for six years, despite seeing a counselor. And the memories still get to me when…" She closed her eyes, and her voice faded.

"Yeah. I can see why." He was quiet for a moment, the popping and crackling of the campfire filling the silence between them. Then he cleared his throat and scooted closer to her.

She glanced up at him as he settled next to her and took her hands in his.

"But you conquered those fears today when you got on the zip line. You didn't let the fears win."

She scoffed. "Really? That's the case you want to make? You do remember how that particular episode ended? I'm not sure that's the best argument to convince me of anything but a full retreat."

Josh screwed up his face and shook his head. "I know it seems that way but…you're here now. You're safe. You did it! You even went first!"

"Which proved bad luck. And I didn't so much go first as I was shanghaied. I blame Dawn for that. And I will get her back for it." She gave a snort of dry humor.

"The point is, you overcame your fear long enough to do something daring. That's a win!"

She forcibly plucked her hands free of Josh's grip, and vigorously shook her head. "Look, I appreciate the pep talk, and the spirit in which it's given, but nothing has changed. If anything, today has proven that I *have* a reason to be afraid of things like…" She waved a hand in the general direction of the zip line and landing platform.

"No!" The severity of his tone surprised her. "I don't accept that. I can't let you think that fear is okay. Fear only holds you back. It cripples you. It keeps you from experiencing life fully. I can't let you give up because of *fear*. You have to get rid of that monkey on your back!"

Kate frowned and drew back from him. "Excuse me? Since when is that for you to decide? I choose how I will live my life and what is worth the risk. Only me!"

"As long as it is *you* choosing and not your fear. You said you used to be adventurous. That is the true you. What you were born with. It's your soul. But your fear has squashed that spirit in you."

"Maybe it's for the best."

He huffed a sigh. "Let me ask you this… Are you happy?"

She grunted her affront and immediately answered, "Yes."

"Are you? Really?"

"I—" She was prepared to repeat her assertion, when a tiny voice in her head whispered, *Don't kid yourself.*

Maybe she was content, *safe*, but was she *happy*? She didn't yet have everything she'd hoped for in life. She still daydreamed about hiking the Grand Canyon or even Machu Picchu. Of hot air balloon rides over the Rhine. Of marriage, children, true love. Was her fear holding her back from pursuing the things she longed for? The tickle at the back of her neck was unsettling.

Josh took her silence as her answer. "That's what

I thought. But you have a chance now, on this trip, to start facing down the demons of the past and living the kind of life that will make you happy." His pleading look speared through her. "Finish this trip with me. Say yes, and I promise not to let you get hurt."

There was that unpromiseable promise again. Yet he was so earnest when he made the pledge that she almost believed him.

Kate rubbed her temple. The stresses and abuse of the day had her muscles aching and her head throbbing. Her answer should be a clear and decisive *no*. So why was she wavering?

"Josh," she started and exhaled slowly. "I'm tired. And sore. And…confused."

A muscle in his square jaw flexed as discouragement crossed his face.

"Before I agree to anything…"

His face brightened with hope.

"Tell me about the sabotage. I confided in you. Now do the same for me. What's going on behind the scenes that I should know about?"

He sighed, removed his hat long enough to rake his shaggy hair behind his ears, then shoved the wide-brimmed Tony Lama on his head. He sat back, his expression dark as he said, "Our ranch is in trouble."

"Trouble?"

He nodded, his mouth pressed in a taut line. "We struggle every month to pay the loans and keep the stock fed and healthy. We've had a tough couple of years due to herd loss, unexpected expenses, and…" He puffed out a breath. "Well, someone has been making life even harder by vandalizing the ranch. The sabotage has been directed at the crops, the herd, the equipment.

Things to damage our bottom line. Someone clearly wants us to go under. Out of pettiness or competition or sheer meanness, we don't know. We still have no idea who is behind it. They've been slick about not getting caught."

"Geez, that's low. What about your adventures business? How does it figure in the big picture?"

"Zane, Piper, Brady and I started McCall Adventures as a way to earn some extra cash for the ranch, trying to save our dad from bankruptcy." He dug the heel of his boot into the dirt and frowned. "Zane and I developed the idea based on our love of high-adrenaline sports and the notion that we could share the ranch and our extracurricular love with other people."

"It's a good idea," she conceded. "I've always thought so."

He raised his head only enough to give her a hooded glance. "Even after what happened to the zip line?"

"You said it was sabotage."

Josh nodded morosely. "Pretty obviously so. Someone cut the tree around the plate where the cable had been bolted. With the added stress of our weight when we came across, what wood fibers were left weren't strong enough to hold the line. They splintered and—"

"So you think that whoever has been trying to make your family's ranch go under is now attacking your new business, too?"

"Seems that way. I have no proof, but it doesn't take a genius to add two and two." He snorted derisively. "And come up with *foreclosure*."

"Is that what you and Zane were talking about outside the stable yesterday morning?"

He jerked his chin up. "You heard us?"

She flashed a chagrined smile. "Yeah. I didn't mean to eavesdrop, but you all sounded so upset, and, well, you weren't exactly quiet."

He dropped his chin again and scratched his cheek. "Yeah. A former employee has gone into business, competing against us, with our high school rival funding him. And I damn sure know they stole the idea from us."

Kate thought on that for a moment. "Did this former employee leave under bad circumstances?"

"Sorta, yeah." He slanted a look at her. "And yes, we've considered that he could be behind the vandalism. But the attacks on the business started before he was fired. So…"

"Does he know about this property? That you were planning to make your base camp here? Otherwise, the finger points to someone on the inside of your business. Someone who had access here in the twenty-four hours between your last check and today."

Josh snapped his head up again and glared at her with a furrowed brow. "No way this was an inside job. Everyone involved with the ranch and this new business is family…or as good as."

"Brady?"

"Has a financial stake in the McCall Adventures and is engaged to my sister."

"What about your foreman?"

Josh shook his head. "Roy is Brady's father and has been with my family longer than I've been alive."

"What about the other hand I met? Dave something?"

"Dave has no reason to sabotage our company or the ranch. We are his livelihood. And he's a good guy.

I can't believe he'd do anything to hurt us." He flexed one wrist by pushing back his hand, then traded to stretch the other. "It's possible someone followed us up here. And it's no secret around town that we own this property. We brought our friends up here all through high school for weekend outings."

Kate's stomach clenched at the notion that Josh's family had a mysterious enemy lurking around town, escalating his attacks.

"So you can't think of anyone who might want to hurt your family? Someone who wouldn't care if innocent bystanders were hurt in the process?" She meant no recriminations by that statement, but she saw a fresh look of guilt cloud his face.

"We've been asking that for months. But the sheriff can't tie anyone on our potential suspect list to the incidents."

"Including the high school rival you mentioned?"

"Considered and dismissed. No evidence he was involved, and he's had solid alibis for the timing of the incidents. And since being an ass isn't in and of itself a crime…" He snorted a wry laugh and shrugged. "The authorities have come up with bupkis. The best information we have came from a guy who was stalking Piper earlier this year. And seeing as how he's nutso, I don't know how much stock we can put in his testimony."

"What about a vandal for hire? Maybe your former employee or old rival didn't do the deed himself, but he could have paid someone."

Josh pinched the bridge of his nose. "Anything is possible, I guess." He twisted his mouth and regarded her with a moue of regret. "I hate that you got caught up in this, that you were put at risk. I'm so sorry, Kate."

She held his gaze for a moment, then nodded her acceptance of his apology. She drew the edges of the blanket closer around her. Despite the fire, the evening air had grown chilly. Her mind skipped back to his earlier question—his plea, really, for her to continue on the trip.

She watched him stoke the fire, adding another log and stirring up the coals. He'd said quitting would be letting the vandal win. She understood why he believed that.

"It's clear how much the vandalism, the harm to your home and livelihood bothers you. Understandably so."

He nodded.

"But…" she continued, and his hand stilled, his gaze lifting to hers. "Do your concerns warp your perception of reality? Can you promise it hasn't clouded your ability to make the right call about continuing the trip?"

He seemed startled by her frankness and didn't say anything for a moment as he "um"-ed and "er"-ed.

"I mean, we want to make the right call—to go on or not. And just like you don't want me to base my decision on my past and my fears, I don't want you pushing ahead out of anger or frustration or a way to somehow spite the vandal…who may never know what choice you make anyway."

He stared at her, silent and unmoving for a few seconds, before he answered softly, "Honestly?"

"Complete honesty. We are sharing confidences tonight. Right? True confessions by firelight?"

He chuckled. "Are we going to exchange stories of losing our virginity next?"

She barked a laugh. "Let's save that one for another night."

He gave her one of his charming grins. "Deal." Then, sobering, he added, "The truth is, I'm not sure what the strongest thing motivating me is. It's all kinda muddled up in me. I really want this adventure business to succeed. For a lot of reasons."

She pinned a hard look on him. "Enough to take unnecessary risks?"

His brow dipped in offense. "*No.* I promised you I wouldn't let you get hurt. I meant it. Kate, I've been doing this—" he waved a hand around the campsite "—all the sports on this property for years. I know what I'm doing and how to manage the risks."

She drew a slow, measured breath. "All I will agree to tonight is that I'll go as far as the end of the rafting. After we get off the river, I'll decide if I go any farther."

The corner of his mouth lifted, dimpling his cheek, and her heart flipped. She knew his devastating good looks had factored into her choice, her attraction to him. But she could kick herself over her shallowness and bad judgment later.

"Good enough?"

He reached for her hand and kissed the back of it. "Good enough."

He spotted his target within seconds of stepping into the hole-in-the-wall bar several miles outside the town limits of Boyd Valley. Setting his shoulders, he strode over to the empty stool next to his target and settled in. He glanced up at the TV mounted on the wall, feigning interest in the baseball game on the flat screen. "Well? What happened?"

"Too much." Grim expression. Guilt?

A chill slithered through him. "Explain."

"The damn zip line fell."

He sent the patron at his elbow a bored look. "And?"

A pause. Jaw tightening. "What do you mean, *and*? Someone could have been killed! The damage was just supposed to frighten them, force them to suspend the tours awhile longer."

"Nothing like the loss of a *beloved* McCall to make them reconsider the venture," he said, his tone dripping sarcasm. He wouldn't lose sleep over any harm that came to the McCalls. After all, they never blinked when they profited from his failure.

A glare. "I didn't sign on for murder!"

He raised a hand. "Calm down. No one died, did they?"

A swig of liquor. "No. The woman on the line at the time survived, but…"

He narrowed his gaze. "But?"

A muttered curse. "I ain't doing this anymore. Not if people get hurt."

"The line falling is your own fault. You did the damage. If it fell, you're—"

"I know!" A frustrated huff. "Damn it, don't you think I know?"

"Keep your voice down." He leaned closer to the other patron. "Don't think you're getting out of this now. I still hold the trump card. Your accident. The girl who died because of you. If I talk to the cops, you go to jail for hit-and-run. Vehicular homicide. Not to mention any charges they want to add for all the vandalism and criminal mischief you've committed against the Double M."

Another bleary-eyed glower.

"Was the zip line your only surprise for them?"

Hesitation, then, "No."

He grinned, picturing the McCalls finding more damage to their startup business. "Good."

The saboteur's hand tightened on a highball glass. "I shoulda never agreed to this. You're the devil."

"Naw, just someone with the power to destroy you if you don't help me get what I deserve."

"The Double M."

"Damn right."

A headshake and dark glare. "You don't deserve squat, you piece of sh—"

"Watch it," he said, aiming a finger at his partner in crime. "If you piss me off, I might decide to go a different way with my plan and offer you up to the cops. My sacrificial lamb."

Bleary eyes sharpened with hatred. "If I go down, don't you think I'll take you with me?"

"Not if I cut a deal. I have friends in the sheriff's office, you know. Face it, I've got your fate in my hands, friend. Get me what I want, and I'll keep quiet. Screw this up, and you go down."

The bartender finally ambled up. "What'll you have?"

"Nothing," he said. "I'm done here." He stuffed a bill in the bartender's tip jar, then strode out.

Josh waited until he thought Kate was asleep to use the satellite phone, the best way to communicate with the ranch given the remoteness of the base camp, and call Zane. He walked a good distance from the campsite, giving himself privacy for the discussion, hoping not to wake Kate. She'd been mentally and physically exhausted and would need a good night's rest before the journey he had planned for tomorrow.

In his head, he rehearsed the case he would lay out to Zane. His by-the-book, legalistic and practical brother would tell him they had to quit. He knew that already. But Josh would rather walk on coals or be skinned alive than admit defeat. He *needed* to wrench some measure of success out of this disaster in order to face himself in the mirror.

In his bones, he believed the making or breaking of this excursion would be the making or breaking of the fledgling McCall Adventures, of the Double M, possibly even of the family's financial future. And the weight of that success or failure rested on him like a thousand-pound bull on his shoulders.

Running the adventures smoothly had been his responsibility. He was the one out here with Kate, the only one who could salvage everything that had gotten screwed up on his watch. And if he could do something to help Kate overcome the phobias that had been born during her childhood trauma, all the better. He couldn't say why he was so compelled to do this for Kate. Maybe as expiation for the accident today that not only retraumatized her but could have cost her her life. He owed Kate, big-time.

He cherished Kate's reluctant agreement to continue with the trip. He considered it a tiny vote of trust. A gift. An opportunity he couldn't waste. He wanted to revive her spirit of adventure more than he could explain, even to himself. He saw something in Kate that spoke to a secret part of his soul, something just beyond his grasp of understanding.

When Zane answered his cell, Josh could hear the fatigue and stress in his brother's voice. "It's me," Josh said. "What's happening on your end?"

"A crap storm. That's what."

Josh rubbed an eye with the heel of his free hand. "Tell me."

"Our insurance company is suspending our coverage until a full investigation can be made. If they find reason to believe we were negligent, they could cancel our policy. No one will write us a policy with that on the books. Not for a price we can afford."

"Did you explain about the sabotage? That we didn't—"

"No, Josh," Zane said dryly. "I forgot." He snorted. "Of course I told them. And they want to see the police report as part of their investigation. I'm scheduled to accompany the sheriff's deputy out there first thing in the morning. We'll bring you two in then. Y'all okay overnight?"

"Yeah, we're okay. But, uh…we're planning to keep going."

"No." Zane's tone was flat and final. "Absolutely not. The cops want to talk to both of you, get your statements. You both need to be checked by a doctor."

"We're fine. Just scraped up some." He rubbed his sore shoulder, refusing to tell his brother exactly how banged up he was.

"Regardless, man. I'm pulling the plug on this trip. We'll get you first thing tomorrow."

Josh chafed at his brother's dictate. "You don't get

to make the decision unilaterally, Zane. What do Brady and Piper say about this?"

"They want what's best for the company, same as I do."

"And I think scrapping this trip is a mistake." He paced a small clearing in the trees and angled his head to look up at the nearly full moon. "Kate and I talked tonight. She's agreed to keep going, at least a little farther. If I can show her the potential of the business, I can—"

"She's a marketing rep, Josh. Not an investor or travel guru whose disapproval versus her endorsement will change the course of our launch."

"So you're saying she doesn't matter?" Josh replied testily.

"What matters is if she decides to sue us. We need to put a cap on this situation quickly. All evening, her coworker has been up in my grill about bringing Kate back to the ranch, and asking what we were going to do to, quote, 'make this right.' I've been trying for hours to appease her, handle the insurance rep's questions, make arrangements with the cops and convince Mom that I didn't leave you dead at the bottom of the ravine."

"I get your reasons for wanting to quit. But I've spent the evening talking with Kate, getting to know her. I have my own reasons to want to keep going."

"That reason better not be because you're trying to get into her pants."

Josh pulled the phone away from his ear to glare at it as if he blamed the phone for his brother's harsh comment. Putting it back to his ear, he said, "Wow. I can't believe you."

He heard Zane sigh heavily. "Sorry, man. I take it back. That was a low blow."

"Yeah." Josh gripped the satellite phone tighter.

"Josh, I know you're disappointed. But bringing you two in tomorrow is the right call."

Josh clenched his back teeth, and something dark and ugly brewed in his core, expanding and making him sweat despite the cool night.

Throwing in the towel would be easy. Might even be the smart thing to do. But he hadn't earned the reputation of being the reckless twin by always doing the safe, smart thing. As much as he wanted to change his family's perception of him as the ne'er-do-well brother, the black, urgent *something* deep inside him pushed him forward. Calling it quits chafed his pride, his ambition, his desire to get things right for his family's sake. Stopping now was tantamount to admitting defeat and resigning to failure. He couldn't do it. Just the thought of what quitting would mean to the business, his family, sucked the breath from him. He paced faster, trying to burn off the edgy, raw feeling that gnawed at him.

And what about Kate? He couldn't let her go home thinking she'd failed in any way. He wanted, *needed* to prove something both to himself and to her. He couldn't leave her with this horrible memory, let her go home with an even deeper fear of taking risks.

No, quitting was not an option for him. "Zane, I can still salvage…*something* from this mess. I know I can. Trust me to fin—"

"Decision's made, Josh." Zane interrupted. "I'll be out there with the cops around eight in the morning. Be ready to leave when we get there."

He grunted, frustration roiling deep inside him.

He disconnected without agreeing to Zane's order. He balled his free hand in a fist and fought the urge to throw the satellite phone. *No. I can't quit.* When his brother arrived with the cavalry at the base camp in the morning, he planned for him and Kate to be gone.

Chapter 5

"Kate? Kate, wake up. Time to get moving."

The whisper nudged her out of sleep. The unfamiliarity of the voice and her lumpy bedding confused her. When she rolled over to blink the morning into focus, her stiff muscles protested, and she groaned.

"I know. It's early, but I have coffee made and your choice of granola bars for breakfast," the warm male voice said.

She angled a bleary-eyed glance at the parted flaps of her tent. Josh's bright smile greeted her, and he reached in to grab her toes in friendly encouragement. "Come on, sunshine. We need to be on the trail in the next thirty minutes."

"Be advised," she grumbled, her voice thick with sleep, "I'm not a morning person."

"I'm getting a sense of that," he said with a wink as he disappeared, letting the tent flap close again.

She wiggled the zipper on her sleeping bag down and made more disgruntled noises when chilly air rushed into her snug cocoon. She sniffed the fresh air, though, and caught the aroma of both coffee and bacon. Worth getting up for. If she had to.

She used both hands to scratch her head and finger comb her hair. Then, while she worked up the motivation to leave her bed, she listened to the shuffling sounds outside as Josh moved around the campsite, the twitter of the birds in the trees, and the crackle of the revived campfire. Judging by the thin amount of light in the tent, she knew it had to be quite early. Apparently, Josh kept rancher's hours even away from the ranch.

"Okay. Let's do this," she muttered to herself and rolled to her knees. Her entire body was sore and tight from the trauma of her fall and the extreme tension she'd been through yesterday. She arched her back like a cat and rotated her head, stretching her neck muscles. She wanted a hot shower at least as much as she wanted coffee, but she guessed that wasn't in the picture. Crawling to the fresh clothes she'd set out the night before, she dressed as quickly as her stiff muscles and half-awake brain could manage.

"Why are we in such a hurry to get going this morning?" she croaked loud enough to be heard through the tent flaps.

He didn't answer right away, and she was about to repeat the question louder when he said, "We want plenty of time to reach the pickup point before dark."

She paused in buttoning a blouse over her T-shirt. "We'll be rafting *all day*?"

Another hesitation before he answered. "Not exactly. So, how do you take your coffee? I'll fix you a cup."

She pushed back the tent flap and crawled out. "Cream and sugar, but I'll make it." Nodding to the bacon sizzling in the pan on a rack over the campfire, she asked, "You sharing that manna?"

"By all means." He looked her up and down, his gaze lingering on her breasts as she stretched her back and raised her arms over her head. "How did you sleep?"

"Like I was in a sleeping bag in the woods where it was twenty-five degrees colder than I like my bedroom at night." She smiled at him to soften what he could have taken as a complaint. "Not too bad, once I fell asleep."

"We'll be hiking a bit to get to the point where we'll launch the raft. How sore are you today?"

She poured herself coffee and rolled her shoulders as she added sugar. "Stiff, somewhat achy. If you have any around this campsite, I'll take a side of ibuprofen with my breakfast."

He rose to dig through his backpack. "Each of the backpacks has a small first aid kit included. Mine's more elaborate, but if you need another tablet later today, you should have a packet or two in your kit." He offered her the small bottle of pain medicine, and she shook out a dose.

"Thanks." She swallowed the tablets with a sip of hot coffee, savoring the warmth and the flavor. "Ah, nectar of the gods."

Josh chuckled. "No arguments here." He lifted the pan from the fire rack. "And nothing goes better with nectar than bacon."

They ate their breakfast of bacon, granola bars, bananas and coffee, sharing companionable conversation about trifling things. Kate noticed a certain restlessness in Josh that mirrored the uneasiness she had about what might lie ahead as they traveled on today. Was he jumpy because of what happened yesterday or had something else made him antsy?

As soon as they finished eating, he doused the fire and packed up his backpack in short order. Within minutes he was ready to hike out. Kate, who moved slowly most mornings, rushed to brush her teeth and jam the last of her supplies into her pack.

"All righty then." He gave the campsite one last sweeping glance as they left. "We're off." But they hadn't gone more than a few hundred feet into the woods before he asked her to wait while he did one last thing at the camp.

She obliged, using a fallen tree as a bench to wait on him. Josh returned in a few moments, his expression oddly guilty-looking and his smile strained.

"Is everything okay, Josh?" she asked as she fell in step behind him.

"Sure. Why?"

"You seem anxious or restless somehow."

He glanced back over his shoulder, sending her a quick grin. "Just eager to get going. It's going to be a great day."

The sooner they booked it outta there, the better. Josh knew Zane would be pissed that he didn't follow the plan his bossy twin had laid out. Josh could only hope that Zane would not press the issue and come after them. He'd written Zane a note in his tent after

Kate went to sleep, hoping to explain his reasoning, but Zane could be as stubborn as Josh was. That was one trait they shared, even if they were different in many other ways.

He'd concluded his note,

Don't follow us. I know what I am doing, and I can handle anything that comes up. I'll be alert for more vandalism. You probably think this is a mistake, but as part owner of the business, I have a right to disagree and make my own call. I just cannot justify giving up. I believe this is what is best, not only for McCall Adventures, but for Kate, as well. Have Dawn explain what I'm talking about. I'm convinced that if Kate doesn't face her fears now, if yesterday's events are left to fester in her head, she'll only end up with greater and more paralyzing fears down the road. I can't in good conscience let that happen. I know I can help her find her courage again. I need to help her.

My plan is to meet you at the takeout point on the river this evening around dark. But if Kate agrees to keep going after the rafting, we may be out here another day or two, so don't panic if we don't show up at the pickup spot. I'll call for pickup when we have accomplished what we set out to do. Josh

After leaving the note where he was sure Zane would find it, he hurried back to meet up with Kate and put some distance between them and the campsite before his brother showed up.

Because, yeah…Zane would be plenty pissed.

* * *

Once Josh returned, they set out hiking. Kate trudged along behind him, regretting the fact that his large backpack hid most of his glorious backside from view. When he said nothing for several minutes following his return, she said, "Josh, are you sure everything is okay?"

"Um…yeah. Of course."

The brief hesitation before his pat response was the most telling part of his reply.

She sighed and squared her shoulders as she walked. "Listen, I have a request. No, it's a nonnegotiable condition."

He paused and turned to face her. "A condition for what?"

"For continuing with you today and any farther I may go."

He narrowed his eyes, clearly stunned by her high-handed pronouncement. "What sort of condition?"

"I expect you to be one hundred percent honest with me at all times. If I ask a question, I don't want a soft sell or caginess. I want straight answers and complete disclosure. I may be nervous about this trip, but I'm a big girl, and I can handle the truth even when it's unpleasant."

He arched a black eyebrow and gave her a measuring scrutiny. A beat later he lifted the corner of his mouth. "I see."

"So…will you do that?" She met his pale blue eyes, which even in the shade of the trees and shadow of his wide-brimmed cowboy hat had a piecing brightness about them that made her pulse scamper. "Will you promise to give me the full, unvarnished truth from here on out?"

He ducked his chin once in agreement. "I will."

Satisfied, she motioned to the trail. "Good. Onward, then."

They hiked for more than an hour, traveling mostly downhill, and her stiff muscles loosened up with time and use. Her bruises had turned a scary blue-black but only hurt if she pressed on them. The cut on her forehead had scabbed over, and she removed the bandage he put there, giving the wound air to heal faster. The farther they got from the campsite, the more Josh seemed to relax, and he engaged her in conversation about her job, Dallas sports teams and funny stories about growing up on the ranch as one third of triplets. He'd apparently always been something of a daredevil and capable of finding mischief without effort.

"One time I filled Piper's boots with manure."

"What!" Kate squawked, half amused and half indignant on Piper's behalf. "Josh!"

"She was so mad. They were her favorite boots, too." He shook his head as he laughed. "Zane, being the rule follower and responsible one, ratted me out."

"That surprises me. I'd have thought as twins you'd have had each other's backs."

"Oh, we did. There was plenty of stuff we had on each other, and there were ways we protected each other, but he felt bad for Piper. We have a pretty strong bond with her, too. And when Mom gave us the stink-eye, wanting to know who did it and threatening to take away our Game Boys, he caved. I did lose my Game Boy for a week, but Zane let me share his."

"I'm guessing Piper got new boots?"

"Naturally. Better than the original ones." She could hear the smile in his voice. "You know, she's talking about wearing boots under her dress when she and Brady get married."

"Fitting for a ranch wedding, I'd say. When is the big day?"

"Late June."

"Ah, a June bride. June weddings are supposed to be good luck."

"That's fortunate, but not why she picked the date."

"Why then?"

"By then we should have the additions to the herd branded, the sorting done and all of the animals moved out to their summer pastures." He stopped long enough to pick a stem of some sort of wildflower growing by the trail. Bringing it to her, he tucked it in her hair, the stem propped on her ear. The back of his fingers brushed her temple, and a sensation like static electricity shot through her. He smiled as he surveyed his handiwork, and the tingling feeling spread.

"Once the spring season jobs are done," he continued, "they'll have a few days for a honeymoon before the summer haying work starts."

To mask the discombobulation his touch had stirred in her, Kate chortled a wry laugh, adding, "Squeezing a wedding in between branding and haying. Isn't that romantic?"

"Maybe not, but it's life on a working ranch." Turning ninety degrees, he pointed ahead of them. "The river is just up here. If you listen, you can hear the rapids."

She'd been seeing glimpses of the river through the trees for the last several minutes, but when she stopped and focused her attention on the noises around her, she picked the sound of rushing water out over the rustling leaves and birdsong. A thrum of nervous tension flowed through her.

Josh pulled out a canteen and took a long drink before offering it to her.

She shook her head and waved it off. "No thanks."

He extended it closer. "Rule of thumb in hiking and outdoor sports is eat before you're hungry, drink before you're thirsty and rest before you're tired."

She considered the axiom. Good advice, she figured, so with a nod, she pulled out her own canteen and drank.

When he took another drink, her eyes were drawn to the arch of his throat, the movement of his Adam's apple as he swallowed, the fine sheen of sweat that made his sun-bronzed skin glisten. The clench in her belly this time had more to do with her sexy guide than her qualms about the impending challenge of white water.

"Your backpack has protein bars, packaged cookies and gorp for snacking," Josh said as he stashed his canteen. "Try to eat a little every hour or two to keep your energy level up and feed your muscles."

"Gorp?"

He drew a plastic bag from his pack now and held it up for her to see. "Voilà! Gorp. Granola, oats, raisins and peanuts. G-O-R-P. Plus we add pretzels and M&M's."

"So...trail mix."

He flashed a lopsided grin. "Yeah. Hikers' nickname for trail mix." He opened the bag and held it out to her. "Have some."

She took a small handful and nibbled as they continued hiking. Josh shifted the conversation to explain how the rafting would work. Basically, he'd steer, and she'd provide extra paddling as needed. He told her what equipment she'd receive (one paddle, a helmet and life jacket) and how to handle mishaps (falling out of the boat, overturned raft, hitting an obstruction or getting stuck on a sandbar, to name the most common) should they arise.

A tiny squeak of worry escaped her throat before she could catch it. He slowed his pace and faced her, adding, "I'm not saying any of those things will happen, but you need to know ahead of time that they could. If you are prepared, these things are much less of a big deal. It's when you panic and react the wrong way—like fighting the current—that problems arise."

She placed a hand over her belly and took a slow breath, telling herself to calm down. "I'm okay," she said as much to convince herself as to reassure him.

At the launch spot, a small hut that looked like it had been built many years earlier sat on the rocky bank of the small river. Vines had grown up the sides of the hut, and some of the wood appeared to be newer than other pieces, clearly marking spots where repairs had been made. The front of the hut had a wide door with a hasp and padlock, intended to keep the door closed. Except the hasp had been ripped free of the outer wall and dangled at an angle. The door stood wide open.

"Damn!" Josh muttered as he approached the hut. "What now?"

Chapter 6

Kate's pulse picked up as she studied the damaged lock and the concern darkening Josh's face. "This wasn't an accident. Was it? You're thinking it was more sabotage."

"It's certainly suspicious, but the jury is still out." He ran a hand over the hut where the hasp had been ripped free. Scarring on the wood around the broken hasp gave evidence of the efforts by someone, or something, to pry the metal closure from the door.

After sliding the straps of his large backpack off, he set the pack on the ground and fished out a flashlight. He shone the light through the opened door of the hut, and together, they took in the disarray of the contents. Plastic storage tubs had been opened and tossed, paddles scattered. Spread throughout were granola bar wrappers and shredded cracker boxes.

"What the hell?" Josh said, picking up one of the torn boxes.

"Y'all were keeping food in here with the equipment?" Kate asked, aghast. "Even I know that's like asking bears to ransack the place."

Josh's mouth tightened as he threw the box aside with more force than necessary. "Hell, no, we didn't keep food in here. Besides bears, it would attract mice and insects and—"

"Well, clearly somebody..." she allowed her voice to trail off as she caught up to his apparent line of thought "...planted it. Trying to attract bears?"

"As good of a guess as I've got." He examined the scarred door again. "Sure looks like the work of a bear."

"So we're back to sabotage. They wanted a bear to get in there and mess up the equipment." She turned full circle scanning the terrain, wondering where that bear had gone.

"And being on the riverbank where they knew a bear would likely come anyway, they upped the likelihood one of the beasts would smell the snacks and tear into the place."

"Smart. And completely devious." She slid her own pack off and rolled her shoulders. "What are you going to do?"

He shook his head as he began digging through the tumbled rafting equipment. "Nothing."

She frowned. "Nothing?"

"Nothing I can do at the moment. Damage is done." He heaved a deep breath and gave her a strained smile. "So we move on."

She hated that whoever was vandalizing the McCall's

ranch was getting away with destroying so much, hurting Josh's family and threatening their business. Not to mention the lives the saboteur had put in danger. Including her own. Anger swelled in her, bringing a hot flush to her skin and a roil of acid in her gut. She refused to dismiss this destruction as easily as Josh.

But as she watched Josh pull one of the bear-battered rafts out of the shed, she came up with little. Frustration tangled with her anger, and she knew Josh had to be feeling the same cocktail of hard-edged emotions.

Kate dug into her pack, took out her camera and snapped shots of the damage, zooming in on the claw marks on the wood door, the scattered food wrappers and the chaos in the shed.

Josh knocked a cobweb off a paddle, then tossed it onto the rocks. "My dad helped Zane and me build this storage shed like fifteen years ago. And we've never had the first problem with animals bothering the stuff. We took precautions. We sealed up things that were vulnerable to mice and weather. And we never left food here."

He seemed to be venting as much as explaining to her. She continued snapping pictures, and he sent her a hooded glance. "I hardly think these are marketing-worthy shots, Kate."

"Well, like you photographed the zip line yesterday, I thought I should record the damage for any authorities that may need to see this evidence."

"Right. Of course." His shoulders drooped, and his expression broke her heart. His family was under attack, and he had no clue how to protect the people, the ranch, the lifestyle he loved. After a moment spent staring at the ground with tension radiating off him in waves, Josh released a sigh. "Good thinking. Thanks."

He went back to work, dragging out a large rubber raft that had been deflated and rolled up for storage. "There should be an air pump in here somewhere. Give a shout if you see it."

She stopped him with a hand on his arm. "You okay?"

He pulled a face that reflected his surprise, then gave her another smile that left his eyes blank and flat, the muscles in his cheeks taut. "Sure. I'm okay."

He tried again to move into the hut, and she tightened her grip.

He avoided her gaze, so she stepped in front of him and raised her head to meet his eyes. "I'm sorry about all this." She slid her hand down his arm to wrap her fingers around his hand. He'd provided comfort and support to her yesterday, and she couldn't bear to turn her back on his obvious distress now. "You don't have to put on a good face in front of me or pretend this isn't tearing you up inside. If it were my family, my ranch, my startup business under attack, I'd want to rage and cry and kick some vandal butt over this." She waved a hand behind her to the destruction.

Josh's hand squeezed hers. "Hell, yeah. But there's no vandal butt handy to kick at the moment."

"How about a hug instead?" she said, wrapping her arms around his neck. She rubbed his back and felt the shudder that rippled through him. "I can't imagine how maddening it must be to see someone hurting your family and be unable to stop it."

"Oh, he'll be stopped." His tone was low and cold. "I've reached the end of my patience with the sheriff's pitiful efforts finding this guy. When we get back to the ranch, I *will* find a way to stop him."

An hour later, they finally found an undamaged raft and had it inflated and ready to launch. Josh plucked two useable life jackets, two paddles and two helmets from the tumbled contents of the shed, and because they'd had such rotten luck lately, he put an extra paddle in the raft, just in case they lost one. Next, he secured his pack with the satellite phone in the raft, covered with tarps to protect it from the spray as they traversed the rapids.

Once Kate had loaded her backpack and taken her seat at the front of the raft, paddle in hand, he pushed the inflatable boat into the water. He hopped in the back just as the current caught it.

"Forward left!" he called to Kate, instructing her which side of the raft to paddle on as they set their course downstream. The first rapid of the trip was rather tame, no significant obstructions or drops. A good opportunity to ease Kate into the adventure of white-water rafting. In fact, with the exception of a couple of class 3 rapids near the end of the stretch of river they'd cover, the river never got rougher than class 2. Good enough to give a beginner a thrill but rather boring for him. Maybe one day they'd make the Arkansas River's class 3 and 4 rapids part of the adventure. Assuming there was a McCall Adventures left after this trip.

Gritting his back teeth, Josh shoved the depressing thought aside. He needed to focus on steering the raft, ensuring that Kate made it home safely from *this* trip.

He'd no sooner finished that thought than he heard Kate gasp.

"Kate? What—"

"Look!" she said in a stage whisper, pointing to the grassy hillside above the river, where a pair of elk grazed. He smiled and silently thanked the elk for making an appearance. Enjoying encounters with the abundant wildlife and beauty of the Colorado landscape was one of the bonuses they'd hoped to share with clients.

Kate set her paddle across her lap and dug her camera from the top of her pack. She snapped a few shots of the elk as they floated past and sent him a smile full of wonder.

Something deep inside him flipped as he met her bright eyes. She was breathtaking—her skin aglow in the sunshine, her hair windblown and shimmering with golden highlights, her face radiant with the simple pleasure of their encounter with the majestic beasts. Au naturel, Kate was prettier than any model with full makeup and coiffed hair. Seeing a hint of pink on her cheeks, he asked, "Did you remember sunscreen this morning? The air may be cool, but the sun is relentless out here on the river. It reflects off the water, too, for a double whammy."

She twisted her lips into a frown. "Shoot. I forgot."

After re-stashing her camera, she dug into her pack for the tube of sun protection, and he openly stared as she dabbed it on her chin, cheeks and forehead, then rubbed the cream in. She squirted a dot onto her finger and coated her puckered lips before moving on to her arms. Watching her dab and caress and smooth the lotion was about as erotic as anything he'd seen in recent days.

She was his idea of real beauty. Seeing the purple columbine blossom she still wore tucked in her wheat-blond hair tugged at something deep inside him. A possessiveness? As if the flower marked her as his? He gave his head a little shake and shoved that notion away.

They might have been through some harrowing events together yesterday and shared some personal conversation around the fire last night, but she was a long way from "his." And what in the world was he doing thinking in terms of *any* woman being his? While his family was mucking through this financial crisis, searching for the saboteur and fixing the mess this first adventure trip had turned into, he had no room in his life for a romantic relationship.

But his private remonstrations didn't stop him from wondering what it would be like to kiss Kate. More than once today he'd found his gaze straying to her lips while his thoughts ventured beyond the idea of just a kiss. When he'd held her yesterday, he couldn't help but notice how good she felt in his arms. No bony, flat-chested runway chic, Kate had curves in just the right proportion, and when the high emotion of their crisis had passed yesterday, he'd noticed the soft crush of her bottom and pillow of her breasts when she'd sat in his lap, trembling. At the time, he'd known his thoughts were inappropriate for the circumstances, but that didn't stop his libido from rearing its adrenaline-fueled head.

Now, in the light of a new day, with some distance between them and the scene of the disaster with the zip line, he appreciated her shape again. Maybe when they got back to the ranch and some of the pressure was off them both, he'd see if Kate was interested in a vacation fling. And Piper, with her talk about the advisability of mixing business and pleasure, could go jump.

After a couple of hours of paddling, Kate's shoulders began to throb. Rafting clearly worked muscles her regular visits to the elliptical machine at the gym didn't. A fine sheen of sweat had popped out on her brow. No, she mentally corrected herself, in Texas, women didn't sweat. They *glistened.* The euphemism brought a smile to her lips as she paused from paddling to wipe her forehead with the back of her hand.

"Are you hot?"

Kate glanced back over her shoulder. "Pardon?"

Josh chuckled. "Okay, I know you're sexy as hell. What I mean is, do you need a break? There's a spot just ahead where we can swim if you want to cool down."

Sexy as hell? Kate goggled at his assessment before reminding herself, *He's a player. Flirtatious talk means little coming from him.* She cleared her throat and used the pads of her fingers to catch the moisture beading in front of her ears. "Yeah. I could use a break."

"All right. The place I mean is just around the next bend." She heard some rustling and glanced back to see him pull out the satellite phone from his pack. Turning back to search the bend ahead for obstructions in the water, she listened to his end of the conversation.

"Yeah, it's me. Just wanted to tell you we're fine, but we're going to make a stop at the bluff for a swim. Yeah, I know." He fell quiet for a moment. "Maybe around dark." She could hear a male voice, one that didn't sound happy, coming through the line, before

Josh replied, "It's all good, Zane. We'll talk later. We'll see you when we see you. If it's dark or…hell, tomorrow even, don't have a cow. I know what I'm doing."

He disconnected and stashed the sat phone in his backpack again.

"Tomorrow? Why would it be tomorrow?" she asked, her stomach flipping.

"I just said that because Zane was being an ass. He's a control freak and nothing bugs him more than not getting his way." He sighed. "He knows I know what I'm doing out here. This, the rafting and hiking and adventures, is the part of the business that I'm supposed to be in charge of, but he's micromanaging from the ranch."

"Well, the accident yesterday threw everything and everyone into a little chaos. Maybe you could cut him a little slack for being worried about us?"

Josh grunted. "Maybe. But he should trust me more. I know why he's mad, but…"

He didn't finish the sentence, and Kate sensed the unspoken words told a whole lot about Josh. She felt a prick of disappointment that he didn't share the rest with her. She'd thought that after the promises they'd exchanged this morning, he might be more open to confiding in her. And why did confidences with Josh matter so much to her? Because she'd told him about her worst days, the nightmare that still haunted her, and she wanted to balance the scales? Or did it mean she craved a more intimate relationship with her devastatingly handsome guide?

She pushed that notion aside. She would not, could not repeat the mistakes that had burned her before. A long-term, meaningful relationship with Josh was geographically and practically unlikely, and, therefore, had to be off the table.

They paddled on a bit, quietly, and she drank in the beauty of the snowcapped peaks in the distance, the spring wildflowers along the riverbanks and the pale, clear blue of the Colorado sky. Warmth swelled in her chest. The sky was the same blue as Josh's eyes…

Stop it! She rolled her eyes at how easily her brain had drawn the sappy analogy, and her physical response to the thought of him. She was acting like a besotted school girl. Yes, he had breathtaking blue eyes, an engaging grin and a tempting tush, but she needed to draw the line at simply admiring the man's striking features. Like one would appreciate a beautiful painting at a museum, she could only look, then she had to move on.

In an effort to refocus her thoughts, she said, "You didn't tell him about the destruction at the shed."

"Naw. He'll learn soon enough. Didn't want to get into *that* conversation until we can talk in person."

After giving her shoulders a hard rub, she started paddling again. As they drifted around the turn in the river, they reached a widening in the water where a still pool had formed in an inlet to the side of the current. Following Josh's directive, they paddled to the flat, rocky bank below a bluff where trickles of runoff dripped in small rivulets. Trees grew out from the hillside, casting shade over parts of the natural pool, while the sun sparkled on ripples and dragonflies zipped over the surface of the water with a soft hum of their wings. Kate drank in the tranquil spot and smiled. "Wow. I need to get pictures here for sure."

"Agreed. This has always been one of my favorite

spots. Piper, Zane and I would come up here to swim every summer when we were growing up." Having removed his boots at some point, Josh hopped out as they drifted into shallow water and tugged the front of the raft onto the bank. She laid down her paddle and swung her backpack onto her arm. When Josh held out a hand to help her step out, she gripped his fingers and climbed from the rubber boat. Her legs ached from being cramped in the raft, and she stretched the muscles in her back.

He took the pack from her, grabbed his boots from the back of the raft, then dropped it all on the bank, away from the water. Tossing his hat on top of the items, he took her hand again. "Come on. You'll love this."

"Wha—"

He set off at a jog, towing her with him as he sprinted up a narrow, rocky path that ascended the embankment to the top of the bluff. Cresting the hill, he led her out on an outcropping of granite where they had a view of the quiet inlet from thirty feet above the clear pool. Kate cast her gaze around the peaceful scene as a yellow butterfly flitted past. "Amazing. But my camera is in my bag, and my bag is down by the raft where you left it."

He walked even farther out, tugging her toward the edge of the rock. After pulling off his shirt, he tossed it aside, and while she gaped, distracted by his broad, muscled chest, he said, "There'll be time for pictures later. First we swim."

Then, with a wink, he unzipped his shorts and kicked them off, as well, leaving him in only his navy boxer briefs.

Distracted as she was by the sight of his nearly naked and toned physique, she almost missed his added, "And the best way to get in the water is to jump."

Chapter 7

After a second of delay, his words sank in, and she blinked at him. "Jump?"

"Yeah. It's only about a twenty-five-foot drop. And the water's plenty deep in the pool. We did this all the time as kids."

Her mouth dried, but she wasn't sure if the aridness was due to trepidation over his proposed leap or his dishabille. "Look, Josh...I know what you're doing, and I appreciate that you want to help me. But...I'm not jumping."

He paused, arching one eyebrow as he sent her a cocky grin. "What I'm *doing* is showing you the most fun you can have with your clothes on."

She returned a wry look. "Then why are you taking your clothes off?"

His cheek dimpled as he smiled at her. "Because

I don't want to spend the rest of the afternoon in wet clothes." He hitched his head toward the drop-off. "Come on. You can do it. It's not a huge jump, but it is incredibly fun."

She twisted her mouth as she considered his suggestion. She'd had a favorite swimming spot near the family farm in Missouri where she and her brother had swung by a rope on a tree branch to hurtle themselves into the pond. They'd yelled like Tarzan and dared each other to attempt flips. The memory made her smile. Fear hadn't dogged those summer days with her brother. Before…

Her heart ached for the lost courage, but Kate shook her head. "I don't know."

Josh's expression reflected his disappointment in a flicker before he shrugged and moved to the edge of the drop-off. "Are you sure? I'd hate for you to pass it up and regret the missed opportunity later."

Kate felt her chest tighten with anxiety. Without knowing it, he'd cut to the heart of her inner turmoil. For years since her accident at the silo, she'd let so many things pass her by, including a high school class trip that included a ropes course and an opportunity in college to go skydiving. She'd listened to her fear, given in to her doubt and allowed moments to slip away that she could never get back. Chances her inner child, her free spirit cried out for, but her wounded soul squelched.

"I…can't."

He gave her a level, patient look. "You can. And you should." He paused a moment, letting his comment sink in, then added, "If you change your mind, I'll be down there waiting for you." With one last puckish grin, he saluted her. "YOLO!"

He took a small step back, pivoted, then took a long leap forward, off the bluff, whooping his delight.

Kate rushed forward in time to see him splash into the water. A moment later he broke the surface, swiping his hair back with his hand, and giving another joyful hoot of enjoyment. He tipped his head back to gaze up at her, and his face split with a wide white smile. "That was better than I remembered!" He motioned with a big swoop of his arm. "Come on, Kate! The water's only a little frigid."

She snorted a laugh. "Oh, yeah, that'll change my mind. Telling me the water's frigid."

"Only a little frigid." He ducked under the surface again and came back up with his face tipped up so that his hair slicked back over his skull. Water glistened on his shoulders and dripped from his chin. "What do I have to do to convince you to jump? Huh?"

She shook her head. "Josh, I'm just not ready."

"How about a reward?" he shouted up to her. "You jump, you get a prize."

She chuckled and shook her head. "What kind of prize?"

"Oh, ho ho! So I've got your attention now with the lure of a reward?" As the sun beat down on his chiseled cheeks and stubble-dusted jaw, his expression radiated good humor and teasing. Her heart thumped harder as she gazed down at his handsome face and his tempting lips quirked in a lopsided grin.

"No. I'm just…curious. What do you have to offer? A granola bar? A glow stick?" *You.* Her heartbeat became flustered at the possibility that flashed through her brain. "I have all the same things in my pack that you do."

"No, not a granola bar. Something better. But you'll have to come down here to see what it is." Was she just imagining the sparkle of mischief in his oh-so-blue eyes?

A pang wrenched deep inside her at the idea of disappointing him. He'd been so kind and thoughtful the past two days. He'd truly taken care of her in every way. He'd comforted and encouraged her. Kept her warm, made her laugh, shared his private pain. She hated that her reluctance meant she'd let him down.

Close behind that thought, something hot pricked her heart. Call it stubbornness or guilt or the desire not to fail in this moment.

In an instant, determination surged in her. Acting quickly, before her fear caught up to her and stole her initiative, she scuttled back from the edge of the bluff and toed off her tennis shoes.

Josh's heart sank as Kate disappeared from the top of the rock. Retreating again. "Kate?"

He waited a moment for her to return to his view at the edge of the outcropping of rock. When she didn't reply or reappear after a few seconds, he called again. "Come on, Texas. You can do it!"

He tried to keep his tone light and encouraging, but in his chest, frustration weighed heavily on him. He'd felt sure he could help Kate find her lost spirit of adventure. He needed to know he'd done at least that much for her, since everything else about this trip, his new business venture, his attempts to help save his family from financial disaster had been such a failure. He needed a win, damn it! He needed just one thing to go—

A high-pitched cross between a scream and a squeal pealed from atop the hill. His heart stumbling with alarm—was Kate all right?—his gaze shot to the top of the bluff. *"Kate?"*

Stripped down to her bra and panties, she came racing out to the edge of the bluff, took a running jump and hurtled out into the air. Her cry tuned up an octave and a few decibels as she windmilled her arms and tucked in her legs on the way down. She splashed into the water about ten feet from him, and without hesitating, he headed toward her before she even came back up to the surface. He realized he was holding his breath when, at last, she erupted from the water with a shriek.

"Kate?"

She shouted a curse and blinked the water from her eyes. "A little frigid, my eye! It's *freezing!*"

He couldn't help himself. She looked so miserably cold, so irritated with him, so…breathtakingly beautiful, his relief and happiness burst from him in a belly laugh. He swept her into his embrace, their legs tangling as they treaded water, and he seized her mouth with his.

She seemed startled by the kiss, her body stiffening briefly before she wrapped her arms around his neck. But he was the one who was shocked. He hadn't expected the jolt of pure pleasure, the to-his-core electric charge. Sure, he'd been aroused kissing other women— and there'd been plenty of kisses in his past. But holding Kate, celebrating this victory over her fear with her, sharing *this kiss* filled Josh with something more than the physical.

His brain was a bit too stunned by his reaction to analyze what he felt beyond the sweetness of the moment, the power of the connection and the desire to deepen the kiss. Which he did. Operating on impulse, his go-to mode, Josh slanted his mouth over hers and cradled the back of her head with a splayed hand. His legs scissor-kicked automatically, keeping them afloat while he explored the seam of her lips, the tip of her tongue with his own. Heat suffused his body, chasing away the chill of the water.

Several moments later, she tore her mouth from his, panting for a breath. He allowed his gaze to travel down to her soaked bra, a simple, flesh-toned satin number that clung to her erect nipples, and the exposed curve of her breasts just beneath the surface of the water. Another wave of lust slammed him, and he couldn't stop the growl of approval that rumbled from his throat. "Damn, Kate, you are one sexy woman."

She raised her green gaze to his and tugged up a corner of her mouth. "You're not bad yourself, cowboy."

Her compliment sparked something at his core. He'd had women ogle him for years. In truth, he relished the attention. But knowing she returned his feelings of attraction was deeply satisfying in a way he'd never experienced before.

He nipped lightly at the tip of her nose. "You did it."

She drew and released a deep breath before a bright smile lit her face. "I did it."

"I knew you could."

Her grin twisted in irony. "I didn't."

"So what convinced you?" he asked, wiping drips of water from her eyebrow with his thumb.

She chuckled and shook her head. "I don't know.

You. My old moxie. Who knows? I didn't take the time to overanalyze it when the courage came. I just... jumped."

"I knew you had it in you."

Her expression softened. Warmed.

He leaned his forehead against hers and whispered, "Ready to go again?"

Go again? Oh, yes. So long as what they repeated was that toe-curling kiss.

She tipped her head to the side as she eyed him. "If I jump again, do I get another reward?"

His crooked grin said that her request pleased him. "Count on it."

When Josh pulled away from their embrace, taking with him his body heat, she was reminded just how cold the water was. And of her state of undress. And his. A tingle shimmied through her as she skimmed her gaze over his chest and savored the brush of his hard, bare thighs against hers as they treaded water. She became awkwardly aware of the way her nipples had reacted to the icy inlet...and his touch.

She was no prude, but coupled with the amorous kiss she'd returned, she worried that he would read her actions and responses to his overtures the wrong way. Or...maybe her real concern should be that he was reading her exactly the *right* way.

Her body wanted him. Her heart might even be leaning toward further exploration of their sizzling attraction. But her head wasn't on board yet.

Josh was a womanizing flirt who lived three states away from Texas and whom she'd likely never see again after she and Dawn finished working on the

McCall Adventure Ranch campaign. A fling with Josh would be just that. Another fling that went nowhere and left her at loose ends, possibly—no, probably—heartbroken. That sobering reality check more than the frigid water cooled her passions as they swam to the bank and sloshed out of the river.

Barefooted, they picked their way over the rough ground, littered with rocks and stems. Seeing her careful, slow progress, Josh waited for her to catch up to him.

"How about this?" he asked as he swept her into his arms, carrying her cradled against his chest.

"Oh!" She looped her arms around his neck with a gasp. "That's…good actually. I'm kind of a tenderfoot as well as a chicken, I guess."

"Nope. Not a chicken."

She scoffed her disagreement.

"My mother liked to tell us, 'Labels lie.' If you keep calling yourself a chicken, you're giving yourself permission not to prove otherwise."

"But what if it's the truth?"

He lifted a shoulder in dismissal. "You jumped, didn't you?"

"So? I was scared to the point of shaky knees. Still kinda am." Although the quiver in her belly at the moment had more to do with having his arms around her and her body cradled against his bare chest. His skin was warm and smooth and glistened in the sunlight with diamond droplets of water. *This chivalry should be in the promotional brochure*, she thought with a secret grin. *Women would buy out every trip.* Her inner grin shifted to a frown, and a prick of jealousy poked her at the thought of Josh carrying any other woman.

They'd reached the top of the hill, where tufts of grass, smooth rock and packed dirt made for easier barefoot terrain. He set her on the ground and rolled his shoulders to stretch the muscles.

Muscles that flexed and rippled in the most delicious way. Kate pressed a hand to her belly where, in addition to butterflies jumping again, tendrils of desire curled as she recalled their kiss. Clearly she'd lost her senses. Kissing Josh when she knew nothing could come of it was tempting fate.

Tempting...

She released a slow breath. Yes, the word fit well. Josh was definitely tempting...

"A chicken doesn't *do*." He had his arms akimbo, and his gaze drilled her. "You did. You *did* today, and you *did* yesterday. The fact that you were scared just makes you all the braver in my book."

The lack of teasing in his countenance stopped her. He had, in fact, a tender sincerity about him, and she caught her breath as he stared deeply into her eyes. This wasn't flirting or patronization. She saw an earnestness and compassion that caught her off guard. Josh, it seemed, was much more than the adrenaline junkie, playboy cowboy she'd pegged him to be. She shouldn't have been surprised. After all, *labels lie.*

Josh stepped closer, and she shivered. Not because of the cool breeze that buffeted her wet skin, but because of the new insights she had about her traveling partner. In the last few minutes, she'd confirmed his incredible kissing talent, and she'd uncovered a depth and kindness to his personality that made him easier to like...and to fall for.

She didn't need any more reason to find him attractive. She was already struggling to keep her heart at arm's length from his charms.

"Now, let's go prove how *brave* you are again. Together." He laced his fingers with hers and led her to the edge of the bluff again.

Looking down, she experienced another wave of heebie-jeebies. The height seemed so much *more* from this vantage point. An intimidated squeak wiggled loose from her throat, and he squeezed her hand.

"Together on three. Okay?"

She met his eyes. Nodded.

"When we jump, you have to say, 'YOLO!'"

She arched one eyebrow. "Why?"

The corner of his mouth twitched. "It stands for 'you only live once.' And it's McCall triplets tradition."

"I'm not a McCall."

"Today you are. Ready? One, two..."

He'd distracted her with his talk of tradition, and she had no time to brace or balk before he squeezed her hand and shouted, "Three!"

Her legs sprang forward as if on autopilot, and she shouted with him, "YOLO!"

They splashed into the water, still holding hands, and the renewed shock of cold, a spike of adrenaline and a spurt of happiness shimmied through her.

As she surfaced and gulped in air, a giddy giggle bubbled up in her chest. Using the grip he still had on her hand, Josh towed her close, and they laughed, while blinking at each other through wet, spiked eyelashes.

Something hot and dangerous curled inside her as she reveled with Josh in the simple thrill of their leap, the beauty of the sunny day and the notion that for once, she'd conquered her fear.

The water sloshed around them, the crest of the waves they'd created slapping the base of the bluff and rocky bank.

"So…" Josh said, a devious twinkle in his eyes.

She screwed her face in a teasing scowl. "*So* what?"

"So…I think we've proven that you're not a chicken." He smoothed back the dripping ends of her hair and grazed his knuckles along her cheekbone.

She hummed a low note of disagreement. "I set aside my qualms for a low-risk jump. One jump doesn't mean I've miraculously overcome my childhood trauma."

"Two jumps. And point taken. But it *is* a start. An important step. Yeah?"

She drew and released a deep breath, allowing the smile that budded in her chest to blossom on her lips. "Yeah."

His returned grin was confident and adorably smug. "Yeah."

Slipping his hand behind her head, he tugged her close and kissed her again with the same breath-stealing, fantasy-sparking finesse he'd employed before. Kate leaned into him, enjoying the kiss. She'd earned it, hadn't she? After setting aside her inhibitions to leap from that bluff, didn't she deserve to indulge in Josh's kiss?

When she canted back from him, catching her breath, she twisted her mouth as if in thought and said, "Well, that kiss was okay, but I think I'd rather have the granola bar."

Josh quirked an eyebrow. "Ouch!"

"Kidding." She laughed and slid her hand across the water to splash him. Earning a tidal wave in return. She sputtered and launched herself at him, and he ducked, only to come up with her on his shoulders.

"Josh, what are you—?" she started, but he tossed her into the water, dunking her.

The horseplay continued for several minutes, and Kate savored the sound of Josh's deep, musical laughter. He hadn't had much to laugh at in the last day or two, and she sensed the chance to cut loose was as welcome to him as to her.

Finally, after a raucous water battle where she managed to get water up her nose twice, she sputtered, "Uncle! I yield!"

"And I claim as my prize, a kiss!" Josh took her by the wrist and reeled her close again.

But one kiss led to another…and another.

When their legs bumped while treading water, he murmured, "C'mere."

Shifting to his side, he swam toward the sunny bank where large rocks were submerged, forming steps and platforms that allowed them to stand instead of treading water. He claimed one of these boulders and leaned back against another, smiling broadly at her as she joined him. He reached for her hand and drew her close. "Now, where were we?"

Then they were tangled in each other, the rest of the world forgotten. Kate lost herself in Josh's lips, which roamed leisurely from her mouth to her throat, to the shell of her ear. She basked in his touch, his hands stroking her face, massaging her nape and trailing down her spine to cup her bottom. She responded with her own curious exploration, nibbling his earlobes, tracing his collarbone with her tongue and greedily measuring the expanse of his corded back and shoulders with bold strokes of her palm.

When she lifted her head, inhaling a breath tinged with his earthy scent, she tipped her gaze toward the sun and squinted against the bright light. She could almost hear Dawn's applause and *attagirl*.

Decision time. She had the opportunity to put a stop to this seduction. Her mind briefly flickered to past dalliances…and the resulting heartache. She'd sworn to herself not to go this route again, but his kisses had turned her knees to jelly, her resolve to dust, and she found herself pressing into him, snuggling her body against the heat radiating from his. The proof of his arousal strained against his wet underwear and fit far too well in the V of her legs, where her own need throbbed and begged for more.

Stroking a hand up her spine, he paused at the clasp of her bra and skillfully unhooked it. Evidence that he had experience in these matters. Another warning bell clanged in her brain. She didn't need a crystal ball to know Josh was not in this for the long haul. He'd take his pleasure and bid her a polite goodbye when the adventure trip was over.

An uneasy flutter stirred in her gut, even as Josh slid her bra down her arms and cupped her breasts in his palms. The callouses on his work-roughened hands lightly abraded her nipples, sending ribbons of sweet sensation to her womb. When he ducked his head to suck one sensitive bud into his mouth, the jolt of pleasure was so pure and intense, she moaned her satisfaction. Her knees buckled, and her body sagged closer to his.

Josh's hands roamed from her bottom down her

thighs, then up again to caress the sensitive skin at the small of her back. He seemed to know exactly where to touch her, and how, to ignite her passion. She clung to his broad shoulders, returning his kisses, as he explored and aroused. Heaven help her, the man knew what he was doing, and he did it well!

And still the voice of caution battled the growing desire that thrummed in her veins. She was on fire. Weak with wanting. Burning from the inside out. She wrapped her legs around him when he lifted her to straddle him.

His fingers hooked in her panties, ready to finish her disrobing, and he murmured, "Say you want me, you want this."

Let go. Give in. Follow your desire, her heart whispered.

Remember Jason, her head said.

A shudder rolled through her, and she rasped, "No."

He stilled, raised his head and blinked at her, confused. "Kate?"

Tears burned her eyes, and she shook her head. "I'm sorry. I—I can't. I—"

She felt the tension enter his body, the effort he made to rein in his desire before he set her down, easing away from her. Disappointment was plain in his face. "All right," he said, his voice gruff.

Her grip on his shoulders tightened, and she resisted when he would have pushed her back. "I want you, Josh. I do. I just...can't—"

He gave her a tight smile and stroked her cheek. "It's okay. I know that a girl's *no* means no. You don't have to explain."

"But I do. I—"

"We should get going." He levered away and snagged her bra from the rock where he'd tossed it. "Zane'll be waiting on us."

"Josh!" She tried to catch his hand. He seemed more than just frustrated or disappointed that she'd stopped him. Not mad exactly, but…could he be hurt?

For him to be hurt that she'd called a stop would mean he cared. She already suspected there was more than met the eye to Mr. Happy-Go-Lucky McCall, and his pensiveness as she donned her bra and watched him roll tension from his neck and shoulders supported that theory.

She followed as he dived back into the water. They swam around the bluff, toward the shore where they'd left the raft, and Kate stumbled out on weak legs. Her thigh muscles quivered from fatigue and lingering desire.

She was still musing about the interlude, when Josh drew her back to the present with a grumbled curse. As she slicked water from her arms and belly, she sent him a cautious glance. "What's wrong?"

He raised a hand and motioned to the bank in general. "Look around. Notice anything different?"

Frowning, she cast her gaze about them, and a sinking feeling settled in her gut as the truth dawned on her. "The raft is gone!"

Chapter 8

Kate waded back out into the water, searching up and down the visible stretch of the river for the raft. The raft that held most of their supplies, she realized with a fresh beat of panic. "Where did it go? What happened?" She sent Josh an anxious look as a new possibility occurred to her. "Was someone here…while we were—?" She flapped a hand in the general direction of where they'd been kissing and swallowed hard, imagining someone spying on them. Someone with evil intent. "Did someone take it?"

Josh swiped a hand over his hair, wringing out some of the water. "I doubt it. It's more likely this is my fault." His jaw tightened, and his face reflected his self-disgust and frustration.

"Your fault? How?" She walked back onto the bank, and she hugged herself as a breeze cooled her skin and the reality of their situation chilled her spirit.

"I must not have beached the raft well enough." He shook his head, his toe kicking at the marks on the dirt where the raft had left drag marks. "This should have been good enough. The water's not that choppy, and there's almost no wind. I don't get it."

But she did. "I'm guessing you didn't account for the waves."

He glanced at her with a furrowed brow.

"The waves we made when we jumped…especially when we jumped together. The water fight? Couldn't that have dislodged it?"

An acknowledgment of her assertion morphed his expression from confusion to defeat. Despite her own concern about their predicament, Kate ached for Josh, knowing this setback only dug deeper into the pit of blame he'd already carved for himself. He fisted his hands so tightly his knuckles blanched, and his silence belied the internal turmoil she could read in his eyes. Remembering how supportive he'd been during her meltdowns, she was compelled to offer some comfort or acquittal to his guilt.

She stepped closer to him and placed a hand on his shoulder. "Josh, don't blame—"

He jerked his gaze up as if he'd forgotten she was there. Pulling away from her touch, he scrubbed both hands over his face before regarding her with a strained smile.

"It's okay. We'll be all right. Inconvenienced, but we'll be all right." He inhaled a harsh breath. "I'm sorry, Kate. I know I promised we'd be back to the pickup spot tonight, but without the raft, without the sat phone, which was in my pack, we're gonna have to hoof it outta here."

"Hoof it? You mean *walk*?" When he nodded, she added, "How far?"

He rubbed his fingers on his forehead, his brow wrinkled as he thought. "Probably another ten miles from here." He paused, rubbing a hand over his mouth as he thought. "Considering the terrain, the late hour, and—" he gave her a quick, apologetic look "—other factors..."

"Meaning my inexperience and limited physical capacity?" she wagered.

He gave a small nod. "We'll have to camp along the way tonight, but we should make it to the pickup point tomorrow before nightfall."

"Camp?" She gaped at him. He was serious. "But when we don't show up at the pickup spot this evening, won't they come looking for us?"

He nodded. "Possibly. Don't forget, the last word they had from us was that we were making a pit stop here and would be late. And most of the area we'll be traveling is pretty inaccessible except on foot. So even if they did mount a search, who knows how long it would take to find us? And we'd still have to walk out."

She mumbled an unladylike word under her breath.

"Hey," he said, offering her a lazy grin. "What happened to trusting me? This is just a diversion. A different sort of adventure. We'll be fine."

Kate narrowed her eyes, suspicion tickling her spine. "Did you do this on purpose? Did you push the raft off when I wasn't looking?"

He raised both hands, palms toward her, his expression slightly offended. "Swear to you, I didn't. Just trying to stay positive. Make the best of the circumstances. It's really not as bad as you think. We'll hike along the river, snuggle tonight to keep warm—" he added a suggestive eyebrow wiggle that prodded a chuckle from her "—and be back at the ranch tomorrow night."

"What will we eat? What about wild animals?" The worrier in her was working overtime as she considered the logistics.

His shoulders dropped, and he took a slow breath. When he raised his head, he pinned a steady gaze on her that burrowed to her marrow. "Kate…" He walked closer and framed her face with his hands. "I promised not to let you get hurt. I've got this."

She opened her mouth to ask another of the dozen queries buzzing around in her brain, but his next question stopped her.

"Kate, do you trust me?"

A small voice deep in her soul wrestled its way through the doubts and fear. When she answered, she knew she meant it. "Yes."

True to his word, Josh found a way to feed them, catching a trout with a fishing line made from a loose thread from his shorts and sanitizing water from the river using tablets the ranch had supplied in her backpack. Josh sent her out to gather sticks and fallen limbs for a campfire while he cleaned the fish, telling her, "Okay, Texas, the rule of thumb is, gather as much wood as you think you'll need, then gather that much more. You generally will use way more firewood than you think you will, and you don't want to have to find more after dark."

She saluted him. "Aye, aye, captain. A double portion of firewood coming up."

"And stay within eyesight of me and the river. It'll be dusk soon, and you don't want to get lost."

She cast a wary eye to the dense woods and nodded. "Way ahead of you, cowboy."

As directed, Kate gathered a large pile of small twigs for kindling, dragged a few larger dead limbs over for Josh to break up. She surveyed the pile she'd made, then went back to gather more. Once the campfire was going, she settled on the ground, leaning against her backpack while Josh stretched out on his side, propping up on his elbow. One of the greener forked limbs she'd found served as a roasting stick to cook bites of the trout. Even without seasoning, she decided the fish was as tasty as any she'd ever eaten. Hunger had a way of replacing seasoning on the flavor scale.

They saved the protein bars and small bag of gorp from her backpack for their hike the next day, but enjoyed the packaged cookies for dessert.

As it had the night before, the glow of the fire created an intimacy that evoked reflection and sharing. Tonight, having shared the ups and downs of the day—not to mention the smoldering kisses and erotic caresses at the swimming hole—Kate sensed an even deeper bond with Josh than just twenty-four hours before. A personal connection that had real weight and substance behind it. Her mind shied away from labeling it the *L* word. Affection, maybe. But she could not, *would not* allow herself to fall for another man she'd known such a short time and would say goodbye to in a few days.

Just the same, the campfire's bubble of light in the middle of the night's infinite blackness narrowed the world to two people. One tiny golden pocket in the expanse of wilderness. But before long, even the fire was not enough to keep the night's chill from settling in Kate's bones. She blew in her hands to warm them and scooted closer to the flames.

"C'mere," Josh said, waving her over with a flick of his hand.

Cocking her head to the side, she gave him a leery look. "What are you thinking?"

"Only that two can create better body heat than one." He winked at her, adding, "But I'm game for whatever naughty ideas you're suggesting."

She chuckled and tossed a twig at him. "I'm not suggesting anything. What I said earlier today still applies."

"No hanky-panky," he said with a serious nod. "I understand."

She rolled to her knees to crawl closer to him.

"No knocking boots. No riding the stallion. No sham-bam-a-lam."

She snorted a laugh as she settled next to him. "Stop."

"No getting lucky, no making the beast with two backs…"

"Oh, ho ho! Shakespeare. Impressive."

"I went to school." He slid his arm around her, snuggling her closer. "I may not have made straight A's like Zane, but when my lit teacher started laying out Shakespeare's euphemisms for sex, this randy teen was all ears."

"I can imagine."

"Pop quiz. When is *dying* not really death, but something much more pleasurable?"

She arched an eyebrow. "Really?"

"According to Mrs. Nesbit. And who am I to doubt her?"

"Wow," Kate said with a throaty chuckle. "Gives *Romeo and Juliet* a new light."

He raised a hand. "Don't get me started. Double entendres flying everywhere in that one."

She cleared her throat. "Can we change the subject? All this talk about sex is making me…" She fumbled for her own euphemism.

"Hot?" Josh suggested, no remorse in his teasing tone.

She play-growled.

"But wasn't warming you up the goal here?"

"Not that kind of warm."

He grunted. "You started it."

"What!" she sputtered, laughing, and he finally chuckled himself, the rich, low sound rumbling from his chest, a vibration she could feel as she nestled against him.

She could easily see how Josh had earned his reputation in the family as the cut-up. The impetuous charmer. But Kate knew he was so much more.

Evidence of that truth came a few moments later. When their lighthearted banter quieted and after a few moments of listening to the fire crackle and the river murmur beyond the circle of light, she said, "Penny for your thoughts."

"Penny, huh? Did you know that the U.S. government loses money minting pennies? It costs more to make a penny than it is worth."

"Interesting factoid, but that's not what you were thinking about."

"You're sure about that?"

"Pretty much."

"You're right."

"So..."

When she angled her head to look up at him, he thumbed a wisp of her hair out of her eyes. "The guy who vandalized the zip line had to know someone could get hurt, even killed. In the past months, he's damaged property, poisoned cattle, but he never endangered our family, per se." Josh drew a slow breath. "He's escalating. Getting more dangerous."

She shivered. "That's...frightening."

"I keep wondering—if he's not found soon, what will he do next?"

Chapter 9

"You're afraid he'll hurt your family." A statement, not a question.

A shudder rolled through Josh. His family was everything to him. Even the hint that this jerk could turn his viciousness on his parents or siblings—anyone at the Double M, for that matter—left a cold pit in his stomach. "Yeah."

The succinct response grated from his throat. Could Kate hear the fear in his tone that he did? Not that it mattered. Somehow, he knew his most private thoughts and emotions were safe with her, a first for him. In fact, sharing things with her was so easy, it felt ordained. Meant to be.

Nestling her closer, he laid his cheek on the top of her head. Despite their swimming jaunt and the day's perspiration, he could still smell the lingering fruity scent of her shampoo. Peach, he thought. Summertime. Fresh and sweet. Like her kisses.

His adrenaline spiked just a bit, making his heart thump harder when he considered how much he cared for Kate, the natural ease of his rapport with her. She was unlike any woman he'd known before. Or at least he related to her better than any other, wanted more from her than anyone else. So…what did that mean?

He'd teased Piper about having a fling with Kate, but what he was feeling was deeper than that. He could see himself in a long-term, committed relationship with her. He could fall for her.

The truth surprised him. Maybe it should have even scared him. Josh McCall, whose superpower was avoiding responsibility and anything that required a commitment longer than the expiration date on his milk, was not the settle-down-with-one-woman-for-the-rest-of-your-life sort. Or so the stories around town went. He'd been fine with living up to that reputation until now. He'd not met anyone that challenged that concept.

But Kate was different. Kate—

"Josh," she said now, pulling him from his musing, "you keep saying 'he' when you talk about the vandal. But couldn't the perpetrator be a 'she'?"

Josh blinked his surprise. "A woman?"

She spread her hands as if to say, *why not?* "One of you sexy cowboys at the Double M could have attracted a femme fatale. A jilted lover? A jealous secret admirer? Couldn't it as easily be a woman trying to drive you out of business as a man?"

His grip tightened on her, and he angled his head, gaping.

A woman? He turned the notion over in his head. "I— But who?"

"Well, that is still the $64,000 question, isn't it?"

He sat up and narrowed a squinty-eyed frown on her. "$64,000 question? What does that mean?"

She pushed up on an elbow. "You know…the quiz show from the '50s?"

He gave her a wry look. "A little before my time."

"But the saying has endured. My grandmother used to say it all the time. And they made that movie about the scandal…" She waved a hand. "Never mind. My point is the same. You should consider that a woman could be getting her revenge for a broken heart or—"

"What are you implying about my brother's and my love lives?" He curled his cheek up in a half-teasing grin. "What kind of guys do you think we are?"

"Hey, no judgments. I'm just saying maybe a woman has a beef with you—"

"No pun intended?" When she gave him a blank look, he added, "Beef? Cattle ranch?"

She rolled her eyes. "Will you be serious?"

He wanted to tell her just how seriously he took the unknown saboteur. How the threat haunted his sleep at night and ate at his gut by day. That teasing and humor were how he kept his sanity. Instead, he gave her a nod. "Sorry. You were saying?"

"Just offering a different perspective. Maybe the preconceived idea that it is a man is what's holding up the investigation."

"I suppose a woman could be involved but…a few months back, when this guy was stalking Piper—"

"What!"

Another truth he hated to dwell on, because knowing how close he'd come to losing his sister drove ice to his bones and made him want to put his hand through the jailhouse wall to get at the lowlife who'd terrorized Piper. Instead, he raised a hand to put Kate off. "Another story for another time. Anyway, this cretin, when the sheriff's department interrogated him, copped to certain things, but swore up and down he wasn't guilty of burning up our field with the winter feed. But he says he saw a man in the area just before the fire started. He could only give a vague description. Cowboy hat. Jeans. Dark hair. Nothing that doesn't describe every guy at the Double M, but it's our only lead."

She stared at him, her brow furrowed. Her gaze shifted slightly to nothing in particular, but the crease at the bridge of her nose remained, telling him she was deep in thought. Processing. Analyzing.

A weird sensation, both light and expansive, filled his chest as he studied her by the firelight. He could see pink on her cheeks and a few new freckles on her face thanks to their day in the sun. He wanted to kiss the delicate sun spots, smooth away the wrinkle of consternation in her brow. He wanted to make love to her, but he would respect her *no* for what it was.

After a moment her eyes found his again, and she said simply, "Wow. I wish I knew what to tell you. You gotta believe that the police will catch the guy before anyone gets hurt."

"Do I? Don't forget, if not for a lot of luck on our part, either one or both of us could have—" He caught himself. Why was he reminding her how badly the ziplining had gone? He wanted to embolden her, not keep her locked in her fear. He muttered a curse darkly and lay back on the ground.

She said nothing, but she curled next to him, her hand on his chest and her cheek on his shoulder.

He inhaled deeply, just…savoring. He liked having Kate there, next to him. She anchored him, soothed the rough edges of his frustrations and anger concerning the vandal. The babble of the water over the rocks in the river, the stars overhead, the scents of earth and smoke and the woman beside him…this was his idea of paradise. He could almost draw a box around that moment, isolate himself and Kate in this place and time, separate from the rest of the world, the events of the last thirty-six hours, the concerns that weighed on his family. For a little while.

"Jason," Kate said without preamble.

He arched an eyebrow. "Uh. It's Josh."

She patted his chest. "Jason is the name of the guy who taught me not to indulge in vacation flings."

He snorted. "I hate him already."

She fell silent again, and after a moment, his curiosity got the better of him. "What about Jason?"

"I was just remembering him. Reminding myself why it would be a bad idea to have sex with you like I want to."

"You want to?" Parts of his anatomy took notice.

"You really have to ask? I'd have thought the way I was climbing on you at the swimming hole put that question to rest."

Josh couldn't help it. He smiled. "So there's hope? It's still a possibility?"

She chuckled. "Oh, Josh…if only…" Her fingers curled into his shirt, and she said, "I met Jason on a business trip. We were on the same flight from Dallas, and it turned out we were attending the same conference. I was there to learn, and he was there repping his company at one of the vendor booths. When we saw each other at an opening night cocktail party, we ended up talking for a while, then going to dinner together, and then..."

The *and then* made Josh tense. He didn't want to think about Kate with any other man. Especially when he knew the story ended badly for her. He clenched his back teeth and kept quiet as she continued.

"One night led to another and another. Basically, we spent every free minute of the weeklong conference together. Dinners out. Wine. Sex. By the last morning, I figured we'd started something we would take back home with us. I raised the question of where things would go, and he—"

"Said it was over?" Josh guessed. An easy enough blank to fill in.

"Actually, his phone rang at that exact moment, and he took the call...from his wife."

Josh couldn't contain the groan of disgust that rolled from his throat. "Aw, Kate..."

"He'd never given me a clue. Wasn't wearing a ring. I was stunned. Sick to my stomach."

"I hope you kneed him in the family jewels and gave him some scratches on his face to explain to his wife."

"I wish I had, too, sometimes. But me being the chicken I am, I snuck out of his room while he was in the bathroom on the phone with her. I never saw him again."

Acid pooled in his gut, not just because this bastard had used and hurt Kate, but because he was unable to do anything about it. Not punch the guy in his piehole, not take away her humiliation and heartache. Nothing. That inability chafed his innate protective instinct.

Instead, all he could think to say was "There you go again with that chicken label. You chose the less confrontational response to the situation, but…you were in shock, hurting, angry. Maybe you made the wise choice. Have you considered that?"

She harrumphed her disagreement.

They lay quietly for another moment or two, though he could feel a new tension and distance stringing her tight. He vibrated with pent-up frustration, as well, as if that Jason punk had come and wedged himself between them, ruining the peace and happiness of their private campsite haven.

Fix this. Maybe he couldn't erase Jason the cheater from Kate's past, but he would do what he could to neutralize the power he had over her in the present. Squeezing his eyes closed, he tried to think about what the people in his life that he trusted for advice would say. His parents, Roy, his siblings…what would they tell her? After a moment of dwelling on the subject, one truth more than any other filtered its way to the top.

He cleared his throat. "You realize that by letting your bad experience with Jason guide your choices, he's *still* hurting you." Yep, that's what his mom would say. And Piper would add, "You're…still giving him power, letting that old heartache hold you back from what could be your destiny."

She stilled, then slowly sat up, twisting her body to face him. "If I didn't know you were using that line to get me to sleep with you, I'd say that was one of the most perceptive arguments I've ever heard."

Josh rolled to a seated position and threaded his fingers through her hair. "Yeah, I want you to sleep with me, *but*…not because of any *line* I give you. And I'm not saying *I'm* your destiny. I just hate to see you squander opportunity because of something that happened in the past." He paused, ducking his head a little to meet her gaze straight on. "Remember, you only live once."

"YOLO…" She tipped a grin at him. "That really is your motto, isn't it?"

He lifted a shoulder. "Never really thought of it as my motto. I just don't want to live a life where I end up with regrets."

She hummed thoughtfully as she slid a hand along his jaw, stroking his cheek with her thumb. "You really are something, Josh McCall. For someone who claims to be the less scholarly twin, you're very deep. Wise." She met his skeptical look with a smile. "Thank you."

Drawing him closer, she leaned in and gently kissed his mouth. At first tentative, then harder, deeper.

He let her set the pace. As he'd told her, anything that happened would be because she wanted it, not because he'd cajoled or pressured her. He didn't want Kate to have any regrets either.

But when her tongue teased his lips and she canted against him, he wrapped an arm around her and eased back on the ground, holding her as she settled against him. Desire pounded in his blood, but he lassoed the wildness and held it back. He'd be patient if it killed him. And judging by the heat that licked his veins and the pulsing pressure that built inside him, he just might die from unspent need. He grunted a short laugh. *Die*…

Those Shakespearean-era poets and playwrights might have been onto something.

Kate moved her kisses from his mouth to his chin, then along the curve of his jaw to his throat. The sexy nibbling of her lips left a trail of heat that sizzled and sparked every nerve ending. His entire body hummed and pulsed. Her fingers wound in the hair behind his ears and teased the nape of his neck.

An owl hooted, and with a flinch and breathy gasp, she raised her head to listen. "What was that?"

"Just an owl."

She released the breath she held. Nodded. "Cool."

"I know. Right? There's all kind of wildlife out here. All around us. It's one of the things I love about out-door sports—being out in nature."

In the glow of the firelight, he saw her brow dip, and she cast a wary gaze toward the dark beyond their campsite and shivered. "All around us, huh?"

He chuckled and caught the back of her head, lifting his lips to hers for a smacking kiss. "Don't worry. I'll protect you."

The corner of her mouth twitched, and she snuggled close to him again. "No doubt. I'm just not a fan of things that go skitter and growl in the night." Her fingers bunched in his shirt. "Did I mention earlier the mice that were in the silo with me as a kid? If the pain, hunger and isolation weren't enough, I had to share my little prison with horrible beady eyes and scrabbling claws that would climb on me at night." She gave a full-body shudder.

He shifted his gaze to the backpack he'd strung up from a tree branch, a few paces beyond the circle of the campfire light, in an attempt to keep critters of all sorts from the gorp and other snacks that would be his and Kate's breakfast tomorrow. He wouldn't tell her that, even now, he'd wager animals of all sizes were lurking around them, drawn by the scent of their dinner and the food in their backpack. Instead, he pulled her closer, stroked her hair and whispered, "I've got your back, Kate. I promise."

Kate woke the next morning to the music of songbirds and the early rays of sun peeking through the branches overhead. She was cold, but she was still snuggled next to Josh, her head pillowed by his shoulder. In the grand scheme, not a bad trade-off. She hated to move, to stretch her stiff muscles, knowing it would wake him. She tipped her head back and angled her gaze to study his perfect profile. Full lips. Straight, narrow nose, scruff-dusted jawline. A wisp of his raven hair fell over his forehead and tickled his closed eyelid. Silently, moving slowly, she reached up and brushed the hair back, smoothing it into place with the rest of the hair tucked behind his ears.

He opened one eye, and his mouth curled up in a smile.

"G'morning," she whispered, surprised to realize she meant it. She, who usually hated mornings, was happy to greet the new day. And especially happy to greet the man beside her.

"Hi." He inhaled deeply and stretched his arms over his head before drawing her close again. "See. Told you I wouldn't let any critters get you."

She grinned. "My hero. Though I did hear some odd, rather frightening noises in the night." She placed a finger on her pursed lips. "Oh, wait...that was you snoring."

He winced. "Sorry. Hope I didn't keep you awake."

"Not much. And I think it helped scare the wild-life away, so..."

He laughed.

Flashing an unrepentant smile, she leaned in for a kiss. Then another that lingered and stoked some-thing wild and hungry in her core. Oh, yes. She could learn to love mornings if she were to wake every day to Josh's stubble-darkened mug and tempting kisses.

But you won't. The cold voice of reality jarred her like a clanging bell shattering the calm. In a few days, she'd be back home, and he would just be a pleasant memory. No more.

With that stark reminder washing away the golden haze she'd draped over the moment, she pushed away from his grasp and stiffly climbed to her feet. "I guess there's no coffee today, huh?"

"No." He eyed her with a disappointed look she knew had less to do with the dearth of coffee and more to do with her abrupt departure from his arms. He rolled to a seated position and pointed to the backpack hanging from the tree. "But chocolate has caffeine if you want to eat all the M&M's out of the gorp."

She finger combed her hair, and finding leaves and moss clinging to her, she plucked the bits of nature from the mussed strands. "Naw. I'll survive. I'll be grumpy for a while, but I'll survive. Now, if you'll ex-cuse me—" She cast an eye around the wooded area, deciding the best path to take to find some privacy. "Nature calls."

"Avoid the plants with three leaves," he called to her as she marched away from their camp.

"Got it!" She called back. Poison ivy was not what worried her as she walked a short way into the cover of the trees and scrub brush. Snakes, spiders and other creepy crawlies were her main concern. Along with her own foolish heart.

She'd been alone with Josh less than two days, and she could already feel herself falling for him. She sighed and batted a branch aside as she waded deeper into the woods. Kissing Josh had been a mistake. Knowing how tender his touch could be, how sweet his lips tasted, how she thrilled with the press of his body against hers, *that* was the real danger. Because he left her wanting more. So much more.

And the deeper personal connection she felt with him following their fireside conversations and late-night confidences made her attraction to him much more than physical. She saw his caring heart, his sense of humor, his earnestness and passion that radiated from his core. A loyal family man, a protector and hard worker, Josh was an intriguing mix of rugged cowboy, daring adventurer and soulful charmer. Her first impression of him had been so wrong. Josh was complex, and she longed to spend days, months, years peeling back his layers.

She grunted and kicked at a rotting log, irritated with herself for dwelling on what couldn't be. Hadn't Josh as much as said he wasn't looking for anything long-term last night? *I'm not saying I'm your destiny.*

Shoving her frustrating line of thought aside, she hurriedly finished her business and returned to the campsite. Josh had dumped water on the lingering coals of the fire and seemed eager to start their hike. He donned his cowboy hat, shouldered the backpack and glanced around the small clearing. "Did we leave anything?"

"Doesn't look like it. Lead on."

He swept a hand downriver. "After you. We'll largely follow the river, only leaving the bank for the woods in a few spots where the terrain gets tricky."

She set out, picking her way along the edge of the water, careful not to slip on the damp rocks or mud. She saw now why he thought the hike would take most of the day. Their progress was slow, at times arduous, scaling boulders and tree roots along the river or struggling through dense underbrush and vines in the woods. Either way was rugged, but beautiful. Even though the day had grown overcast soon after they started walking, the clouds couldn't tamp Kate's enthusiasm for the wildflowers and majestic landscapes. She was charmed by the animals they encountered including chipmunks, marmots, a beaver, butterflies and two eagles. On one occasion a wood frog startled Kate as she answered nature's call midmorning.

To his credit, Josh had rushed to her aid when she'd yelped at the amphibian that had jumped on her. She'd managed to yank her shorts back up and semi-recover from her alarm by the time he reached her, and when she told him of her frog visitor, he doubled over laughing.

"I'm not scared of frogs," she defended herself. "It was his rude and unannounced appearance when I was most vulnerable that got me."

"Oh, Texas, I'm sorry. I don't mean to make light,

but you have to admit, you'll laugh about this when you tell it back home."

She lifted a grin and marched through the scrub brush to follow him back toward the riverbank. They rested by the water long enough to eat a protein bar and drink some disinfected river water.

"I'm not sure I understand why you have to use those tablets in the canteen before we drink. The river looks so clear."

He took a swig from the canteen, then handed it to her. "It may be clear, but likely loaded with all kinds of bacteria and parasites. Trust me, you don't want to deal with giardia."

"What's giardia?" she asked as she eyed the water flask warily.

"A parasite that will give you a nasty, weeks-long stomach bug with all the trimmings."

She wrinkled her nose and held the canteen back out to him. "Maybe I'll pass."

He pushed her hand back toward her. "That's what the tablets are for. Drink up. You don't want to get de-hydrated either."

She took a few hesitant sips and recapped the bot-tle before handing it back to him. "Well, I'm ready to head out again. How much farther?"

"Hard to say. I doubt we've come more than three miles so far."

She goggled at him. "Three?"

"At most."

She blew out a fatigued breath and stretched her back. *"Oy vey."*

"A bi gezunt."

Kate cocked her head. "What?"

"I thought we were switching to Yiddish." He held out a hand to help her over a large rock as they got underway.

She chuckled. "How do you know Yiddish?"

"My school friend Adam."

She nodded. "And you said…?"

"It means basically, 'Don't worry. You still have your health.'"

"Ah." They trudged on, making small talk and teasing banter as the temperature dropped and the clouds increased. After another long stretch of walking, climbing and picking her way along the trail, Kate stopped to take another swig from the canteen. As she rested, she tipped her head back, listening, inhaling the clean air. "What kind of bird is that I'm hearing?"

Josh took a turn with the water, and he, too, angled his head as he listened. "Hmm…"

"I can't recall ever hearing a birdcall like that around Dallas. I was just curious."

He scratched his chin and twisted his mouth in deliberation. "Well, that'd be the Striated Floofle Flapper."

Her gaze darted to his, ready to question him about his identification when she saw the corner of his mouth twitch. "You clown!"

He laughed. "I have no idea what bird that is. Birdcalls are not my specialty." He held up a finger, his face brightening. "Oh, except for the whip-poor-will." He demonstrated the easily recognizable birdsong, and she shook her head, her grin wry.

They began walking again, and she scanned the highest branches, searching for the feathered creature she could hear but not locate. "Whatever it is, it sounds mad. Like it's fussing at its kids for being late coming home for dinner."

Josh didn't answer at first, but when he did, his voice sounded wary. "Yeah. It does sound upset."

Kate lowered her gaze from the treetops and slowed her pace, puzzled by Josh's tone. "What's wrong?" She caught up to where he'd stopped walking to cast a glance upriver and into the forest. "Josh?"

"I may not know what bird it is, but I know that when the birds sound upset it could mean a predator is nearby." She joined him in turning slowly, peering into the deepening shadows as the sun sank. "Could be a rival bird or something messing with her eggs," he continued as she spotted something large and dark moving out of the tree line where they'd just been hiking, "or it could be something more like a mountain lion or—"

"Bear!"

"Yeah. Maybe."

She raised a shaking finger. "No, definitely. There!"

Josh whipped his head around to look where she pointed. A large bear lumbered out of the woods. Headed toward them. When it spotted them, the animal reared up on its back legs and sniffed the air before continuing toward them.

Biting out a curse word, Josh yanked Kate behind him. After clapping his hands loudly, Josh waved his arms and shouted, "Hey! Go on! Get outta here!"

But the bear kept coming, pausing only once to huff and sway its head.

With another muttered obscenity, Josh took a step back. "They don't usually approach like this. Those huffs are aggressive. It's warning us away."

"So I vote we go. Run."

"*No.* Do *not* run. Find a branch to wave. We have to look bigger than we are, make it think we are bigger than it is and scare it off."

While she scurried to comply, Josh shouted again and waved his arms.

Finding a thick stick on the bank behind them, she grabbed it, but as she rose, a whining sort of grunt caught her attention. She lifted her gaze and spotted a cub on the other side of the river, trying to wade across the swift stream, then doubling back when it found the current too strong, the water too deep.

"Oh, no," she muttered, her heart rising to her throat. "This is bad. Josh, she has a baby. That's why she won't leave."

He turned his head to look for the cub.

And in that fraction of a second, the sow charged.

Chapter 10

"Any word from your brother?" Michael McCall asked his son when he found him brooding behind his desk in their home office.

Zane looked up at his father and shook his head. "Not since yesterday morning. I've called the satellite phone three times and got no answer."

His dad frowned. "You think something's happened or that your brother is purposely ignoring you?"

"I think Josh is just being Josh. Reckless and short-sighted." Zane slapped his hand on the desk. "We started this company to save the ranch, and on our first trip out, Josh is ready to ruin us with his little rebellion."

His father opened a file drawer and began flipping through papers. "Isn't *ruin* a little harsh? He's doing what he thinks is best for the company, misguided though he may be."

"The insurance company told us to stand down. If anything happens to him out there—if anything happens to Kate Carrington out there—we've got no coverage! I'd say *ruin* sums it up."

"What he's doing is risky, yes. But your brother thrives on risk." He pulled out a document, slid his reading glasses from the top of his head, and held the paper close to his nose to examine it. Then, tucking the pages under his arm, he closed the drawer and returned his attention to Zane. "Give him some credit. We've got enough trouble around here without borrowing any from tomorrow."

"Exactly! I'm trying to fix things, save our ranch, and his going rogue doesn't help anything!"

Michael reseated his glasses on top of his head. "Zane, I truly appreciate what you're doing for the family and why, but you don't have to carry this burden. The ranch's failings, the financial difficulties… I got us into this, and I'm going to get us out."

"I want to help."

"I know you do. I thank you for your efforts, and I'm proud of you for this adventure business you've started with your siblings. But I have a plan of my own that I'm working on."

Zane sat taller in the seat. "What plan?"

His dad put him off with a wave of his palm. "No need to worry yourself about it. I have it in hand. I just want you to know you don't have to carry the world on your shoulders. Trust your family to share the load. That's what we're here for."

"So you're not going to tell me what you have up your sleeve?" Zane asked.

His father gave him a mysterious smile. "Nope. You don't need anything else to worry about."

"Josh!" Kate shrieked.

Josh's pulse spiked as the bear ran at them. He mentally scrambled to remember anything he'd learned about defending himself from bear attack.

But the bear was on him in an instant. Survival instinct took over. Protective mode.

Save Kate.

"Back away, Kate!" He raised his arms to protect his face as the bear reared up, growling. He could feel, smell the animal's fetid breath. The sow took a mighty swing, which Josh ducked to avoid as if he were boxing. The next swipe of the sow's paw came while he was still bent over. The bear struck his left shoulder from the back, the animal's long claws gouging his flesh.

Over the whoosh of blood in his ears, he heard Kate shouting, the sound muted as if from a distance. Shock only numbed him for a heartbeat, before a blinding pain streaked from his shoulder down his arm. He felt a pop. The hot sting left by the claws.

The force of the blow and the breath-stealing agony radiating from his shoulder knocked Josh to his knees on the muddy bank. The dark form of the bear rose over him again. He flattened himself on the ground, tried to protect the back of his head, but his left arm wouldn't move. The bear stomped her front paws near his head, huffing and grunting.

A piercing, primal scream reached him through the veil of his adrenaline-fueled haze.

Kate! Had he shouted her name? He wasn't sure, but protecting her became his focus. He rolled, trying to find a way to his feet again. Kate stood right beside him. Within range of the bear's swiping paws. A chill raced through him. "Kate, go! Back away!"

"Nooo!" she yelled. But not at him, he realized. At the bear.

Kate had a thick stick, and she swung it at the bear. He heard a thud…and another as she struck the sow. The bear backed up, shaking its head. Huffed and stomped its front paws again.

Josh hurried to his feet while he had the chance. His shoulder throbbed, and his arm hung at a weird angle. Dislocated. Damn it! But he positioned himself between Kate and the bear again, determined to keep himself in the fore of any attack.

A squawk-like cry came from near the water, and with a quick side glance, Josh saw the cub scramble onto the bank and bound toward its mother.

Kate stepped around his left side and swung the stick at the bear's nose. The mother bear grunted and backed away from Kate, who continued to shout, "Nooo!" in strident tones. Finally, seeing her cub amble into the woods, the bear turned and loped off after her baby. Neither Josh nor Kate moved for a moment, too stunned at what had happened to do more than pant for air with terror-tightened lungs.

Shoulder throbbing, Josh kept a wary gaze in the direction the bears had run until they both disappeared from view. They weren't likely to return. A black bear wouldn't typically mix it up with humans if they could avoid it. This sow, having gotten bonked a few times with Kate's stick, was likely hightailing it for home.

"Holy crap," Josh mumbled after a few seconds and turned stiffly to face Kate. "Are you okay?"

Her green eyes were wide, her cheeks pale, her bottom lip trembling. But she swallowed hard and nodded. "Yeah." Her gaze dropped to his injured arm, and her expression darkened. "But you're not."

Now that the imminent threat was gone, and his pulse was returning to normal, the searing ache from his arm and back captured his full attention. "No, I'm not. How...how bad is my back?"

Her eyebrows lifted a bit, as if startled by the news his back had injuries, but she eased around behind him. And gasped. "Oh, my God, Josh! You're bleeding. Badly."

"I figured as much." He grimaced as he moved to sit on a fallen tree trunk. "First order of business is getting my arm back in the shoulder joint."

She drew a shaky breath, her face so white he thought she might pass out.

"Kate?" He narrowed a worried look on her. He gritted his teeth, knowing what he had to ask and hating it. "I...need your help."

Josh needed her. As scary as the bear attack had been, now was *not* the time to fall apart. She had to rally herself, concentrate, and be there for him the way he'd taken care of her over the last day and a half.

Kate closed her eyes, gave her head a sobering shake, and blew out a cleansing breath. "How? What do I need to do?"

He slid off the tree trunk where he'd been resting and started to lie back on the dirt.

"Wait!"

He hesitated, frowning at her when she stopped him. Quickly she stripped off her shirt and spread it on the ground behind him. "If you get dirt in those cuts, you're just asking for infection." Of course, Lord only knew what kind of bacteria and other nastiness was already in his wounds from the bear's claws. Kate pressed a hand to her stomach. Disinfecting and wrapping the deep wounds was her next battle. One thing at a time.

Josh nodded his thanks to her and rolled back until he was flat. "Move my arm to a ninety-degree angle, then pull straight out."

She followed his instructions, wanting to cry when he screamed in agony. When she let up on her tugging, he shot her a side glance. "Don't stop. It's not in yet."

"But I'm hurting you!"

"Yeah, like hell," he grated through clenched teeth. "But it can't be helped. Pull hard. Brace your feet on my side if it will help." Sweat had popped out on his brow and upper lip.

Mustering her strength, both physical and mental, she gripped his arm again, positioned one of her feet against his ribs, and pulled as hard as she could. He roared in pain, and she joined him in a guttural howl of exertion and distress, her heart aching for him. She felt the *thunk* at the same moment he gasped, then panted a few breaths as he groaned softly.

"That's it. Thank God." He slanted a look toward her. "Thank you."

She nodded. "Now, what do we have for disinfecting the claw marks on your back?"

He continued taking slow, heavy breaths, his jaw tight, his brow furrowed in pain. "First aid kit…" He grimaced. "No. Damn it. The main kit's in my pack… which was in—"

"The raft," she finished for him, fighting a feeling

of defeat and helplessness. Now was not the time to quit. Josh was counting on her.

She dug in her pack and found her personal first aid kit, barely larger than a deck of cards. In it, she found a couple of Band-Aids, a plastic packet with one dose of ibuprofen, and a small foil packet with one use of antibacterial cream. It wouldn't be nearly enough. Mentally, she steeled herself, focused her energy on thinking outside the box, searching for resources and the stamina to see Josh through his injury.

She returned to her pack and dug deeper. In the plastic zip-seal bag that held their roll of toilet paper was a small bottle of hand sanitizer. Perfect!

Pulling it out, she infused her tone with a note of optimism for his sake. "Voilà!"

"First Yiddish, now French," he said with strained humor flitting across his face. "You're like the UN, Texas." He glanced at the bottle, and she could read the resignation in his shadowed eyes. Treating the open cuts with the alcohol solution would sting like the dickens, but they had no better option at the moment. His wounds had to be disinfected.

He sat up and turned his back to her. After using a clean sock from her pack to wipe the wound, gently brushing away as much debris, blood and torn skin as she could, she squirted a liberal amount of the hand gel directly on his cuts.

He let loose a creative curse that sounded anatomically impossible and brought a lopsided grin to her lips.

"I hope you don't talk that way in front of your mother," she teased, as she dabbed with the second clean sock to spread the antibacterial gel and mop up the fresh blood that seeped from the wounds.

"Where do you think I learned those words?" he deadpanned.

She paused from her ministrations and leaned forward to peek at his expression. "Excuse me?"

He lifted a corner of his mouth. "Kidding."

She reapplied the hand sanitizer and wiped again. "That should do it for now. I'll save some to clean them again in a few hours." Sitting back on her heels, she snapped the top of the hand gel closed and stowed it in a side pocket of the backpack where she could retrieve it easily later.

Next she gathered up the shirt she'd spread out for him, dusted off the loose dirt and pine needles and pulled it back over her head. The shirt was stained with bright streaks of Josh's blood, which she tried to ignore. As much as she wanted to wear a clean shirt, she knew she needed to save her last unworn T-shirt to bandage Josh's wounds. She pulled the clean shirt out of the pack and tugged at the seam.

He turned when he heard the tearing cloth. "Kate, what—"

"Turn back around. Let me wrap the shoulder, and then I'll make a sling."

The tendons in his jaw flexed as he regarded her. "Was that a sentimental shirt for you? A favorite? I'll replace it and all your other losses—"

She gripped the wrist of his uninjured arm. "Unimportant in the big picture. Just…get well, and…get us back home. Preferably without any more scares or injuries."

Kate kept her tone as light as she could, but she saw the shadows that flitted across his face. He was hurting, mentally as well as physically, though she knew he'd do his damnedest to hide both from her.

"That was really brave, what you did, taking on the bear like that," she said, hoping to boost his morale.

"Some would call it stupid. Reckless."

She paused, frowning at him. "I'm sensing a trend here. And I think you've fallen into the trap you advised me to avoid."

"Huh?" he grunted, clearly distracted.

She took hold of his chin and met his gaze to be sure she had his attention. "The labels you allow yourself to believe. I think you were told you were reckless or irresponsible as a kid and you believed it."

His brow dented. "I…I don't think those words were ever used to my face. But…"

He fell silent and finally she prompted him. "But…?"

He pulled his chin free of her grip. "Well, if you hear often enough how great your twin brother is, you can read between the lines. We're supposed to be the same. We have the same DNA. But I'm not the model student and businessman. I don't have his knack for details."

"Who says you have to be the same? Being twins doesn't mean you have to follow the same path in life." She took one of the clean strips of T-shirt and began wrapping his shoulder. "You have your own strengths. Just because you don't excel where he does doesn't mean you're…deficient somehow. Like you told me, you are not your label."

"Actually, I earned my label. I did things as a kid and teenager that…I'm not proud of."

She hummed an acknowledgment, remembering some of the tales he'd told her of his mischievous stunts. "But were you maybe…rebelling? Seeking attention in a way that would set you apart from Zane?"

He scoffed and wagged his head. "No." Then, a beat later, "Not intentionally." Then, after a moment when she could all but see the gears turning in his head, "I don't think so."

Josh tipped his head as he looked at her with an expression that said her suggestion was taking shape in his head, and he was readjusting his perspective on events in his past. She gave him a moment to process her point, taking the time to fit the T-shirt strips and tie them off.

"For the record," she said as she finished her bandaging and worked on creating a sling from the shirt she'd worn the day before, "what you did with the bear was not recklessness. She came at us. You had no choice." She stilled, her hands going limp in her lap as she replayed the events in her mind and shuddered. "And I know you put yourself in front of me on purpose." Her throat clogged with emotion, and she had to clear it before adding, "You saved my life…again."

Gratitude and affection swelled in her chest, to the point of pain. The emotion tightened her lungs and choked off her air. A longing pounded through her veins with an urgency she couldn't deny. Plowing her fingers into his hair, she cupped the back of his head and hauled him closer. She took his mouth in a hungry kiss, and at her core, ribbons of desire unfurled and flowed through her.

Josh returned her fervor, framing her face with one palm and slanting his mouth to deepen the kiss. Unable to maintain the awkward angle of her body, she toppled onto the mossy, vine-strewn floor of the woods. Josh followed her down, covering her body with his, bracing his weight on his good arm.

Kate shut out everything but the warm, satin feel of his lips on hers, the press of his hard body pinning her against the cool earth, the insane sense of security she experienced in his arms. Which was totally crazy, considering they'd just been attacked by a bear.

But he'd protected her. And she'd dived in to rescue him without a thought to her own safety.

She must have made some small sound of humor or pleasure, because he lifted his head to look deep into her eyes.

"What?"

She shook her head, confused. "What what?"

"What were you just thinking about?" he asked, his thumb stroking her cheek. The soft rumble of his voice mesmerized her, and she had to shake off the muzziness to answer his question. "Just replaying it all. The bear, the sounds…"

"Well, stop. Don't dwell on it." He kissed her temple.

"I hit a bear with a stick," she murmured in awe. Then, because it was so insane-sounding, she repeated, "I fought off…a bear…with a stick…"

He smiled at her, his eyes glowing. "You did. You're a total badass."

"Or insane." A fresh ripple of fear rolled through her when she realized how terribly wrong things could have gone. If the cub hadn't rejoined his mother, if the sow hadn't given up the fight as quickly as she did, if she hadn't found a sturdy enough stick to swing at her…

A prickle chased through her, and she shifted her

head left and then right, casting a wary gaze around. What if the bear came back? What if—

A shudder seized her, and Josh's hold tightened.

He shook her gently. "Kate, you're doing it again. Letting the fear hijack you. Living in the *coulda been*s instead of holding on to the reality. *We're okay*."

She snorted and motioned to his shoulder. "A mauled and dislocated shoulder is okay?"

He ignored her sidetrack. "You found the courage you needed when it counted, and we are fine. This—" he indicated his injuries with a tipped head "—is typical for me. A bull bumps you when you're working the chute, a colt bucks you when you're breaking him, a jump on a dirt bike doesn't go quite the way you planned..." He lifted his good shoulder in dismissal. "I've had plenty of broken bones and bruises in my day."

She stroked his bristly jawline. "It must drive your mother nuts."

He flashed an unrepentant grin. "Used to. Now she pretty much expects it."

"That doesn't mean she doesn't worry."

Another one-shoulder shrug. "Ready to move on? We still have about four miles to go to the pickup point."

About an hour later, the first drips of rain splattered on them from the gray sky.

She slowed her pace, and tipping her head back to glower at the clouds that were literally raining on their parade, Kate said, "I should probably warn you. My hair tends to frizz when it gets damp."

Josh moved up beside her and raised an eyebrow.

"Thanks for the heads-up, but, well, that horse left the stable a few hours ago."

She met his gaze, her nose wrinkled in confusion for a split second before his meaning dawned on her. With a gasp, she smoothed her hands over her hair and could feel the kinks and waves that had already popped out from the humid air.

Josh circled her waist with his good arm and hauled her in close for a kiss. "Don't sweat it, Kate. I love that look on you."

"Oh, you have a thing for hags?"

He laughed. Then, letting the backpack thud to the ground, he kissed her again—a deeper, lustier kiss. "Not hags. Just one particular beautiful woman in her natural state. Wild and without pretense. Her cheeks warmed by the sun, and her eyes full of life and lit with the spark of adventure."

She wrapped one arm around his waist, the fingers of her other hand combing lazily through his own windblown and rapidly dampening hair. "You're no poet, Josh McCall," she said, laughing. "But…I love it anyway." *And I love you.*

Her heart leaped when the words sprang so easily to mind. Fortunately, she caught them before she said something so ill-advised. Had she really gotten so lost in Josh's charming smile and hot kisses, his protection and comfortable rapport, that she'd allowed some part of herself to believe she was in love with him?

Rather than give any further credence to the mental slip, she captured his mouth again in another lip-lock that chased sidetrack ideas from her mind. She poured her full attention into the silky glide of his tongue as he caressed the recesses of her mouth. She flattened her hand against his chest and focused on his body heat that seeped through his rain-chilled shirt and the strong and steady thudding of his heart beneath her palm.

A moment later, Josh backed away from the kiss, regret heavy in his expression. "As much as I hate to end this, you need to put on your poncho before you get wetter."

"Poncho?"

He gave her a half smile, half scowl. "Did you not inventory your backpack supplies like you were asked to? Every hiker pack includes a rain poncho."

She squatted to rummage through the pack he'd dropped at their feet. "I inventoried." She shoved aside the first aid kit, which still sat at the top of her supplies, dug past the plastic bag with snack bars and sack with her dirty socks. "I just didn't remember seeing…" She found a small plastic pouch with a picture of a woman in a rain cape and extracted it. "Aha. No wonder I didn't remember it. It's tiny."

"I thought women believed size doesn't matter…" He flashed a naughty grin. "If it gets the job done."

Arching one eyebrow at him, she opened the pack and began unfolding the tightly compressed layers of plastic. As the proof of the rain poncho's size became more evident with each new flap that was unfolded, Josh's smirk brightened, as well. "You see? Sometimes the packaging can be deceiving, and what's inside might be bigger than you imagined." He waggled his eyebrows as the rain splattered his face. "Much bigger."

She couldn't help it. As if by its own volition, her gaze slid down to the fly on his hiking shorts. Her brain conjured an image of him at the swimming hole, when his wet underwear kept few secrets about his…er, size.

He'd also hidden no secrets from her backside that morning when they'd woken, spooning, snuggling to ward off the morning chill. Heat flashed through her now as it had then, and she curled her fingers into the plastic drape so hard she almost tore a hole in the protective covering.

To mask her reaction to his teasing, she snorted a laugh and shook her head. "Yeah, yeah, sport. Help me get this thing on, huh?"

With his good hand, Josh helped her tug the poncho over her head and straighten the folds.

"What about you?"

He shrugged his right shoulder. "I guess I get wet."

"But…" She fumbled for words, a sense of selfishness weighing on her. "You'll freeze!"

"Better me than you. I have more muscle, more body heat. And you're the guest. This whole boggled trip is on me." He picked up the pack again, slung it over his good shoulder and started walking.

"You didn't cause any of this to happen," she argued, falling in step behind him. The patter of the rain on the hood of the plastic rain gear made it harder to hear his response, but she caught, "I can't…blame… job to…home safely."

She shook her head, knowing that Josh would feel guilty for the many ways this trip had gone off course no matter what she said. Yet when she analyzed her perspective on the past few days, she saw so much in a different light now.

While his fledgling adventure company bore the primary responsibility for the failure of the zip line, saboteur or not, she still held Josh in high esteem for the way he'd rallied in every situation. He'd been truly devastated by the zip-line disaster, rattled to his core and desperate to make amends. She knew, having seen some of the notes he'd made in a small notebook the first night, that the company would be making serious operational changes as a result of the tragic experience. Since the accident he'd been far more careful, and he'd put her needs, her safety first.

He'd even made her mental health, her battle between her old fears and her buried longing for adventure, a priority. She acknowledged that she'd made small strides in understanding her phobia and chipping away at the doubts that held her back. She had Josh to thank for that.

A sweet mellowness filled her chest. Her feelings for him, she realized, were more than gratitude and a sense of security. She liked him. He was kind, funny, encouraging…and, of course, sexy as hell.

I love you. Heaven help her, she thought, remembering how easily those three simple yet complicated words had come to her just moments before. Her pulse spiked as she trudged along behind her cowboy guide. Despite her better judgment, she *was* falling in love with him!

As they trekked farther downstream, Josh noticed that the water level in the river was rising at an alarming rate. He slowed for a moment and turned full circle, casting a hard look around them and trying to pinpoint where they were, how much farther they needed to go to reach the spot where he'd told Zane they'd meet him.

Kate moved up beside him, and she studied him with a penetrating stare. "Is something wrong?"

"Mmm, not really," he replied distractedly.

"Josh?" Her tone was stern. "You promised full disclosure. Remember?"

He angled his head to meet Kate's gaze, and he expelled a harsh sigh. "I was just noticing the rising water. This river is fed by a number of streams from the mountains. Runoff from all the higher elevations to the northwest."

She sent a side-eye glance to the roiling rapids. "And?"

"Well, judging from the dark clouds behind us and the increased volume of water in just the last half hour or so…" He bit the inside of his cheek, hedging mentally. He didn't want to alarm her.

She stepped closer to him. "Josh? Spit it out!"

He gritted his back teeth for a moment, then decided she deserved his candor. "The conditions are good for a flash flood through this river valley." He scratched his chin as he eyed the water. "Thanks to the bowl shape of the terrain in this stretch of the river, with the bluff on one side—" he aimed his thumb at the sheer rock wall "—and the steep hill on the other—" another flick of a finger toward the dense trees and boulders that rose at a sharp angle to a jagged peak "—the rising water has nowhere to go. It can only flow so fast, and so the runoff will get deep and turbulent quickly."

She surveyed the landscape with wide eyes. He read her understanding of their predicament in her creased brow and flared nostrils. "You're saying we could drown."

Chapter 11

"That would be an extreme case," he said, adding a brief grin. But indirectly, yes, he was saying that, although he wouldn't give the threat any power by speaking the words. Such bluntness would only frighten her needlessly. Impressing the urgency of a hasty retreat from the area was good enough.

Josh adjusted the backpack on his shoulder and took her hand. "What I'm saying is we need to pick up our pace. There's no telling how much or how quickly the water will rise, and I don't want us to get trapped or caught up in a washout."

Almost as soon as he finished his explanation, the skies opened, and rain poured down on them in sheets of fat drops.

Kate gasped as the cold rain soaked her head. She hunched her shoulders and blinked as the rain splashed in her eyes. "Was rain even in the forecast for today when we left the ranch?"

Josh removed his hat and shoved it on the crown of her head. It would help shield her face from the worst of the downpour. "If I remember right, there was like a thirty percent chance. But you know how quickly a forecast can change in the spring."

"I do. Texas is notorious for strange weather shifts."

She looked especially fragile, peering at him from under the wide brim of his cowboy hat, her hair wet and feminine curves lost under the man-size poncho. *Vulnerable* came to mind, though he was learning just how much of a misnomer that was for her. She'd proven tougher and more capable than even he'd imagined when they started the trip. The kind of hiking they were doing was far more difficult than a tourist's day hike. She'd roughed it without a tent, sleeping bag, decent supper or bathroom without complaint. Yep, Kate Carrington definitely had a core of strength and courage. If only she could see it, believe it about herself.

They hiked on for several minutes in silence, hunched against the rain and deepening chill. He kept a wary eye on the river flow and didn't like what he saw. He stopped and faced her when he realized how swift the current was getting.

"Things are already picking up." Josh swiped his own soaked hair back from his eyes and studied the water, the depth, the available stones for crossing the river, weighing it against what he knew of the terrain ahead, and the location of the pickup spot. "We need to cross to the other side before it gets deeper."

She gaped at him, then at the river. "Cross the river?" Squinting against the driving rain and angling her head to look past him, Kate appraised their surroundings. "But won't hiking be easier on this side?"

"For now." He forcefully swallowed his impatience. Her skepticism was understandable, but it chafed that she still didn't trust him enough not to question him. "The landscape changes not too far ahead, and by the time we hike that far, the river might be impassable. Besides, we have to be on the other side to reach the pickup spot."

Her gaze shifted to the swift water, and resignation shadowed her face. "All right." Her tone was weary, her posture defeated. "How do you propose we do this?"

He gripped her hand as he led her down to the water's edge. "We'll use these rocks as stepping stones," he said, pointing out the ones he meant, "until we get to that gap in the middle. It looks like there's a sandbar where it won't be as deep, and we can wade through until we get to that big rock over there." He aimed his finger toward the far bank.

He felt her shiver, though he couldn't be sure if the shudder was from the cold or from fear. But she squared her shoulders, gave a tight nod and followed him onto the first rock without protest or hesitation.

They leapfrogged from one slippery rock to another, their feet sliding a bit with each jump, but with some tottering and foot-shifting to catch their balance, they made it to the midpoint. But when Josh stepped down into the river, midstream, the water was deeper than he'd anticipated, reaching his waist. And faster. And colder. He'd forgotten that the runoff from the higher elevations would include a large amount of snowmelt. The chill stole his breath for a moment, and he was considering a different way across when Kate splashed down into the river next to him.

Her gasp had a note of distress behind it, a mewl of shock. But more important, the current caught her off guard, and she stumbled, almost going under as the water knocked her from her feet.

Josh snaked his arm around her waist just in time to keep her from going under. But his injured arm had been the one closest to her, and he reacted, slipping it free of the sling, without thinking it through. The tug on his shoulder as he caught her weight and pulled her back to her feet shot a lightning bolt of pain from his shoulder to his fingernails. His grunt of pain brought her worried gaze up to his.

She gripped a handful of his shirt, still fighting the current and struggling to find purchase on the slippery rocks and stay upright. "Josh?"

"I'll be all right," he replied, wincing, but refusing to release his hold on her. "Are you okay?"

"Unharmed, but the water is too strong. I don't think I can cross without it knocking me over."

A legitimate concern since she was several inches shorter than he was, and the river reached midchest on her. What's more, the water pulled at the loose plastic of the rain poncho like wind in a sail. Considering how wet they already were and how moot the cape had become, he moved his hat back to his head, pulled the poncho off over her head and jammed it in a side pocket of the backpack, praying it didn't work loose and wash downstream.

"Okay, here's the plan." He shifted the small backpack to his bad shoulder and gritted his teeth against the ache. He could endure the discomfort for a few minutes, and he wanted his stronger arm free to help Kate. Getting her safely across was his priority. And the sooner the better. The water was dangerously cold. "You hold on to my belt, and I'll hold on to you. Small steps and lean into the current. We'll cross together."

She nodded, and he noticed her bottom jaw trembling from the chill. *Hell*. He couldn't build a fire in this rain. All their clothes were wet. And they were at least forty-five minutes from the rendezvous spot. Assuming Zane was even there. Considering he'd had no communication with his brother in the last twenty-four hours, they'd likely have to find a way to get back to the ranch on their own.

He made a mental note to add *Keep a vehicle at end campsite* to the list of changes and additions he intended to make to the business plan.

One tedious step at a time, they waded through the swift water. Even Josh, worn down by fatigue, pain and the numbing effects of the cold water, had trouble keeping his feet under him. But with Kate snuggled against him, his arm supporting her, encouraging and guiding her, they eased across the river and dragged themselves out on the opposite shore. He found a spot a few yards downstream where a small rock outcropping created a canopy of sorts to protect them from the worst of the downpour. He stopped there long enough to remove the sling, awkwardly strip off his wet shirt and wrap the thin rain poncho around them both. The plastic, thin as it was, would do the best job of trapping what body heat they had. He pulled her down, settling with his back against the rock wall and pulling her onto his lap. Holding her shivering body against his chest, he rubbed her arms and tried to chafe some heat into them.

"D-don't we need to keep m-moving?" she asked, her chin quivering. "The water's s-still rising."

"In a minute. I want to warm you up a little first." A chill raced through him, and his body shuddered. If he was this cold, she had to be freezing. She was already battling early stages of hypothermia. The need to get her out of this river valley and back to civilization grew more urgent every minute. He weighed the risk of staying put a few more minutes in order to infuse her with what little body heat he could versus the danger from the rising water and the delay in getting her real medical help.

If only they had...*heat packs!*

He reached around her to fumble open the backpack and rifle the contents. Obviously he was suffering the early effects of hypothermia, as well. He could tell his thought process was muddled. He'd completely forgotten about the heat packs that were part of the guests' backpack supplies.

He found two of the rectangular plastic packets that, when crushed, mixed chemicals to create a small amount of heat. After activating the first one, he handed it to Kate. "Tuck this somewhere in your clothes."

Heating her torso was the most important goal.

She took the packet but dropped it as she tried to work it under her shirt.

He smashed the second heat pack, and after savoring the heat on his own hands for a few seconds, he took over for her, raising her shirt and shoving the heat source into her bra.

Under the circumstances, he shouldn't have found the soft swell of her breast against his fingers so arousing. But he noticed. And he stored the memory away to examine at a more appropriate time.

"Y-you've just been waiting for a chance to c-cop a feel. Haven't you?" She twitched a lopsided grin at him, and he chuckled, relieved to know she still had the presence of mind to crack a joke.

"You got it, sweetheart. All part of my master plan to seduce you." He took the second pack from her and tucked it next to the first one, hoping the packs would help warm her blood as it flowed to and from her heart, carrying the heat to her vital organs.

She turned to face him and raised one icy hand to his face. "You don't need an elaborate plan. All you have to do is ask."

With that, she placed a soft kiss on his lips, then snuggled back in against him, her bottom nestled intimately against his crotch.

Two things occurred to Josh. One, she hadn't stuttered this time. He hoped that meant she was starting to warm up. Two, just ask? In any other circumstance, that would be all the invitation he needed. His mouth dried, and he struggled not to think about how good her fanny felt rubbing against his manhood.

Last night by the fire, she'd told him she didn't want a vacation fling. So had her opinion changed? Or did she believe he could give her more than a fling? Or was it the hypothermia talking?

Regardless of which one was true, he couldn't take her up on the offer. Certainly not now, when they needed to get moving, get out of this river valley before it flooded, get warmed up before more damaging cold settled in their cores. And not when he knew she was vulnerable, worn down by the trip, the stress, the cold. Which sucked, because he really wanted Kate. In a powerful, marrow-deep way. Right now, just holding her close, her delicate scent in his nose and her soft breath on his neck were about as erotic as anything he'd ever experienced. But it was more than just lustful, mutually satisfying one-night-stand sexiness. He'd connected with Kate over the past few days, bonded with her. He *liked* her. Her gumption and wit, her gentleness and insight, her intelligence and compassion.

He drew her closer, pressing a kiss to the top of her head. She was the kind of woman he wished he could find in Boyd Valley. Someone he could build a relationship with.

He blinked as that thought filtered through his head. Whoa. A relationship? Kate had worked some potent magic on him, if he was considering a relationship with anyone. He felt a bit like he'd been kicked in the gut by a bull—winded, a little dizzy, mentally reeling.

He tried to picture himself settling down with one of the women from town whom he'd dated. Nice gals, all of them. But the image didn't crystalize or feel right until he put Kate's face on the woman. A restlessness fluttered in his chest and spurred a rush of adrenaline to his blood.

Why was Kate the only woman he could see in his future? And why was he even considering such nebulous issues when he had more pressing concerns like getting them back to the ranch in one piece?

A rumble of thunder roused him from the distracting thoughts of having Kate in his bed, not just for a night but for a lifetime. He cleared his throat and nudged her. "Feeling better? Think you can walk?"

She raised her head and gave him a nod. When she reached into her bra for the heat pack, he stopped her.

"Leave them there. They stay warm for a few hours." He helped her climb to her feet. Then, stretching his stiff, cold muscles as he stood, he hitched his head, signaling the need to get moving. The water level had risen a good foot just in the few minutes they'd been hunkered down under the outcropping. As if to punctuate their situation, a louder growl of thunder rolled through the valley, echoing off the rocky bluffs.

Josh returned his hat to her head, took her hand and sent her a grim look. "Bigger storms are moving in, Kate. We need to haul ass."

For the next several minutes, they all but jogged downstream, stumbling over loose rocks and slipping in the increasingly slick mud and wet rocks of the riverbank. As Josh predicted, the water rose quickly, lapping at their feet and forcing them to move to higher ground every few minutes. But each move took them to steeper terrain with larger boulders to maneuver over or around. Josh helped her navigate, picking the best foothold and easiest paths across the rough landscape. Even with his help, his hand holding hers to steady her, her feet slid on one of the mossy and rain-drenched rocks, and she landed hard on her butt.

"Kate!" Josh was at her side in an instant. "Are you okay?"

The taste of blood filled her mouth, telling her she'd bitten her tongue. She dabbed at her mouth, and, realizing how dirty her fingers were, she immediately regretted it. She spit out the grit and blood on her tongue and gave him a shaky nod.

"I think so." The spike of adrenaline in her blood left her trembling from more than just cold as she pushed back to her feet. Other than a sore bottom and wounded pride, she was uninjured.

The fall did make her more careful as she picked her way along the muddy bank. But careful also meant slow, and Josh gave her a frown after a few minutes.

"I know the fall shook you up, but we need to move faster." He cast a meaningful glance to the river, where the water level had crept up another foot in the last half hour, and the current seemed swifter by the minute. She readjusted Josh's hat, which had been knocked askew when she fell, and gave the narrowing strip of navigable terrain a glance. Not only was the water rising, but the forested hillside on the opposite bank had changed to a similar landscape of boulders and sheer rock wall, narrowing the gulch that the river traveled through.

"How much farther?" she asked, not wanting to complain but eager for some gauge of their progress.

"Not far. A few more minutes. Thirty at best." He swiped at the rain dripping from her eyebrows and gave her a smile that warmed her inside, better than the heat packs stuffed in her bra. "Would it sound patronizing if I said I was proud of you?"

She blinked and tipped her head in surprise. Of all the questions he could have asked, that was way down the list somewhere close to, *Have you ever met a purple penguin?*

"You're proud of me?"

His face brightened. "Hell, yeah. This trip has been

a clusterf—" He stopped and cleared his throat. "A *challenge* from the start."

She gave him a wry grin for his alternate word choice.

"It's been far more difficult and more arduous than we ever intended," he continued, "and you've soldiered on admirably. You've risen to the occasion every time I needed you to and sometimes when I'd never have expected you to. You've been a—"

"Halt." She flung her hand up and shot him a teasing scowl. "If you call me a trouper, I'll puke."

"I wasn't." He cocked his head. "But your aversion to the word is intriguing." He adjusted the backpack on his good arm and turned to keep walking downstream. "I'd love to hear the story why that word bothers you when we're not trying to get out of a gulch before it floods."

"No story," she called to him, "just a term that makes my teeth hurt."

She stared at his back as he headed out, mulling his praise. He was proud of her? Maybe she should consider that condescending, but he hadn't said it in an ironic or snide way. His sincerity touched her. Her heart swelled, and his kind words buoyed her spirits and energized her to continue walking, despite the chill in her bones and her aching muscles.

Josh continued to surprise her. She'd originally assessed him as an adrenaline junkie playboy whose flirtatious charms were not to be taken seriously, but he'd shown himself to be a man of convictions, courage and a generous soul. Her heart thumped realizing that her first impressions of him, her snap judgments about him before she knew his heart and mind, were exactly the kind of labels he'd been pegged with his whole life. People misread his joviality and love of adventure as proof he had no substance, no commitment, nothing to contribute to the family business beyond his workaday ranching skills. And after hearing it repeated enough times—or implied through actions and attitudes—Josh had bought into it himself.

But his love and loyalty to his family were abundantly clear in his desperation to save them from financial ruin. She could see that he was attempting to prove his worth to the family through his contributions to the adventure business. The passion behind his attempts spoke of his internal pain for the years he'd believed he didn't live up to some false measuring stick of success and value in his family. Before she left Colorado, Kate vowed to tell Josh exactly how she viewed him, how his dedication impressed her and how his protection and encouragement when she needed it had meant everything to her.

Set in her resolve, she squared her shoulders and ducked her head, watching her footing carefully and allowing his wide-brimmed hat to shield her eyes from the worst of the stinging rain as she trudged on behind him. The rain had let up some, but one look over her shoulder told her another band of heavy rain was headed their way. And if it was raining hard upstream, they could expect the river to continue its rapid rise. They were already wading through floodwaters in low spots along the bank, and the swift water carried increasingly larger debris from washouts upstream.

Her gaze was focused on next steps ahead of her when she ran into his back. He caught her elbow to steady her balance, then dropped the backpack on the tiny strip of rocky shoreline that wasn't part of the swirling floodwaters.

"Okay. This is it," he said.

Kate raised her head, tipping the hat back from her face so she could get a better look around. She gave the surrounding area a sweeping gaze. "Here?"

She'd expected to reach a widening in the river valley, a flat spot where Zane or the ranch staff could drive a vehicle in to pick them up. The terrain here was no different than anywhere they'd been the last two hours. "But where are—"

Her words lodged in her throat when she saw what hung from the sheer rock cliff beside them.

Chapter 12

Josh knew the exact moment she spotted the ropes anchored to the rock face of the bluff, because her sentence cut off and her cheeks paled. She turned an accusing look on him.

"You didn't say anything about rappelling to get to the pickup place!"

"Technically this isn't rappelling. Rappelling means you're going down the cliff. This is climbing, because we'll be going up."

Her expression said his explanation of the difference only irritated her further.

"Look at it this way. Our transport back to warm, dry clothes and a hot meal are at the top of that cliff."

Her face modulated some, but clearly she wouldn't let him off the hook easily. "I asked you to be completely honest with me."

"I never lied." He shot her a guilty look. "I just didn't—"

"It falls under the full disclosure part of the promise. Remember that?" She looked pointedly at his injured shoulder. "And how do you propose to climb with your bad shoulder?"

"Well…" He rubbed the joint in question, which ached even at the thought of the task ahead of him. "It will be tricky. No denying. But I have no choice."

"No choice," she mumbled, giving the bluff and ropes a wary scrutiny. "Are you even sure Zane's up there?"

"I— No." Josh angled his face to look up toward the top of the rock face, then cupped his hands around his mouth. "Hey! Zane? Brady? Anybody up there?"

They waited, holding their collective breath, and he strained his ears to listen for a response over the drumming of the rain and roar of the rapids behind them. The river water had overflowed its natural banks, and wind-driven waves lapped at their feet. Another line of hard rain was just behind them, and an urgency to get up the ropes and out of the path of the floodwaters gnawed at his gut.

When he got no response from above, he shouted again, and Kate added her voice. He hated the note of anxiety that he heard in her tone. The despondent, discouraged underpinnings bore into his soul. He'd wanted what he thought was best for her, tried so hard to take care of her. But look at them—limping home, chilled to the bone. Defeated.

And his family still had to find the culprit behind the vandalism, before anyone got hurt.

"No one's there," she said quietly. "Now what?"

"Maybe they left a vehicle for us. I don't know." He swiped rain out of his eyes and gritted his teeth. "First things first. We go up, then we deal with what is or isn't waiting up top."

She held his gaze for a moment, her nerves evident from her pinched lips and lowered eyebrows. But she gave a resolute nod and turned to face the cliff. "Show me what to do."

"Before anything else, I'm going to check that the anchors are still solid and secure, that no one has messed with them."

Kate's already pale face blanched a shade whiter.

He stepped closer to her and squeezed her upper arm. "It's okay, Kate. I will make doubly sure it is one hundred percent safe before you hook on. I will get you to the top unharmed. I promise."

She nodded. "I trust you."

Having her faith was a double-edged sword. While it filled him with a tender ache and deeper affection for her, he also saw it as an honor that bore the highest responsibility and gravest consequences. He could not, *would not* betray the trust she'd placed in him.

He moved the backpack to a boulder, out of the path of the rising water. Their safety harnesses were already attached to the climb ropes, and he unhooked them and handed her one, showing her how to wear it around her legs and seat it at her hips. Then, wrapping the main climb rope around his hand, he pulled hard, adding more and more of his body weight as he leaned back, testing the anchors. He favored his good arm, knowing that during his ascent he'd have no option but to put stress and weight on his injured shoulder. He shoved that thought down. He'd work through the pain. Deal with what came up. He had no choice. Tugging as hard as he could on the ropes with one hand, he grunted with exertion, wishing he could give the rope a fuller test before Kate started climbing.

Without his asking, Kate stepped in front of him, grabbed onto the rope and added her strength to the test pull. As if she'd read his thoughts. As if she understood him and his needs before he spoke them.

Don't be stupidly sentimental, man. She was just doing the obvious thing to help.

But he still felt a twinge of gratitude, a deepening bond with her. A sense of teamwork and connection. A feeling of… He shook his head. *Focus, McCall. You can get poetic and mushy after you get her back home safely.*

Even with both of them pulling, leaning to put their combined body weight into the tension on the rope, the anchors, fixed in a three-point redundant system, held.

Thank God. Finally something went right.

But Josh wanted to make doubly sure everything was functioning. "I'm gonna go up a little ways and come back down, just to be extra sure everything's working right."

She shivered, a nonverbal reminder to him that they needed to hurry, then bobbed a nod of agreement.

As he prepped for his test climb, he showed her the Grigri, carabiners and belay loop on his harness. He clipped on all the gear and explained her job as the belayer for his climb. A drysack with climbing gloves of various sizes had been hung ready for use with the harnesses, and he found a pair that would fit her hands.

"It's essential that you keep your brake hand on the dead rope at all times." He demonstrated the method by which she'd pull in the slack from the live rope as he ascended, then tugged the rope through the Grigri while maintaining her grip with her brake hand.

"What happens if you fall?" she asked, her eyes dark with worry. "I'm not strong enough to hold your weight."

"I'm not going up very far. Just enough to test that the anchors will hold, that no one's loosened them. Just pull in the slack."

He could see in her eyes that his answer hadn't told her what she wanted to know, that she suspected he was keeping something from her. But telling her she'd be lifted off the ground if he fell would only make her more nervous. And he really was only going a short way to test the ropes for trouble.

As part of their preparation for the trip guests, he and Zane had spray-painted the best handhold and foothold spots. The bright blue and neon-orange markings stood out against the gray gloom of the rainy day. But Josh had climbed this rock so many times he figured he could probably do it blindfolded.

"On belay?" he asked.

"What?"

So much for traditional terminology. "I'm ready to climb. Are you ready?"

She braced her legs and flexed her grip on the rope. "Yeah."

He leaned over and smacked a kiss on her mouth. "For luck."

She blinked, then closed the distance between them. With a hand behind his head, she dragged him in for a long, serious lip-lock. One full of heart and meaning. Or at least that's how he chose to interpret the heat behind the kiss. She'd come to mean more to him than just a guest of his fledgling business. His protection of her had become personal. Possessive.

When she finally pulled back, she said in a low voice he could barely hear over the rush of the water, "If we're looking for luck, no need to shirk. Right? We need all the luck we can get."

"True."

She pressed her mouth against his one more time, and he could have gone on kissing her for hours. But a loud rumble, a crack and splash drew their attention to the river. A powerful, muddy wave of water roared toward them. The wave was heavily cluttered with large branches and other debris.

"What the...?"

"Probably an obstruction, a dam of deadfall gave way upstream," he said.

She edged backward, closer to the rock wall as the river gushed up and swallowed their feet. Her anxious expression echoed his own concern for their need for haste.

"Right, then," he said. "Here I go. Ready?" He faced the bluff, looking for his first handhold.

"Josh, look!"

He turned, following the direction of her pointing finger. Something small and brown was in the water, coming their way. Flailing, scrabbling to get onto a swirling bit of drifting limb. His heart squeezed for the woodland creature caught by the turbulent water, but the flooded river was too swift, too dangerous. They could do nothing to save—

But Kate was staggering into the deeper water, her intention obvious.

"Kate, no!" Josh shouted, his voice panicked. Clipped in for the climb, he could only move a few feet toward her before the rope grew taut and brought him up short. "Kate, come back!"

She wobbled, fighting for balance against the current. His cowboy hat tumbled off her head and washed downstream as she fought for balance on the slick rocks. Then, in a matter of seconds, the animal reached her. She scooped it into her arms and tucked it against her body. Immediately she turned, folding the tail of her shirt into a pouch around the animal, and waded back to him, with the trembling animal snuggled against her.

He grabbed her shoulders. "Are you crazy?"

"I couldn't let it drown!" she cried.

Josh wanted to both shake her for her recklessness and kiss her for her courage. He opted to hug her in relief that she was safely out of the fastest part of the current. "Geez, woman. You scared the hell outta me!"

"I'm sorry about your hat. I'll g-get you a new one."

He held her closer. "Forget it. I'm just glad you're okay."

She pulled back, and they both stared down at the tiny creature in her arms. A rabbit. The poor thing was breathing hard, too tired from its swim to do more than lie limp in her arms and shiver.

"You are one damn lucky bunny, dude." Raising his gaze to hers, he asked, "Now what do you plan to do with it?"

"I—I don't..." Clearly she hadn't thought it through. She'd simply acted, tossed practical sense out the window and followed her compassion for the waterborne animal in need. And reckless as it was, he admired her for her act of humanity.

Kate squared her shoulders. "We'll put it in the backpack until we can get to the top. Then…warm it up and release it?"

Her idea was as good as any he had with no time to spare, so he snagged the backpack from the boulder and unzipped it. He took out some items they no longer needed, and they wrapped the rabbit in one of her dirty shirts before tucking it in the main compartment of the pack and zipping it closed.

"Okay, Bugs is secure," he said, resuming his position, ready to climb. "Let's get on with this." When she signaled she was ready, he reached for the first handhold and shoved his toe into a notch in the rock to begin his climb. Hand, foot, hand—he grimaced when he pulled himself up using his injured shoulder. Fiery sensations shot through his shoulder, his arm trembled, and his grip slipped. He gritted his teeth against the throbbing and swallowed the groan that swelled in his throat. Quickly he found his next foothold and pushed up, easing the tension on his bad arm. Josh paused and caught his breath before he moved higher. Strong hand, foot, weak hand, pull—the weakened tendons in his shoulder gave out. Lightning streaked down his arm. He shouted in pain. Lost his hold on the rock wall. Fell.

Kate's scream rang in his ears just before he crashed on his backside in about a foot of swirling water. The landing shuddered through his bones. The icy water stole his breath. But the impact shoved his loosened shoulder back in the socket. The searing ache subsided, but his head was muzzy. Shock. He didn't move for a moment. Needed to assess.

"Josh!" Kate was at his side in an instant. "Oh, my God! I'm so sorry. I tried to brake, but when I got pulled up... I didn't... I—" Her voice caught, and she sucked in a deep breath. "Are you hurt?"

He slowly sat up. Moved one foot, then the other. Rolled to his knees. He was sore, but felt no significant damage. He shook his head. "I'm okay."

More than a test of the top anchors—which passed— the short climb had proved a test of his ability to scale the rock wall. And he'd failed.

As much as he hated to admit it, he couldn't depend on his left arm for the climb. He forced his dazed brain to work, to figure out his next step, the plan B.

Holding his injured arm close to his body, he pushed to his feet. Swayed.

Kate wedged her shoulder under his armpit and slipped an arm around his waist. "Easy there. Take a minute."

He exhaled and braced a hand on the cold rock bluff. "We don't have a minute." Slow breath. "It's going to get harder and harder to fight this current. The logs and debris are dangerous." He placed his hand on her cheek, and met her wide-eyed gaze. "You need to go up. Now."

He felt her shiver, but rather than balk, she straightened her back, held his stare and nodded.

"Right." Her eyes brightened, and her fingers curled into his soaked shirt. "If there is a vehicle up there waiting for us, maybe I can use it to pull you up."

His cheek twitched in a weak grin. She was thinking of him, how *she* would rescue *him*. Was this the same person who'd started this trip? The terrified woman he'd held while she shook and cried after her near miss? Somehow, at some point in the last two days, she'd shed the fears that hampered her and found her inner strength. Found that something that compelled her to save drowning rabbits and put her doubts aside to figure out how to help *him* scale the bluff with his injured arm.

Tipping her chin up, he kissed her again. "Kate Carrington, you are amazing."

His assessment earned a smile, and the warmth of it filled her face and burrowed deep inside him.

A chunk of wood hit his leg, jarring him back into action. "Pulling me up with a vehicle is one option. But just in case there's no truck up there, here's what you'll need to do."

As quickly as he could, he talked her through tying off to a fixed anchor—a tree or boulder—and showed her as best he could the rope configuration, use of the Grigri and technique to belay him from the top. The current pushed her against him, her feet slipping as the water rose higher, flowed faster. At an alarming rate.

Get her up top. Now! "Look," he said as calmly as he could, "if we're going to escape this flood, you have to hurry."

Her jaw tightened, and her chin lifted. "Right. I can do this. I will get you out. Somehow."

She startled him with another long kiss and a lingering stare into his eyes. "Josh, I lo—"

Another piece of debris clipped their legs, and whatever she was going to say was lost in her yelp of pain.

"Go!" He thrust her toward the rock wall and tightened his grip on the belay rope. "The best foot- and handholds are marked in orange paint."

She nodded, took a deep breath, and began her

climb. He used his weaker left hand to pull in the slack, his right hand for the brake grip. Josh gritted his teeth and set his feet to do his job. Belaying Kate would hurt his injured arm, but he'd let the rope rip his damn arm off before he'd let her fall.

Chapter 13

"You can do this. You can do this," Kate muttered softly to herself as she fumbled and groped for each foothold and handgrip. Pulled herself a little higher, then a little more. Not looking down. Not letting herself think about anything except the next few inches up…and Josh. She had to do this. For Josh. He was depending on her to get them both out of the floodwater and up the cliff. "You can do this. You *have* to do this."

The cold water had sapped her energy and her strength. Her muscles quivered as she pulled herself up, stepped, pushed higher. Her fingers were icy and numb as she searched for each next rock knob or ledge.

She paused once, sending a quick glance up to measure her progress, and was so dismayed by her surprising lack of progress, she resolved not to look again. *Just keep moving.*

"That's it! You're doing great!" Josh called from below, his voice barely audible over the roar of the raging river. Who knew water could be so *loud*?

The violent pounding of her heart, taxed by exertion, made her wonder how far she could push herself before the organ simply burst like an overblown balloon.

You have to hurry.

Faster. Go faster.

Hand, foot, push and pull. Hand, foot, push—

Her hand slipped, and she gasped as she lost her grip. The harness jerked as the belay rope tightened.

Josh shouted something that was drowned by the thundering water and the rush of blood in her ears.

Scrabbling for a grip, Kate panted for a breath and swallowed the panicked mewl that rose in her throat. Her stiff fingers closed over the lip of a thin ledge, and she clung to it as she calmed her tremors. Don't think about it. Just…*do.*

If she let her thoughts distract her, she'd be paralyzed. *Keep moving.*

Hand, foot. Hand, foot, push and pull. Rain dripped in her eyes as she tipped her head back to look for the next painted handhold guide.

The climb seemed to take forever. Her breath sawed from her, and her limbs moved only because of sheer will. Finally, she hoisted herself over the top edge of the cliff and rolled onto her back. Her muscles trembled, completely depleted. Tears of relief spilled onto her cheeks. She was able to discern them from spattering rain only because her tears were warm and made her eyes sting.

Josh.

She had no time to savor her relief or rest her aching body. She had to get Josh up the cliff. Rolling to her hands and knees, she swept the top of the cliff with her gaze. And spotted an old pickup truck.

The windows were spotted with rain and heavily fogged, but she thought she could make out a person inside. Her pulse bumped harder. *Help.*

"Hey!" She waved her arms, then tipped sideways with fatigue and had to catch her balance before she fell over. No one stirred at the truck, and she began to doubt her eyes. Was there anyone inside or...?

Person or not, the truck provided the power to haul Josh out of the river and up the cliff before the flood-waters overtook him. Swiping her soaked hair back from her face, she crawled close to the edge of the cliff and shouted down.

"Josh!"

She heard a muted reply.

"There's a truck here! Hang on! I'll be right back!"

Without knowing if he understood or not, she stumbled to her feet and staggered over to the truck. As she neared the vehicle, she could better see that, yes, a man was inside. But although she shouted and knocked on the driver's window, the man didn't move. He was either asleep...or dead.

Bile rushed up her throat at the notion. Why had such a terrifying possibility occurred to her? Maybe because the vandal who'd been attacking the McCall family had almost killed her with the zip-line sabotage? Or because the man's preternatural stillness seemed all the more frightening on this dreary, wet day?

She tested the door handle. Locked. Damn it!

"Hey! Open the door!" She banged on the window again, and when she still received no response, she circled the truck to the passenger side. The rear bumper had a worn-out Double M Ranch bumper sticker. At least she knew the truck belonged to the McCalls.

The passenger side handle worked when she tried it, and she prayed that when she opened the door, she wasn't swamped by the smells of a decaying body. Swallowing hard, she pulled and was hit by an overwhelming stench…of alcohol. She spied the bottle that had spilled when the man had lost his grip on it. The back seat of the extended cab had empty beer cans littering the floor.

She focused on the man slumped over in the driver's seat and heard a light snuffling snore.

Clenching her back teeth in irritation, she poked the man's arm. "Hey! Wake up! I need your help to get Josh up the cliff."

With a grunt, the man raised his head, and she studied his craggy face. She remembered being introduced to the older man, the foreman at the Double M, and dug in her memory for his name. Brady's father… Summers… Ray? No, Roy.

"Mr. Summers?" She grabbed his sleeve and shook him. "Wake up. *Mr. Summers?*" Then finally yelling, *"Roy, wake up!"*

His eyes opened, and he jerked a bleary gaze toward her. "Huh? Who're you?" Then, looking around him and rubbing his eyes, he mumbled, "Where…" His sentence trailed off in a mumble she couldn't make out.

Anger flashed in her. The man Josh's family had sent to pick them up was drunk. As a skunk. And he smelled almost as bad. She shook his arm again, shouting, "Roy, I need your help! Josh is hurt and can't climb up here. We have to use the truck to get him out of the river water." Another hard shake of his sleeve. "Do you understand?"

"Josh's...hurt?" Roy looked confused. "Naw...they said he wuz 'kay."

"He hurt his shoulder yesterday. A bear—" She stopped herself. No point explaining it all to him now. "Look, can you help me or not? I need the truck to pull him up. I'm not strong enough and...well, you're not sober enough."

"Truck..." Roy sat straighter and put his hands on the steering wheel. "I gotta pick up Josh. And...the lady."

"I'm the lady. And I don't have time for this. Get out! I need the truck." She stretched across the inebriated foreman to unlock the driver's door, then circled the vehicle again to open the door. When Roy stared at her blankly, she grabbed his arm and dragged at him. "Get out!"

Moving slowly, Roy slid from the front seat and wavered as he tried to stand. The cold air and chilly rain seemed to shock him, and his eyes widened. "Josh..."

"Is at the bottom of the cliff, waiting." She nudged him aside and cranked the engine. Throwing the F-350 into reverse, she backed as far as she dared toward the edge of the drop-off and climbed out with the motor idling. The extended cab truck had a bumper hitch, and she used it to tie off the ropes that snaked over the cliff. Walking back to the rock ledge, she peered down to find Josh. He was holding on to a boulder, floodwaters to his waist, battling the current.

Her heart rose to her throat. "Josh!"

He glanced up.

"I have a truck to pull you up!"

He pointed to his ear and shook his head.

"A truck!" She shouted again in frustration. Then inspiration struck. She hurried back to the driver's seat and laid on the horn.

When she returned to the edge, Josh was smiling and giving her a thumbs-up.

"Ready?"

He nodded.

She blew him a kiss and hustled back to the front seat. Her body ached, but having the end in sight, having a means to help Josh buoyed her flagging spirits and reenergized her.

"Go slow," she told herself, knowing that a quick ascent would bump and scrape Josh along the rock wall. He needed to be able to orient himself and push off the rocks with his feet or hands, guide his path.

Holding her breath, she put the truck in gear and eased off the brake. The F-350 crawled forward, stalled. She tried again, giving the slightest tap to the gas pedal. She rolled forward a couple feet, faster than she'd intended. She winced and whispered an apology to Josh. Jerky stops and starts weren't good for him either, so she pushed the gas again, barely. The automatic transmission caught, and she inched forward, fighting her own impatience to get Josh up faster.

"Please, please…" She wasn't really sure what she was wishing for, what her pleas were seeking. But she knew this mess wouldn't be over until Josh was safely above. A shiver rippled through her as she nudged the gas pedal again, watching the rearview mirror for signs that Josh was up. Should she stop and check on him, make sure the plan was going right? That seemed wise.

Putting the truck in park, she returned to the edge

of the cliff. She peered down and spotted Josh dangling a few feet out of the water. As she watched, he managed to use a hand to turn himself and brace his feet against the rock. He glanced up, saw her and gave another thumbs-up.

Releasing a tense breath, she staggered back to the driver's seat, fueled purely by adrenaline. As she prepared to inch forward again, she heard a man shouting, "Josh!"

She glanced in the rearview mirror and spotted Roy Summers, standing at the edge of the drop-off, wobbling as he tried to look over the edge.

Terror streaked through her. Irritated as she was with the foreman, she couldn't let him tumble drunkenly over the cliff. Damn, damn, damn the man!

She slid back out of the truck and stumbled tiredly to Roy. "Get back, Roy!"

Her mother had been a schoolteacher, a strict disciplinarian, and Kate had learned the tone of voice that commanded attention and respect. She employed it now as she seized Roy by the arm and tugged at him. "Get *away* from the edge!"

"Josh...is hurt?"

She dragged him toward a fallen tree and shoved on his shoulder. "Sit. Down."

Roy fell more than sat.

She aimed a finger and a stern warning glare at him. "Stay. There."

Roy fumbled to sit up. "Josh—"

"I'll help Josh. You stay put. Got it?"

"I—"

"Stay. Put!" she shouted.

Roy frowned at her but nodded.

She shook from fury, cold, exhaustion, frantic worry, muscle fatigue—God only knew which, but probably a brew of them all. Kate climbed back in the truck and shifted into drive again. Eased off the brake.

She allowed the truck to roll forward at a turtle's pace, though everything inside her wanted Josh up top *now. Faster. Hurry*. She fought the impulse to gun the engine. Forced her breathing to slow. *Patience. Easy does it*.

Finally, Josh's dark head crested the drop-off, and he hauled himself the last few feet before dropping on his knees and sagging like a rag doll.

Slamming the F-350 into park, she slid from the front seat and raced to him. "Josh! Are you okay? Did I go too fast? Ohmygod!" She nearly knocked him over as she threw herself at him, wrapping her arms around his neck.

"I'm fine. You did great." He returned a strong one-arm hug, kissed her cheek, while she clung to him. She felt a shiver roll through him. He'd been in frigid, waist-deep water for several minutes on top of the chill from the rain.

"You need to get warm," she murmured in his ear. He nodded, but didn't move from the hold he had on her. He seemed as reluctant as she was to let go, but when Roy's voice broke the bubble of intimacy around them, Josh raised his head.

"Josh, you're hurt?"

Josh backed from their embrace.

"Roy, hi. You have no idea how good it is to see you." A warm smile lit his face, then Josh stood and extended his right hand to help Kate to her feet.

Sliding the backpack from his shoulders, he opened

the main compartment, lifted out the wet rabbit and set it on the ground. "There you go, Bugs. Find shelter, buddy."

After a brief stunned moment, the bunny came around and bolted toward the nearest scrubby bush.

Roy blinked as if he thought he was seeing things before he turned back to Josh. "The zip…zip line…" To her surprise, and clearly Josh's, too, Roy began to weep. "You were hurt. She said you were hurt. You coulda died…"

"Hey, whoa. I'm okay. Just reinjured my shoulder. The one I dislocated a few years back. But it wasn't on the zip line. We had a close encounter of the bad kind with a mama bear."

Roy stumbled closer, and with his head hanging, he put a hand on Josh's shoulder. "I'm sorry, son. I didn't… You weren't…"

Josh sent an awkward glance to Kate, and she mouthed, "He's drunk."

Closing his eyes, his expression darkening to disgust and annoyance, Josh backed away from Roy's grip. Roy staggered, swayed but stayed on his feet. Barely.

"Let's get out of here." Josh turned to her. "Kate, I hate to ask, but…can you drive? Between his inebriation and my bum shoulder, you're best suited for the job. I'll sit in the back and keep an eye on him." He jerked his head toward Roy.

She blinked against the rain and swiped a hand across her nose to wipe away the tickling rivulets dripping from her bangs. "Uh, sure."

"Come on, old man." Josh shoved his good shoulder under Roy's arm and led him toward the idling truck.

"Josh is hurt..." Roy mumbled again, then shook his head. "No...he's 'kay."

When he reached the passenger door, Josh wrinkled his nose and scowled. "Damn it, Roy! It smells like a distillery in here. What the hell?"

"Sorry. Sorry...didn't mean to..."

While Josh loaded Roy in the back seat of the extended cab, Kate arranged the front seat to her liking, adjusted the mirrors and buckled her seat belt. Then turned the truck's heater on high, the fan to full blast. She rubbed her hands together in front of the stream of warm air and sighed tiredly. "That feels so good!"

Josh closed the passenger door and settled in the back seat. "There's a dirt-and-gravel road that leads off this mountain. It's narrow and windy, and with all this rain, it'll be muddy and slick."

Kate met his gaze in the rearview mirror. "Just when I thought the dangerous portion of the trip was behind us."

He flashed her a rueful grin. "I'll make it up to you."

She lifted both eyebrows and the corner of her mouth in a flirtatious grin. "Oh, yeah? Do tell?"

Shifting into gear, she headed for the narrow road, following Josh's verbal directions. He hadn't been kidding when he said the road would be twisty and slick. Kate clutched the steering wheel with a white-knuckled grip as they wended down the steep embankment for several miles.

She could feel the tires lose traction once or twice in the mud, causing the back to fishtail slightly, and each time, her pulse would spike.

Neither she nor Josh spoke as she maneuvered down the mountain. She was focused on driving, and he was either allowing her to concentrate or too exhausted to make conversation. When she finally reached the paved road, she glanced over her shoulder and with a humorless grunt said, "Well, that was fun."

"You handled it expertly, though. Good job." Josh reached over the front seat to squeeze her shoulder. "You've risen to the occasion every time it was needed over the last few days."

She shifted on the seat, awkward with his praise. "I wasn't fishing for a compliment. Really."

"Didn't think you were, but you deserved the truth. You've earned my compliments and much more."

Another backward glance told her that Roy had passed out again. He snored softly, mouth slack, and not likely to wake again anytime soon. Kate debated whether she should say anything about the foreman's inebriation. The man's drinking and job performance were ranch business and none of hers. Except that Roy's intoxication today meant he'd been no help in rescuing her and Josh. And the alternately concerned, furious and frustrated looks that Josh gave the sleeping man proved how important the matter was to Josh.

What was important to Josh was now deeply important to her. Her stomach flipped realizing how much she'd grown to care for Josh. "So…" she said softly, and Josh's eyes met hers again in the rearview mirror. "I'm guessing this isn't the first time he's gotten drunk on the job."

Josh puffed out an exasperated sigh and twisted his lips as he studied the foreman. He seemed to be debating whether to say anything, but after a moment he said quietly, "We've known for years that he drank heavily in the evening. It started when his wife died back when

Brady was a kid. Brady says his dad's drinking got worse January before last, when Brady's brother and sister-in-law were killed in a car accident."

"How could his drinking *not* affect his work?"

Josh shrugged. "I think Brady covers for him. Roy confines his drinking to the evenings…usually." Josh glanced at Roy and frowned. "Somehow, for the most part, Roy's managed to keep his drinking separate from his job performance."

She nodded. "I believe the term is *functional alcoholic*." Her gaze darted back to the rearview mirror in time to catch Josh's eyebrow lift in intrigue.

"You have experience with alcoholism?"

"Not in my family, but my best friend since childhood has had to deal with it with her mom. We've discussed her struggles many times."

Josh nodded and shifted his attention to Roy, who grunted, smacked his lips, then nodded off again. With another heavy sigh and a frown, Josh added, "There was an incident a few months back at my parents' anniversary party where he showed up drunk and made a scene."

Kate said nothing, waiting. She could tell there was more on Josh's mind, but she gave him the space to tell it at his own pace.

"He's like family, Kate. No…he *is* family. He's been our foreman for longer than I've been alive. I don't know what we're supposed to do."

Using the mirror, Kate studied Josh's pained expression. "Have you, or your parents—someone—talked with him about it?"

"Brady has, I'm sure."

"Tell me if I'm overstepping here and I'll butt out,

but…it seems to me, if he's like family…and he needs an intervention…you, meaning your family, should insist he get help."

Josh's face reflected defeat…and agreement. "Yeah. I know. We've been kicking that can down the road for a while."

"Avoidance isn't a solution. If you care about him—"

Josh was nodding. "I do. We do. You're right. It's just…hard. And touchy, you know."

"There are organizations out there to support you all, his family, too. Use them," she suggested with an encouraging tone. "And…if you want someone to listen, I'm here."

"Okay. Thanks." Josh said no more, and she took the cue that the subject was closed. Instead, he instructed her where her next turn would be to get back to the ranch.

They debated whether she should drive them to the ranch first or if she should go straight to an urgent care clinic for Josh's shoulder. His priority was getting her back to the ranch and into warm, dry clothes. But Kate was worried more over Josh's injured shoulder. And since she was literally in the driver's seat, she won. She made one stop at the first diner she found to get them all cups of hot coffee. When she returned to the truck, Josh was on a cell phone, presumably Roy's, talking to someone at the ranch, reassuring them that the two of them were safe and would be back at the Double M as soon as the doctor saw to his shoulder.

When he hung up, he said, "My mom insists on meeting me at the after-hours clinic. I told her I didn't need her to come, but she's a mother and she's been worried about us, so…" He lifted a hand as if to say, *What can you do?*

After removing her coffee, she handed Josh the take-out carrier with the last two cups, and he added, "She's bringing Piper to drive you and Roy back to the ranch."

Kate was oddly disappointed not to be the one to stay with Josh at the clinic, making sure he was all right and getting him home. But then, it wasn't her responsibility, was it? She was the ranch guest. Just the marketing advisor. No more. Even if her heart screamed that she wanted to be much more.

But they'd faced so much together these last few days. Didn't that count for anything? They'd shared kisses, touches, embraces that suggested a deeper bond than simply guest and tour guide. And yet she had to consider the fact that the feelings could be one-sided. Josh had said he was proud of her for tackling the challenges they met head-on, but he'd never expressed any personal affection for her. Kisses were just kisses without words of love to back them up.

She took a gulp of coffee that warmed her inside, but a different sort of chill had settled in her bones in the last few moments. The physical danger had passed, but a niggling sense of dread warned her a new danger lay ahead.

Chapter 14

"See that she's given plenty of TLC when you get her home," Josh told his sister when Piper and his mother met him at the medical clinic. "Hot coffee, one of our best steaks, build a fire at the guesthouse and open the best bottle of wine for her."

"I know how to be a good hostess, Josh," Piper countered. "You go be a good patient and do what the doctor tells you."

Their mother tugged gently on Josh's good arm, coaxing him toward the exam room where the nurse stood waiting for him.

"And give her a pair of those fuzzy socks you love so much."

"I will." Piper laughed and sent Kate a look as they headed out to the parking lot, where Roy waited in the back of the truck. "What have you done to my brother?"

Josh puffed out a sigh and turned toward his mother. Her expression asked the same question Piper had raised. He frowned. "What?"

"Did I say anything?" his mother said with a sly smile.

The doctor's exam told him what he'd already guessed. In addition to mild hypothermia—already improving thanks to warm blankets, hot coffee and the dry clothes his mother brought—Josh had dislocated his shoulder. And although he'd popped it back into the joint, the tendons had been strained, the joint was inflamed, and he needed to ice it, rest it and take anti-inflammatory painkillers for several days. The claw marks left by the bear were also checked and cleaned. After getting a steroid injection, a prescription for an antibiotic because of the claw wounds and a sling for his arm, he stopped at the front desk to settle his bill, while his mother headed out to the car.

"Well, well, well. Josh McCall lives to tell the tale."

Josh glanced up from the document he was signing. His gut clenched with antipathy when, at the check-in desk across from him, he spotted his high school nemesis—and, unfortunately, his loan officer—Gill Carver.

"What do you want, Gill?"

"Just making small talk with a client. No need to be nasty." Gill shifted his attention to the woman signing him in. "Mandy has a fever and a sore throat." He put his hand on top of his daughter's head. "Dr. Hayward is expecting us."

The nurse bent to talk to the little girl, then led her down the hall toward an exam room.

"I'll be there in a minute, sugar," Gill called as he

moved his gaze back to Josh. He gave a quick glance to a form he was filling out, but said, "Word on the street is you had a bit of trouble on your first adventure trip this week. In fact, the way I heard it, you nearly killed a woman."

Josh gritted his teeth. "Mind your own business, Gill."

Gill chortled. "Huh. Seems to me, as your banker, the one who loaned you money for this venture of yours, it *is* my business."

Restless and irritated, Josh tapped his credit card on the countertop, waiting for the cashier to return and finish checking him out.

"Your *accident*—" Gill paused, clearly letting the sarcasm in his tone soak in before continuing "—leads me to think you don't know what you're doing with your adventure tours."

"Ma'am," Josh called, waving his card at the billing clerk impatiently. She held up a finger to signal she'd be there in a minute.

"Gill's Thrills, on the other hand, had a great opening weekend. Karl Townsen took a group out rappelling, horseback riding and through a ropes course. No accidents or injuries. Just satisfied customers."

Josh tried to ignore Gill's adolescent taunting. He stared at the paperwork in front of him, the black ink blurring as his frustration and loathing grew.

"Maybe you should hire some professionals to help on future tours. Assuming this disaster doesn't shut you down."

Josh squeezed the pen in his hand so hard it snapped in two. "Maybe you should shut up."

He regretted the words as soon as he spoke them.

Stooping to Gill's level with juvenile retorts was not the way to deal with the jerk.

He drew a slow breath and released it. "Ma'am, I'm in a hurry," he called to the billing clerk.

"Be right there."

"Maybe hurrying is why you screwed up?" Gill said. "Did you throw your adventure course together too fast? Without safety protocols?"

"You know nothing about what happened or the extenuating circumstances," Josh retorted, his jaw tight. He met Gill's smug look with a dark glare, and as he stared at the bullying banker, a tingle raced down his back. "Or do you?"

Gill scoffed. "What?"

"Did you tamper with our zip line, you sleazebag?"

Gill shot a look to the clinic staff, who were shamelessly eavesdropping. "Are you hearing this?" he asked and scoffed. "Hell, no. I don't need to tamper with anything you and your brother do. I only have to sit back and wait for you to screw it up yourself."

Josh wanted to slam his fist into Gill's haughty mug. Before he resorted to violence, he shoved away from the counter and stalked toward the exit.

"Sir?" the billing clerk called.

"Bill me!"

Josh climbed in his mother's car and squelched the urge to punch the windshield. He took a few deep breaths and shook the tension out of his hands before fastening his seat belt and facing his mother.

"I saw Gill go in with his little girl. Is he the reason for this—" she waved a hand at him "—mood you're in?"

He touched a finger to his nose.

"Why do you let him get to you after all these years? You're a grown man, Josh."

"I tried to ignore him, but he's a colossal asshat, and he might even be behind the sabotage of our business."

His mother swung a sharp glance toward him. "What? You have evidence of that?"

Josh groaned and rocked his head back on the seat. "No. Just theories based on his douchiness."

His mother drove out of the parking lot, and with a worried look, said, "Well, you need to get a grip on your emotions before you talk to the police."

He arched an eyebrow, noticing his mother had turned in the opposite direction from the ranch. "Which would be now?"

She sighed and nodded. "I don't like it. I'd rather you went home to rest, but Zane says the sheriff was very clear. He needs to get your statement ASAP. The insurance company is waiting on the final police report, and—"

"All right." Josh tipped up a hand in resignation. "Will they talk to Kate, too?" He really wished he could spare her that drudgery.

"Already have."

He sent his mother a frown. "Huh?"

"Piper took her to make her statement a little while ago. She texted me while you were getting x-rayed."

Josh grunted. "Not exactly the TLC I'd hoped Piper would show her."

Melissa reached over to pat her son's leg. "Kate's being taken care of, as you will be when we get home. I don't like it any more than you do, hon. But…"

"No. It's fine." Josh clenched his jaw and white-knuckled the passenger side door handle, remembering the horror of seeing the zip line fall. Rage pumped heat through his veins. "Whatever it takes to catch the bastard responsible for the sabotage, I'm in."

Josh talked to the police for about an hour. He had little information to add to what was shown by crime scene photos, taken when Zane brought the sheriff to the campsite and zip-line landing platform after he and Kate had headed out. He promised to make himself available should the investigators need to ask any follow-up questions.

"Well?" His mother asked as they returned to her car.

He shrugged his good shoulder and shook his head. "They've got little right now. Just like all the other incidents. All the boot prints and fingerprints they've found belong to the Double M family, no doubt left during the campsite prep."

His mother frowned. "That can't be right."

"The vandal could have worn gloves. Stolen someone's boots. Or done something to hide his tracks. A piece of plywood to walk on?" Josh closed his eyes, beyond tired, heartsick over the setback for the adventure ranch...and missing Kate.

He'd last seen her three, maybe four, hours ago, and yet he already longed to talk to her, to hold her, to reassure himself she was all right.

Behind his closed eyes, he saw her wading into dangerous currents to save a rabbit, laughing as she emerged from the clear water of the swimming hole, staring at him with moss green eyes, both terrified and tenuously trusting. His heart bumped hard, and he had to work at drawing a breath into his lungs. What was wrong with him?

Piper met him at the car, saying, "Kate wanted me to tell you goodnight and thank you and that she'd see you in the morning. She was headed straight to bed after a shower and a quick bite to eat."

Josh cast a glance toward the guesthouse. The windows were mostly dark, and he saw no activity in the dim light of the living room. Disappointment stabbed him. He'd hoped to check on her, satisfy his deep longing to touch her, kiss her and explore the curious mix of emotions knotted inside him.

Josh hadn't been back in the family home more than twenty seconds before Zane was in his face. "Are you pleased with yourself?"

Chapter 15

"Not now, man." Josh tried to brush past his brother, but Zane pursued him.

"Do you have any idea what you could have cost us? What could *still happen* if we don't get out ahead of this mess real quick? Dawn has been making noises about our liability, about lawsuits…"

Josh pinched the bridge of his nose. "Seriously. Can your tantrum wait? I'm exhausted."

"My tantrum?" Zane raised both hands and gave Josh a what-the-hell look. "This isn't a joke, Josh."

Josh paused and gave Zane a sarcastically confused look. "It's not?"

"Stop screwing around!" Zane punched Josh's chest near his injured shoulder. Not hard, but Josh was sore all over and in no mood for his brother's tirade.

"Back off, Zane, or I swear—"

A shrill whistling sounded from the end of the hall, and both of the twins turned toward their father. "Zane, I know you have business to settle with Josh, but it will keep. Let your brother rest and eat, and you can hash out your beef with him tomorrow."

Zane cast Josh a dark glare. Then, heaving a deep sigh, his expression easing, he said, "I'm glad you're all right."

Josh nodded. "Thanks." He rubbed his sore shoulder, then asked, "Have you seen Kate since she got back? Did you all make her comfortable and get her a good meal?"

"Piper pulled out all the stops once the cops finished talking to Kate."

"Good." Seeing his father reminded him of other business he needed to handle before he slept. "Dad, can we talk? In your office?"

Michael lifted a shoulder. "Sure. What is it, Josh?"

Josh hitched his head and led his dad back to the ranch office. He took one of the seats across the desk from his father's swivel chair and waited for his father to sit. Then taking a deep breath, he said, "It's about Roy. He was drunk when Kate and I got to the pickup point."

Josh filled his father in on the details of Roy's condition earlier that day and other incidents he and Zane had tried to keep quiet to protect their foreman. "Kate says, and I have to agree, that we aren't doing him any favors by ignoring his problem. I think time has come for an intervention."

Michael steepled his fingers and tapped his chin with the bridged fingertips. Finally his father sighed. "I've known for years that Roy drinks too much. And, yes, we've swept it under the rug as long as the ranch didn't suffer from it. But you're right. We've kicked this particular can down the road too long. Brady needs to be involved in this…whatever it is we're doing. We need to be unified, firm, but not judgmental or confrontational."

Josh nodded and rubbed the tired muscles in the back of his neck. "Agreed."

A knock interrupted them, and Dave Giblan opened the door. "Sorry. Am I interrupting?" The ranch hand spotted Josh, and his face brightened. "Hey, look who's home! Glad to see you back in one piece."

Josh nodded his thanks, and Dave faced Michael.

"What can I do for you, Dave?" His dad pushed to his feet and then, after flipping through a few envelopes on his desk, handed one to the hand. "Besides give you your paycheck."

"That'd be what I came for." Dave took the envelope, ripped it open as he turned toward the door, then stopped. Faced Michael again. Dave's face was grim, concerned. "Um, I almost hate to mention this again, but…I really need a raise."

Frowning, Michael dropped his gaze to his desk and shook his head. "Dave, I just can't—"

"I know things are tight for you, but they're tight for me, too!" Dave protested. "Since Karl left, I've had more work to do, and no compensation for the extra hours."

"I know, Dave. I—"

"And with this new adventures enterprise," Dave said, looking to Josh, his tone full of frustration, "you and Zane are spending more time with that and less helping with the herd."

Josh shot his father a guilty look. He and Zane had promised their dad they'd not let the adventure ranch interfere with regular ranch business, and for the most part they hadn't. But Dave had a point.

"Last summer when the herd got poisoned, who stayed up all hours tending to sick cows? And when the crop got burned, who went all the way to Omaha to drive in the truck with extra winter feed, even though it was Christmas Eve?"

"I know, Dave," Michael said quietly.

"Last year, you put me off until this year. And I know I've already asked earlier this spring, but…damn it! I'm living paycheck to paycheck and busting my ass for you. And for what?" Dave braced his hands on his hips and glared at them. "It's not right."

Michael said nothing for several tense seconds. Josh could see the weight of all the ranch burdens stooping his father's back and sensed the strain under the surface of his father's flat expression. This stress wasn't good for his father's blood pressure. Josh was about to intervene, bodily remove Dave, if needed, when Michael spoke.

"You're right, Dave. And I'm sorry we've put so much on you."

Dave relaxed his combative stance, exhaled.

"I'll find the money to give you a raise…somewhere. It won't be much, I'm afraid. But I promise you, when the ranch is back on its feet, you will receive a healthy bonus."

"*If* the ranch gets back on its feet," Dave said, his expression grim as he stormed out.

"And where do you think you're going to find the

money to give him his raise?" Josh asked his dad after a few moments of silence.

Michael rubbed a hand on his thinning hair. "Hell if I know. My retirement fund? Maybe the Christmas account your mother doesn't think I know about."

"Dad…"

"Not your problem, Josh. I'll come up with something. I'm good at finding crazy solutions to impossible situations." His father gave him a sad smile. "You remember the way I jury-rigged the hay baler when it quit two years ago?"

Josh grinned and nodded. "American ingenuity at its best."

"I'll figure this out, too. I still have a trick or two up my sleeve. Right now…you go rest." His smile faded. "And we'll talk to Roy tomorrow."

But he didn't want the burden of solving the family's financial crisis to fall on his father. His dad's blood pressure was already threatening his health. Josh wanted, *needed*, in a way he couldn't explain, to be a problem solver for his father, his family. He wanted to protect his father's health, his family's home. Acid bit his gut as he realized that with his disastrous trip with Kate, he'd only made things worse. Losing Roy, even if just for a few months to a rehab clinic, would put an additional strain on the rest of them. Dave would stroke when he learned he'd be asked to do even more in Roy's absence.

Josh paused in the hallway by a family portrait made just before he, Zane and Piper had graduated from high school. He studied the smiles, the faces, noting the changes. His dad had aged so much in the last ten years. And what about himself? How was he any different than the reckless kid who'd earned the reputation for being more a source of gray hair to his parents than a reason to brag? Rodeo trophies didn't help the family business one bit.

He rammed the side of his fist against the wall and made his way to his bedroom. After he took a quick shower, still ruing his past choices, Josh found his mother's cat asleep on his bed. He rolled his eyes and scooted the deadweight fluff ball off his pillow. "Move it, Zeke. I have an appointment with that pillow myself for the next six to eight hours."

Zeke stood and yawned lazily. Then, as Josh settled in the bed, the cat stretched out along Josh's side. He scratched the feline's head, earning a purr. As Josh closed his eyes in search of sleep, he thought back to the night before, lying under the stars with Kate cuddled against his side. His body tightened remembering her seductive kisses, the warmth of her body tucked under his arm. Zeke was a far cry from the woman he longed to be sharing his bed with, but he reluctantly admitted that having the feline's company, the sound of Zeke's low, rumbling purr lulling him to sleep, was better than sleeping alone.

Kate woke alone and disoriented in a dark room. Her body ached, and her head puzzled over the lingering images of a dream about rafting with a drunk rabbit that she had to protect from a baby bear. She sat up in the twin bed and raked her hair from her face. Placing herself only took a few seconds, as her surroundings came into focus.

Wood-paneled walls... A quilted bed cover...

Josh. Her heart lifted, and she smiled. She was back

at the ranch. Safe. And Josh was somewhere close by, probably just waking up himself. She remembered the morning before, the comfort of his arm around her against the misty morning chill. The day had gone steadily downhill after the bliss of waking next to Josh. She shoved that thought aside.

Kate's first order of business this morning was to find Josh, see how his shoulder was, thank him again for everything he did to take care of her over the last few days. Maybe she'd steal another kiss or two. And maybe broach the topic of what, if any, chance they had of building a relationship.

He'd been the last thing on her mind last night as she fell asleep and the first thing on her mind this morning when she woke up. The image of him as he'd looked atop the bluff at the swimming hole, the sun on his hair and his muscular body stripped to his boxer briefs, brought an immediate smile to her lips…and a curl of desire to her core.

She ambled stiffly down the hall, her muscles aching as if she'd spent too long in the saddle. Kate grinned to herself when that particular expression came to mind. She had ranch on the brain, it seemed.

She found Dawn in the kitchenette, already dressed and sipping a cup of coffee.

"I hope you saved me some of that," she said, aiming a finger toward Dawn's mug.

Her friend turned to her, smiling. "Look at you up at daybreak!"

Kate grunted. "Well, when you hit the sack as early as I did and sleep like the dead for nine hours, it's a little easier. I still need coffee, though."

Dawn stepped aside and waved a hand to the coffeepot. "Just finished brewing."

Yawning, Kate moved to the coffee maker and filled a mug. As she added sugar and milk, she cut a side glance to Dawn. "I don't suppose you've talked to Josh or Zane this morning. Do you know how Josh's doctor visit went?"

Dawn leaned back against the counter, cradling her mug in her hands. "Haven't heard, haven't seen them this morning." She sipped from her coffee while eyeing Kate over the rim. "You gonna tell me what happened with you two the last few days, or do I have to torture you with my singing to get it from you?"

Kate arched an eyebrow. "Your singing is that bad?"

Dawn bellowed a few lines of "You Raise Me Up."

Kate nearly choked on her coffee as a laugh sputtered from her. She waved a hand in front of her. "Stop, stop! Please. I'll talk."

Dawn flashed a gloating grin. "Works every time."

"I'll tell you everything about the last couple days, but first, I want to talk to Josh."

Dawn's focus shifted to the window, and she nodded toward it. "Well, there he goes. Now's your chance."

Kate's pulse drummed a little faster as she angled her gaze out the front window and spotted Zane and Josh walking toward the stable together. Josh's left arm was in a sling, but beyond that she couldn't tell anything about his recovery from their physically stressful ordeal.

"Oh, be still my heart. I'm definitely starting to think a threesome with those two would be worth upsetting Dean," Dawn mumbled.

Kate shot her an exasperated look, and Dawn chuckled. "Kidding!" Then under her breath, "Sorta."

Kate took a gulp of coffee, then plunked her mug down. "I'm gonna dress and go catch up with him." As she headed back to her guest room to change into jeans, she called over her shoulder, "And when I see Dean again, I'm going to tell him what you said!"

"I'll deny everything!"

Once dressed, Kate fortified herself with one last sip of java before heading out to the stable. The morning was chilly, but the sun was beginning to peek through the last of the rain clouds, promising a brighter, warmer day to come.

With the earworm planted in her head, thanks to Dawn, Kate found herself humming Josh Groban as she crossed the ranch yard. Ironic that Dawn had picked that song to sing...or rather to screech. Many of her restless thoughts about Josh had centered around how he'd encouraged her, challenged her, pushed her to face down her childhood fears.

Would it sound patronizing if I said I was proud of you?

When the stakes were high, when someone needed you, you acted without reservation.

He had given her a lot to think about. Assuming she could stop thinking about him and their kisses, about his warm body curled around her when they slept by the river, about the way he looked at her and could make her toes curl with just his sexy grin.

She stepped into the stable and paused to let her eyes adjust to the dimmer light, then followed the sound of voices down the alley to one of the back stalls.

"Damn it, Josh, I told you to wait at the campsite! I

told you we'd pick you up there," Zane said, his voice tight with anger.

"And I chose to keep going. You're not my boss or my father. You're my partner and brother. I decide what I do."

A jolt of shock streaked through Kate. What was this? Josh was told to wait at the campsite? She held her breath as she continued listening, stunned by what she was hearing.

"Not in business you don't. Did you not hear me when I said the insurance company told me to suspend operation? We are without coverage until an investigation of the accident is conducted to exonerate us of fault and a new safety inspection of the equipment is completed. Not only were you working without the safety net of insurance, the fact is, none of the rest of the crap that happened to you would have happened if you'd followed my directions!"

"I had my reasons for continuing. I couldn't accept failure as an option."

"You put the business, our family's livelihood at risk because of your stupid pride?"

"That's not what—"

"What happens if she sues us, Josh? We lose everything! The insurance company won't back us, because you went off the grid!"

"Maybe I was trying to make sure she didn't sue!"

Kate stiffened, a numbness overtaking her limbs even as nausea built in her gut.

"If we'd quit when we did," Josh continued, "Kate would have only known the terror of that zip line falling. That's what she would have taken away from the trip. I wanted her to have better memories to hold on to."

"Better memories…such as you seducing her? You thought you could employ your charms on her, because it's harder to bring yourself to file suit against someone you've slept with?"

"We didn't sleep together."

"Semantics. You still took her to the swim hole, got naked with her, made out…"

"That's not what—"

"Come on, Josh. I know you and women. Are you gonna stand there and deny it?"

Kate's heart thudded against her ribs, and her eyes burned with tears. The intimacy he'd shared with her had been a ploy to win her cooperation in not suing the family over the zip-line accident? She'd had her heart broken by men in the past, men who promised commitment and easily changed their minds when the wind blew in a different direction. But Josh took things to a new level. His betrayal, his manipulation of her feelings cut her deeper than she'd ever been cut before.

"So what? She was willing. It was mutual. What are you implying?"

"Oh, I'm not implying anything, Josh! I'm saying it to your face. You were reckless and out of line. You took unnecessary chances and put Kate at risk for no reason but your own stupid, selfish agenda."

"And I'd do it again in the same situation!" Josh shouted back. "I won't apologize, if that's what you're after. I told you I had my reasons, and I stand by them."

"Do you think you hold enough sway with her to get her to sign a settlement agreement? If we ask a lawyer to draw up an offer of some payment in exchange for—" Zane was saying, but Kate had heard enough. She was so ill with hurt and crushed by Josh's deceit she thought she might vomit. She staggered out of the stable, not even being careful not to make noise.

Leave. She had to leave.

She ran on wobbly legs back to the guesthouse, determined to pack her bag and be gone within the hour.

As she stormed into the guesthouse, she made a beeline for the bathroom before she lost what little food was in her stomach. The taste of bile, the sourness her vomit left in her mouth paled compared to the bitterness of her heartache and disillusionment. Josh's kisses had been a lure to win her favor. His soft looks and tender caresses had been tools to earn her trust…so he could manipulate their relationship to save his skin.

I had my reasons.

Selfish reasons. Deceitful reasons. Heartbreakingly painful reasons.

"Kate? What— Good grief!" Dawn came to the door of the bathroom where Kate was heaving dryly. "Are you all right?"

She shook her head and choked on a sob.

"Of course you're not. I can see that." Dawn stepped closer and rubbed a hand on Kate's back. "Stupid question. Sorry."

Kate stretched out a hand. "Will you hand me th-that towel?"

Dawn snagged the facecloth from the rack and passed it to her. "What in the world happened?"

She shook her head. "I don't want to talk about it. I just… I have to get out of here."

"You're leaving?" Dawn sounded startled. "Now? But our flight isn't until tomorrow."

"I don't care." She straightened, wiping her mouth, and pinned a pleading look on Dawn. "Will you call a cab for me? I want to be gone as soon as possible."

"I don't understand. Tell me what happened? Kate, maybe this is PTSD. You went through a trauma and—"

"It's Josh. He betrayed me. I fell in love with him, but it was all fake for him. A ploy. And I have to get out of here before I—"

"That sonofabitch!" Dawn's back stiffened, and she narrowed an angry look on Kate. "What did he do?"

Kate pushed past her friend and stumbled into the guest room she'd been using. "I said I don't want to talk about it. Will you call me a cab or not?"

"I will. If you're sure that's—"

"I'm s-sure," she stuttered through her tears. Kate tossed her suitcase on her unmade bed and began throwing her clothes in, clean and dirty jumbled together. She raked an armful of toiletries from the dresser top and threw them on top of the clothes without putting them in her zippered pouch. Everything in her suitcase was a chaotic jumble—just like her heart.

"Please, at least tell me the sheriff found something at the campsite that tells us who the saboteur is," Josh said, once Zane had finished reaming him out over defying his directions.

"No. Nothing they've shared anyway. Dad's getting especially pissed off with the sheriff. They're still implying with each new incident that it's an inside job. A hoax to scam our insurance company."

Josh kicked at the dirty straw on the stable floor.

"If we don't find the person behind the sabotage soon, the guy will ruin us."

"Tell me something I don't know."

Josh gave his brother a side glance and scowled. "How sure are we that the cops investigating this aren't dirty?"

Zane blinked his surprise. "We've known the sheriff and his deputies most of our lives."

Now Josh gave his brother the *tell me something I don't know* look.

"I'm just saying…Boyd Valley is a small town. Wouldn't there be talk if the sheriff or someone in the department was crooked?" Zane asked.

Josh smacked his good hand on the railing of the nearest stall. "Well, maybe it's because we are *too* small and short on the latest resources and training that they can't find the vandal."

Zane shrugged. "Maybe. And he doesn't have to be crooked to have a blind spot." When Josh frowned at him, Zane added, "You know, divided loyalties or self-interests."

"So what do we do about it?"

Zane shook his head. "Not much that I can see."

"Well, that's not good enough for me. If the sheriff won't do his job, I say we take matters in our own hands."

"Josh," Zane said in a warning tone.

"Damn it, there has to be something more we can do to stop this guy!"

"The last thing we need now is for you to go off half-cocked and get in trouble with the law."

He grunted. "Where has *the law* gotten us so far?"

"I swear, man. If you do something to screw up the investigation…"

"At least I'm willing to act." Spinning away, Josh stormed out of the stable, fuming at Zane's unwillingness to hear him out. For Zane, everything was black-and-white. Every choice had to follow the rules, had to toe the mark. Business trumped personal choice. In the vandalism investigation and with McCall Adventures.

Josh had dared to break the rules, because he saw something in Kate, a spark that needed to be fed kindling and given oxygen. Did he regret the choice he'd made to keep going, despite Zane's directive to stay at the campsite? Hell, no. Because Kate had shown her fire when tested. And he couldn't have been prouder of her.

Lost in his thoughts, he stalked toward the main house.

Kate. Beautiful, fierce, passionate Kate. What would happen now that the adventure trip was over? Would they—

A strong set of hands shoved his bad shoulder, and he staggered a step sideways.

Dawn stood next to him, glaring at him, hands on her hips. He hadn't seen or heard her approach, and her demeanor had him instantly on alert. "Dawn? What—"

"You prick! What did you do to Kate? What did you tell her?" Her eyes were bright with rage, and Josh gaped for a moment, trying to process the out-of-the-blue attack.

"Um…excuse me?"

"She's in there packing to leave!" Dawn waved a hand behind her in the general direction of the guesthouse. "She says you betrayed her. She had me call an Uber out here to take her to the airport."

Josh blinked, his pulse accelerating as her accusations and assertions penetrated the fog of his disbelief. "Betrayed her? How? I don't—"

"She wouldn't talk to me about it, but she was incredibly distraught after talking to you this morning. Throwing up, crying, shaking... What the hell did you say to her?"

Josh gave his head a little shake. "I don't know what you're talking about. I haven't seen her since she left the clinic yesterday with Piper to come back here."

"Oh, really?" Dawn said, her voice sarcastic and highly skeptical.

Josh spread his hands, and he sent a concerned look toward the guesthouse. What was going on with Kate? Should he go talk to her? "I swear."

His expression must have convinced her because her tone changed to surprise and doubt. "Really?"

"I haven't talked to Kate today. I've been down at the stable with Za—" A cold, prickly suspicion raised the hair on the back of his neck. "Aw, crap. Did she overhear me talking to Zane?"

Dawn drew her shoulders back. "I don't know what she heard. I just know she left about a half hour ago to talk to you and came back within fifteen minutes in tears and in a rush to leave. When I asked her about it, the most she'd say was that you betrayed her."

A rock settled in his gut when he thought of what she might have heard. Josh ran his good hand through his still shower-damp hair. "This is bad. She wasn't supposed to hear th—"

Dawn issued a harsh barking laugh. "Spoiled your little ploy, did it?"

"What ploy? Dawn, I don't—" Josh cut his plea off. Dawn was not the one he needed to convince, not the one who needed to hear his explanation. He started toward the guesthouse with long strides. "She's in there now? Packing?"

Dawn grabbed him by his belt and brought him up short. "Whoa, cowboy! You're the last person she wants to see right now."

"I haven't done anything! Not like she thinks." He balled his hands in fists. "I have to tell her why I made the choices I did. She has to know the whole story."

"What story? What happened out there these last few days?" Dawn asked, her narrowed eyes full of accusation.

"Plenty. But right now Kate has a wrong impression about things, and I have to talk to her before she leaves." He pried Dawn's hand off his belt and started back toward the guesthouse. The crunch of tires on gravel stopped him this time. He turned to the main entrance to the ranch to find a dark sedan pulling up the drive.

"Better talk fast," Dawn said. "That's her ride to the airport."

Chapter 16

Kate was shoving the last of her belongings into a carry-on duffel when she heard the toot of a car horn. Her Uber had arrived, and not a moment too soon. The sooner she could get away from the Double M and Josh's memory, the sooner she could start patching her broken heart back together.

She glanced in the mirror over the dresser as she shouldered the duffel strap and hoisted her suitcase. The wet, bloodshot eyes that stared back at her looked as haunted, as bereft as she felt. She shook her head and scolded her image. "Stupid, stupid, stupid!"

She'd known better than to fall for a hotshot, lothario cowboy. She was such a cliché. A vacation fling? Had experience taught her nothing? With a grunt of disgust, she stomped out through the front door of the guesthouse and across the ranch yard to the waiting sedan.

"Kate!"

Josh's voice slammed into her with the force of a wrecking ball. She froze, unable to draw a breath or raise her head to look for him. Only her heart seemed able to function, thrumming and thrashing like a drunken hummingbird.

He appeared beside her from the direction of the main house, Dawn on his heels.

She found the strength to stumble forward. She only had to reach the Uber, and she could escape. "I have nothing to say to you," she grated through clenched teeth.

"Then listen to me." He caught her arm, and she shook him off. From the corner of her eye, she saw Dawn heading toward the waiting car.

"Kate, I didn't—"

"No! I've heard enough of your lies. You have done nothing but deceive me for your own gain for the last two days." She struggled to hold back a fresh wave of tears as she continued marching toward the Uber. The driver took a step toward her, as if to help her with her bag, then stopped and hung back with a dubious look as he took in their spat.

"My own gain? Wh— No!"

"Oh, yes. Please don't make it worse by denying it now. I heard you, Josh. I heard you telling your brother that you defied his directions so you could use your charms on me to convince me not to sue your company over the zip-line failure."

Josh was shaking his head. "That's not what I said. If you'd give me a chance to—"

"To what? Manipulate my feelings some more? To seduce me for the good of the business?" She felt the hot sting of a tear leaking from her eye, damn it. She swiped it away with an angry flick of her fingers. "My own fault, I guess."

"No, Kate." He tried again to slow her down with a hand on her arm.

"I told myself not to fall for you. I knew you weren't a forever kind of guy. But somehow I let myself believe that I sensed something more in your kisses. That I—"

"Come on, Kate!" Josh reached for her suitcase, and she pulled it away. "Give me a chance to ex—"

"No. I don't want to hear a bunch of justifications for what you did."

He took a couple of long steps to get in front of her and block her path. He wrenched her suitcase from her hand, growling, "Just stop for five minutes and listen to me. Please!"

She stopped. Lifted her chin. Glared at him. "Do you deny that Zane told you to stay at the campsite after the first night? That we were going to be picked up in the morning, but you told me we had to keep going in order to be rescued?"

Guilt shaded his face, and he wet his lips. "Yes and no."

"How can it be both?"

"Yes, he told me to stay put, and no, I didn't say we had to keep going."

She stiffened in shock. "So you're saying I'm a liar? 'Cause I'm pretty sure I lived it, and I know what happened."

"Think about it, Kate. I never said we couldn't quit." He aimed a finger at her, and she slapped it away. Raising both palms to her, he continued, "I asked you to trust me. I asked you to let me help you face your fears, and you *did*! You were awesome!"

She blinked hard and gave her head a shake. "Whoa, whoa, whoa! Are you putting this on me? Like I was some charity case you had to save from myself?"

His shoulders drooped. "God, no, Kate. You're no charity case. You're a bright, dynamic woman with so much life and potential. I could see your inner struggle, and I wanted to help you break free from—"

She shoved at his chest. "So you appointed yourself my shrink? My savior? Who asked you to fix me?"

"Um...well, Dawn sorta mentioned—"

She snorted her disbelief and disdain, and he quickly added, "I'm not saying this is her fault! I take responsibility for my choices."

"Good! That's a start." She narrowed her eyes on him and poked his hard chest with her finger. "If you will recall, my condition for going forward on the trip with you was that you be honest with me. You agreed, but then you kept on lying to me."

He shook his head. "No, from the moment I made that promise, I was honest with you. I swear!"

"But you didn't tell me the truth about Zane's directive to stay at the camp, or that we would have been picked up if we'd stayed put that morning."

He looked away, sighing. "No. But, Kate—"

"Goodbye, Josh." She reached for her suitcase, but he refused to let go. "Give it to me, or I swear I will leave without it."

"Kate, I know we had some troubles on our trip, unexpected problems with the bear and the floodwater, but...can you honestly say you regret going ahead with me?"

His question stunned her. "Excuse me?"

"We had some good times, too. You met every challenge I put before you and more. You blossomed, Kate." He reached for her chin and stroked her cheek with his thumb. His touch sent a jolt of tender, heart-wrenching sensations to her core. "And I was *not* faking those kisses."

Her vision blurred as moisture puddled in her eyes. "Neither was I."

He curled up a corner of his mouth in a grin.

"I told myself not to lose my heart. I didn't want to get involved with another weekend romance. A dead-end fling. But somewhere along the way, I fell in love with you, Josh."

He jerked his head up, his body stiffening, his eyes widening. "What?"

"I fell in love with you, Josh."

He fell back a step, his hand lifting to his mouth. "Kate?"

"You want me to stay? To talk this out? I will, if you can *honestly* say you feel the same way. That you see a future for us. That those kisses you weren't faking mean that you love me, too."

He opened his mouth, staring at her with a stricken expression.

"Honesty, Josh," she reminded him. "I swear if you lie about this, I'll never forgive you. Do you love me?"

He looked ready to be sick. His throat worked as he swallowed hard, then he wet his lips and swiped his palms on his jeans.

She barked a bitter laugh. But the terrified look on his face made it clear the joke was on her. "That's what I thought."

If she'd thought she couldn't hurt any more than when she'd overheard Josh and Zane talking, she'd been wrong. Even when she'd offered her heart and soul, risked everything to give Josh one last chance to redeem himself, he'd shown his true colors. A playboy. A tease. A heartbreaker.

"Oh, Josh," she said in a voice barely above a whisper. "You broke the most important promise of all. You promised not to let me get hurt." She pressed a trembling hand to her chest, and squeaked, "But you've broken my heart."

The color leached from his face.

She lifted the suitcase and pushed past him as she crossed the rest of the ranch yard on trembling legs. The Uber driver rushed forward to get the bag from her and toss it in the back of his car. Her driver seemed as eager to leave the emotional showdown behind as she was.

She didn't look back, even when she heard the crunch of boots on gravel coming up behind her. She snatched open the back door of the sedan and tossed her purse on the seat. Dawn only gave her a sorrowful look and a hug before backing away. "Text me when you're home safely."

"Kate! Wait!"

She paused. Glanced back at Josh. His eyes were panicked, his expression pained. "I…like you. I really… I care about you. I do. I—"

Disappointment pinged her heart one more time.

She shook her head and climbed in the car. Closed the door.

As her driver headed down the rutted drive toward the highway, she said, "The Denver airport, please."

* * *

Josh stared at the plume of dust that hung in the air long after Kate's ride had disappeared down the highway. He couldn't move, couldn't speak, couldn't think. His insides sucked at him as if a giant vacuum was pulling him into a black internal void. He shied away from analyzing the sensation, knowing on some subconscious level that naming what he felt would open him to a world of pain and sorrow that would undo him. The empty blackness filled his lungs, stole his oxygen, suffocated him. But in his paralysis, he couldn't draw in air. Until…

Finally, a ragged gasp wrenched from his throat, breaking the vise strangling him and opening the floodgates to a cascade of stinging realities. Gone. Kate had left. Been angry.

You've broken my heart.

And his own. His brain clicked slowly through the bitter words she'd thrown at him, knowing he'd earned her anger. He had deceived her, good though his intentions might have been. He'd wanted to show her what he saw in her, the spark she had buried under her fears. And he had. He thought. But she felt too betrayed to see it.

And what did it matter now? He'd had the chance to tell her what she'd come to mean to him and…choked.

Dawn marched past him without a word, only shooting him a dirty look as she returned to the guesthouse.

Do you love me? Such a simple, straightforward question. All he'd had to say was *yes*, but he'd bungled it with his cowardly hedging and stammering. What was wrong with him? Why did the idea of loving her and building a life with her cause him to freeze like that?

"Josh?"

Given the chance to do that conversation over, what could he have said that would have kept her here, that could make up for the hurt and anger she felt after overhearing his conversation with Zane? Zane, who'd baited him and pushed all Josh's buttons until he'd spewed stupid thoughtless words that he wanted desperately to take back.

"Josh? Do you have a minute?"

He startled from his daze when Brady stepped in front of him, frowning. "Huh? Oh, yeah... I... What is it?"

"Geez, where were you just then? I've been trying to get your attention for like two minutes."

Josh inhaled and blew the breath out, hoping to clear the cobwebs and loosen the constriction in his chest. Instead, Brady's question only brought the truth home. Pain slashed through him, baring his soul and gouging at his heart. He had to clench his back teeth and squeeze his hands into fists to shove the knot of emotion down. He shook his head. "Forget it."

Brady gave him a dubious look but shoved his hands in his front pockets and cleared his throat. "I, uh... just wanted to apologize for yesterday. For my dad. He feels bad about his condition...when you two got to the pickup. He—"

"Stop."

"Hmm?"

Josh worked to loosen the tension in his jaw. "You don't need to apologize for yesterday. Your dad does."

Brady's expression darkened, and he glanced away. "I know. But I—"

"But nothing. You've spent your life apologizing for him and covering for him. I know. But it's gotta stop. Enough is enough."

Brady shifted his weight from one leg to another and gave Josh an uneasy look. "Meaning?"

"No more apologizing. It's time for an intervention. It's time for your father to get help, or—"

Brady drew his shoulders back, his eyes wary. "Or?"

Josh swiped his good hand down his face and shook his head. "Not my call."

"Look, I know he screwed up yesterday, but he's not—"

"Yeah, Brady. He is." Josh pinched his mouth into a scowl and waved his hand to stall Brady's reply. "I can't deal with this right now. I just…"

Brady stared at him silently for a few seconds, then tipped his head. "Are you okay, man?"

Josh jerked his gaze to Brady's, an automatic reassurance on his tongue. But when he met his lifelong friend's concerned expression, he flinched. Rasped, "No."

"What's going on?" Brady asked quietly.

He drew a shaky breath and muttered, "I think I just let my best chance of happiness walk out of my life."

Kate walked up the steps to the front door of her condo, juggling her luggage as she fumbled for her key. She'd flown standby and managed to get on a flight that got her into Dallas six hours after leaving the ranch. Leaving Josh. But not leaving the hollow ache and bitter humiliation of having fallen into the same reckless pattern of giving a vacation romance far too much of her heart. She had no one to blame but herself.

Sure, Josh had used her and betrayed her trust, but she'd known better than to offer up her loyalty and her love to someone she'd known to be averse to commitment. An adrenaline junkie, of all things. What did she think would happen? That she, someone who eschewed unnecessary risks, could live happily ever after with a guy who wanted to make a living off putting himself in harm's way?

She pushed through the front door and dumped her bags to be dealt with later. "Sadie? I'm home, kitty girl!" Thank God. Home sweet condo.

All the troubles and dangers they'd run into on their hike to the pickup point were just evidence that she was not meant to tempt fate. She was safer here in her condo. Safer…even if not happier.

Kate blinked hard and scoffed. Where the heck had that thought come from? She was pretty miserable right now, but she could draw a straight line to the reason for her heartbreak and frustration.

Sadie, her black-and-white rescue cat, trotted into the foyer and, butt in the air, stretched her back as she yawned.

"There's my girl!" Kate cooed, squatting to stroke the cat's glossy fur.

Sadie rubbed against Kate's leg, purring, but when Kate tried to pick the cat up for a snuggle, Sadie wiggled away with a chirp.

"Right, right. You don't do cuddles. But have you ever thought that maybe I needed a hug?" she fussed at the cat. "Maybe after a week away, I missed you and wanted to say a proper hello?"

Sadie returned, again rubbing against Kate's shin but cringing slightly when Kate tried to scratch her cheek. Rescued as a kitten from a grocery store parking lot, Sadie had been a stray, fending for herself during the earliest weeks of her life when human bonding was the most critical. Kate understood that her cat's distaste for being held and overpetted wasn't personal, but having just been rejected by Josh, the feline's snub stung.

But then, the jewelry store commercial hawking engagement rings on the cab radio had stung, the flight attendant's innocent "Are you traveling alone?" had stung and the numerous texts from Dawn checking on her had stung. Everything seemed to remind her that she'd fallen for a man who could only muster a stiff "Uh… I like you" in response to her baring her soul to him.

"Fine," she told her cat, rising to her feet again. "When you're ready for attention, I'll be in my room unpacking."

She marched upstairs, threw her suitcase on the bed and caught the sob that swelled in her throat. *Don't. Do not cry over him. Forget him and move on.*

Mustering a stiff lip, she began sorting through the mess in her luggage.

The thundering beat of cat feet racing from the living room and up the stairs, full tilt, was her only warning before Sadie flew through the bedroom door and launched onto the bed, then the bedside stand, and finally skidded onto the windowsill, where she rattled the lowered blinds as she crashed to a stop.

Kate chuckled wryly at her kitty tornado. "So you are excited to see me after all?"

Sadie's tail twitched, and she chirped before dashing off again down the stairs like a galloping mustang.

A sharp pang stabbed Kate as the analogy brought back memories of Josh helping her with her horse, his hands on her waist when he boosted her into her saddle. She sank onto her bed, giving in to the tears that rose quickly. She'd held them at bay for the entire trip home, but now, in the privacy of her condo, she indulged in a cathartic cry.

She scoffed as she grabbed a tissue from the bedside and wiped her nose. Who was she kidding? It would take more than a bout of pity-party tears to purge her heart of Josh McCall and his betrayal.

Sadie dashed back up the stairs and sprang onto the bed. As if sensing her human's distress, Sadie curtailed her sprint and gave Kate a blinking look before rubbing against her with a chirpy meow and a purr.

"Thanks, Sadie." Sniffling, Kate stroked the cat's back, acknowledging the proffered comfort, but knowing it would take a lot more than feline snuggles to move beyond this heartache.

"We know you've suffered a great deal of heartache in the last couple of years," Josh's father told Roy the next day across the foreman's kitchen table, "but your drinking has become a problem."

Roy's jaw tightened, and he said nothing. The foreman only stared at his hands, flattened against the tabletop.

From his seat at the end of the table, Josh watched the exchange with his own hands fisted in his lap. Guilt pricked his conscience. His father had decided to confront Roy based on Josh's report of the foreman's drunkenness at the pickup spot. But knowing they were doing the right thing for Roy didn't mean he didn't feel a tug of regret and sympathy for the man who'd been a second father to him.

"I know that you were drunk the other day when you were sent to wait for Josh and Kate Carrington," Michael said.

Roy gave Josh a side glance. His eyes held no accusation, but Josh's gut wrenched just the same.

"Your drinking could have cost them their lives," his father continued in a grave but even tone. "As it was, Ms. Carrington had to take the lead in getting Josh to safety. The whole situation could have gone much differently, with Josh getting swept downstream in the flash flood, if she hadn't managed the crisis."

The mention of Kate's name scraped claws over already raw and bleeding internal wounds. He'd tried several times to call, text and email Kate his apologies, his explanations, but he'd had no response.

You promised not to let me get hurt. But you've broken my heart...

Her parting words had haunted him during a sleepless night. Memories of her kiss, her laugh, her courage followed him throughout his day. Thanks to his injured shoulder, he could only do about half of his typical workload around the ranch, leaving him far too much time to replay every painful word of her leaving, every bittersweet moment of their time together.

"So I'm fired?" Roy asked, cutting into Josh's dark thoughts.

Josh cut a sharp, querying glance to his father, then to Brady, who leaned against the kitchen counter behind his father. What had he missed? Firing Roy had never been part of the plan.

"I'm saying you need to dry out. You need to go cold turkey and stay sober. For your own health and well-being. If you can do that, you can stay on. Your job isn't going anywhere. If you can't stay sober—" Michael exhaled, his expression full of regret "—I'll have no choice but to ask you to leave."

Roy's eyes narrowed as he looked up at Josh's father. "After all the years I've been here? All the hours and loyalty and—"

"Dad," Brady interrupted, putting a hand on Roy's shoulder as he pulled out the fourth chair at the table and sat down. "You're not hearing what he's saying. You decide how this goes. He's keeping you on, giving you the opportunity to get yourself help to quit drinking. Once you get sober, you come back to your job. He's even offering to continue to pay your salary while you're in rehab. That's more than fair. It's beyond generous."

Roy was silent, his expression chastened and guilty for several moments. The loud ticking of the Summerses' electric clock marked the seconds as Roy digested what he'd been offered. Finally he said softly, "I don't need rehab."

Brady groaned and muttered, "Dad…"

"I'll do it on my own. I can quit."

"You've promised me that before," Brady said.

"This time, I'll—"

"This time," Brady interrupted, "you'll go to rehab. For me. For Connor. Hell, *for yourself.* Don't you see what you've become?"

Roy lifted a stark look to his son. He began to tremble, then covered his face with his hands, and his shoulders shook as he wept.

Josh squirmed in his seat, seeing the other man's sorrow and pain. He wanted to cry with Roy. Not just because he hated seeing Roy's turmoil, but because Brady's question echoed inside Josh, as well. *What have you become? Have you become the labels that the world assigned you or are you the man Kate fell in love with?*

"I've been in touch with a couple of clinics. Both are viable options. Both within a couple hours' drive from here," Brady said, his hand on his father's shoulder.

"No," Roy mumbled. "I can do it alone."

Alone. Josh's heart raced, panic clawing at him. Was he doomed to spend his life alone? The thought of never seeing Kate again filled him with dread and a profound grief.

"I know you're scared, Dad," Brady said, and Roy shook his head in denial. "But the experts say the first step is admitting you need help."

"I'm not scared," Roy said defiantly, although his countenance contradicted him.

Josh understood Roy's reluctance to admit he needed help, his unwillingness to admit his fear. No man wanted to own up to being afraid. Society saw fear as weakness.

His pulse ticked in rhythm with the Summerses' clock as his answer to Kate's final question clicked through his brain. Why hadn't he told her he loved her?

Because he'd been afraid.

His breath caught. He'd wanted nothing more than to help her find her courage, and when he'd needed to face his own fears, he'd balked.

"Courage is the ability to act, to do what is right, despite your fear," Michael said quietly, and Josh jerked his gaze toward his father. But Michael's focus was on Roy.

Their foreman raised his head, swiped at his face and swallowed hard. "I've let so many people down. I'm sorry."

Josh pictured Kate's tear-stained face as she turned away from him and climbed in her cab. Her disappointment. Her heartache. Her disillusionment. He'd failed her.

"So do something about it," Brady urged his father. "I can drive you to a clinic today. I have faith in you, Dad. You can beat this."

Kate, do you trust me? How many times had he asked her to put her faith in him on their perilous journey? And she had. Josh heaved a heavy sigh. Trust had to be earned. He had to regain her faith, her trust. But how? She wouldn't take his calls, answer his emails or texts.

Roy closed his eyes, bowed his head and whispered, "Okay. I'll go."

And in that instant, Josh knew what he had to do, too.

Chapter 17

Josh stared through the windshield as he drove past the grazing pastures. An all-too-familiar ache settled inside him. He'd taken for granted that the land would be in his family for generations to come, just like it had been for decades before. And yet other ranches in the area had failed. Drought, poor investments, recession. Neighboring ranches had been foreclosed on, stock, equipment and property sold to pay off debt. He'd even accompanied his father to a couple of the auctions as a teenager. They'd acquired one of their best breeding bulls at a foreclosure sale. Josh's gut clenched at the thought of his family's business being sold off piecemeal in that fashion.

"So, what are you going to say to her?" Piper's question yanked him out of his deliberations.

He shifted his gaze to his sister, who would drive the

truck home from the airport. "I honestly don't know. I'm hoping I'll figure that out when the time comes."

"You're just going to wing it?" She seemed stunned. "Don't you think winning her back deserves at least a little thought and preparation? A romantic speech? A grand gesture? A—"

"That's not how I operate. I'm more…extemporaneous." Partly true. He knew some of what he wanted to say, but he wanted Kate to be the first to hear it, not Piper. The rest would come from his heart.

"Well, good luck, Doofus. I want you to be happy. And if Kate is the one…"

"She is. I'm sure she is."

"So, I talked to Zane this morning before I headed to the airport," Dawn said via a phone call as Kate drove home from the office. "Because all business has been suspended until the insurance company officials are satisfied with repairs and reinspection of all aspects of McCall Adventures, our contract for marketing consultation is on hold, as well."

Kate squeezed the steering wheel. She knew this conversation was necessary, but she wasn't ready to deal with the McCalls' account. She might never be.

"Zane has already paid our firm for work done to date. We'll be fine on that score," Dawn said.

"But will the Double M and McCall Adventure Ranch survive this setback?" Kate mused, half to herself, half to Dawn.

"Not our problem, honey. Oh, they're boarding my flight. Gotta run."

Kate bade her friend safe travels and disconnected. Having endured a trying and tiring first day back at the office, she wanted nothing more than to pass the evening with a bottle of wine and mindless TV shows to distract her from the abyss in her heart. She'd spent the day answering numerous questions about her trip, the zip-line accident and the remnant scratches and bruises scattered across her skin, all reminders of Josh and his deception.

She'd brought in Chinese food, which she had no appetite for, and had just settled on her couch with a glass of merlot and Sadie on her lap, when her doorbell chimed. She considered ignoring it. She didn't want to buy magazines from the neighbor's kid or sign for any packages. Sadie raised her head when the bell sounded but didn't vacate her lap, another sign she should ignore the person at the door. But the visitor persisted, ringing her bell again and adding a knock. Her car was in the driveway and her lights were clearly on, so she couldn't very well pretend she wasn't home. Maybe if she—

"Kate?" a male voice called from her front door. "Are you there? Please open the door."

She gasped, startling Sadie from her lap.

Josh? Here?

After taking a swig of merlot to steady her nerves, she headed for the door on shaky legs. In the foyer, she paused and peeked out her peephole to confirm her suspicion.

Heart galloping, she spied Josh's slightly distorted face, broad shoulders and arm in a blue sling.

He rang her doorbell again and banged on her door, sending a fresh wave of adrenaline skittering along her nerves.

"Kate, please! Give me a chance to explain!" he called. "I just want—"

She opened the door, and the rest of his sentence fell away. His expression seemed both relieved and terrified. Or maybe that was just her projecting her own tangled feelings onto him.

"Hi," he said, fidgeting with the cowboy hat in his hands.

She gave him a stiff nod in greeting. She summoned a memory of his hat washing away in the floodwaters and mumbled, "You…got a new hat."

He looked down as if surprised to find himself holding the black Stetson. "Yeah. I mean, no. I had another." He swallowed. "Can I come in?"

Josh was here. In Dallas. At her home.

"How did you find me? Find my house?"

He turned up a palm. "Everything's on the internet these days. Welcome to the age of no privacy."

She sagged against the door. How many times had she wished Jason would show up at her house to apologize for hurting her, to tell her he was getting a divorce and wanted to be with her? Of course, Jason hadn't shown up, and she hadn't dared to hope that Josh would. Why travel down a road that led to deeper despair and a sharper sense of having been played the fool?

But Josh *was* here.

She drew a shallow breath into lungs tight with apprehension. Stepped back. Opened the door wider.

As he stepped into her foyer, Sadie, shy around strangers, scampered quickly past them and up the stairs to hide.

Josh tracked her black-and-white cat with his gaze. "You have a cat."

"Yeah."

"You never mentioned…" He hesitated, then said, "My family has a cat. Zeke. He's a real goofb—"

"I'm sure you didn't travel all the way here to talk about cats," she said, cutting him off. She didn't close the door, still uncertain she was going to let him stay. She was in no mood for chitchat or rehashing how he'd deceived her.

His expression darkened, chastened. "No. I didn't." He exhaled deeply and met her unflinching stare. "I came to say I'm sorry."

She clutched the doorknob tighter, needing the support when her knees wobbled. Moisture crept to her eyes, and she blinked rapidly to fight the tears. An apology was a start, but was that all? She held her breath, waiting him out.

I care about you. His bland reply to her profession of love replayed in her head and opened the scabs on her heart.

"Kate, I know what you overheard me say to Zane in the stable, but…you misunderstood."

She raised her eyebrows and screwed her face into an expression that said, *Really? That's how you want to start this conversation?*

And he balked. "Wait, that's not what I… Can I start over?"

She studied the panicked look in his eyes and the fine sheen of sweat on his brow, despite the mild temperature outside and air-conditioning inside. Flop sweat? Was he that anxious about what he had to say? A pulse of sympathy waded through the tension in her chest.

She closed the door, deciding to give him the benefit of the doubt. "All right. In here."

He followed her into her living room, where she reclaimed her spot on the couch and lifted her wine for another gulp.

"Your condo is great." He cast a sweeping glance around, a nervous grin tugging his lips.

"Thank you," she said flatly. "But please make your point. I'm too tired today for pleasantries and too hurt to pretend your showing up here isn't killing me." Her voice cracked, echoing her assertion.

He lowered himself onto the sofa beside her, setting his hat on her coffee table. His brow dipped, and his gaze softened with regret or concern or some other painful emotion that clouded his sky blue eyes. "I screwed up, Kate. I admit it. I made bad choices that hurt you, and I'm very sorry."

When he paused, searching her face as if looking for an answer, she said, "So you came all this way to apologize?"

He rubbed a hand on his chin. His knee. Through his hair. Clearly he was nervous, and her traitorous heart felt sorry for him. She squared her shoulders when her instinct nudged her to put him at ease. She would not let him off as easily as accepting his apology. "Well?"

Josh cleared his throat. "Partly. And I came, partly, because you wouldn't answer my calls. But mostly because you deserve to hear what I have to say in person."

She reached for her wine, and the merlot sloshed as she brought it to her lips, hand trembling. But even the wine couldn't calm the jitters dancing through her. "And what is that?"

He eyed her glass, wet his lips, and she realized she hadn't offered him anything to drink. *Bad Southern woman!*

But then, this wasn't the typical social visit, and she'd been distracted. Maybe in a moment, once he spit out whatever he was trying to say…

"When I left home to come here, I intended to explain why I didn't wait for Zane at the campsite, why I let you believe forging on was our only option." He pressed his mouth in a grim line before continuing. "I was going to repeat my argument that I hadn't *technically* said we had to go on, but that I'd asked you to trust me, that I'd urged you to keep going because I thought taking on the challenges of the trip would be helpful to you in overcoming your fears."

She shot him an ironic glare. "That's what you were going to say? Seems to me that you just did." She set her glass down with more force than necessary and straightened her spine. "And when exactly did I ask you to be my therapist? For you to put this off on me, as if it were my fault that—"

"No! Not your *fault*. That's not what I said." His tone rose several decibels, and his eyes narrowed. "And for the record, you did face some big obstacles with aplomb and grit." He reached for her hand, and her pulse scrambled. "You showed an inner strength and courage that you should be proud of. You see that, don't you?"

She tried to remove her hand from his, but his grip tightened.

Sighing, she gave a quick nod. "So what? I did what I had to do when I faced no other choice. Anybody would do the same. But that doesn't mean—"

"You didn't have to jump off the cliff at the swim hole. You didn't have to go in the swollen river to save that rabbit. You didn't have to swing that limb at the bear when she attacked."

She snorted derisively. "Like I was going to stand back and let the bear maul you? That doesn't count."

Josh's eyes widened. "Hell, yes, it does!"

She flashed back to the moment she'd raised the thick stick to defend Josh from the sow. She'd been terrified, but a deep-seated need to protect Josh had overridden all else. Because she'd already fallen in love with him by then. Not that she wouldn't have helped anyone else under those circumstances, but Josh—

"If I make only one point tonight," he said, cutting into her thoughts, "if I convince you of only one thing before you kick me out, please let it be that truth." He brushed his fingertips along her cheek, and the affection in his eyes raked her with bittersweet longing. "You are so much more than you give yourself credit for. So much braver and resourceful. Resilient and strong. You proved that on our trip many times over. And for that much, I'm not sorry."

"I—" she started, then took a breath. Took a moment to really reflect. To remember the events of the trip, not through the lens of heartache for his betrayal and lies, but from a deeply personal perspective.

The stark fear of the zip line breaking, then the comfort of Josh's arms after he rescued her. Reliving the events of her childhood tragedy as she confided them to Josh and sensing that the memories were loosening their grip on her. His challenge to jump off the rock wall at the swimming hole and sharing with Josh the kind of exhilaration she used to seek out for thrills.

On the flight home, in an effort to occupy her mind, she'd flipped through a travel magazine and read an article about scuba diving in underwater caves. And the idea hadn't unsettled her. She'd been intrigued. Titillated. Tempted. She hadn't considered the implication of that reversal before now, but the old adventurer of her childhood had stirred to life again. And she wasn't shrinking away with the doubts and nightmare flashes that used to haunt her.

"Kate?" Josh angled his head and gave her a querying look after a few moments of her reverie.

"Okay," she said with a nod. "I'll give you that. I have made progress in staring down my fears, my past. I did things on our trip I never would have thought I could do. And—" she cracked a smile "—I *am* proud of myself."

His own lopsided grin warmed his face. "Good."

"But—" She aimed a finger at him and lowered her brow. "That doesn't excuse you lying to me. And it doesn't change my hurt over—" *falling in one-sided love with you.*

She bit her tongue, swallowed her words. She really had no right to blame Josh for her losing control of her emotions. He'd never made promises or professions to her. Losing her heart to him, when experience and caution warned her otherwise, was on her.

He scooted closer to her, until his knee bumped hers and he could cradle her cheek with his good hand. "Which brings us back to my reasons for being here." He took a deep breath, and his face filled with strain and…was it fear? Grief?

Her heart bumped harder.

"All of what I just said is what I originally planned to say, but I've recently realized I owed you more. And I had to be truly honest with myself in order to find what I needed to tell you." She felt a shimmy from his fingers as they cupped her cheek. "On the plane, I realized that the real, bare-bones truth of why I ignored Zane's directions to stay at the camp, why I refused to give up on the trip… I was scared." He huffed a laugh with no humor. "Me, the fearless McCall triplet. The risk-taker. Mr. YOLO himself was scared." He paused and shook his head. "Ironic, huh? I told myself I was defying Zane because I didn't want you to be scared anymore, but I was the one who was terrified."

She peered deeply into his eyes. "Of failing." She said it matter-of-factly, and he raised his eyebrows.

"Well…yeah."

"And not just of losing your new business venture or even your family's ranch. Am I right?"

He blinked at her, his expression stunned. "Yeah. It's more about everything that losing the ranch would mean to my family. My dad already has high blood pressure. Losing the ranch could be devastating to his health. I've heard of ranchers who had to sell, file for bankruptcy, and they ended up killing themselves out of a sense of despair and failure."

She gripped his wrist, her chest aching, "Oh, Josh. How terrible!"

"And my mom… The ranch has been in her family for four generations. It would crush her to have to sell." He shook his head. "Not to mention the people who'd be out of work, without a home. People I care about, people who are family to me."

She could see his concern and compassion written in the lines that bracketed his eyes and mouth. The cowboy she'd presumed to be a shallow, womanizing thrill seeker had proven again and again to be a deeply caring, protective man who put others first.

"My sister just moved home to be part of the adventure business that I dreamed up. I owe it to her to make the business a success." He was talking faster now, the words spilling out like a pump that had been primed and now poured forth all that had been hidden in the well of his soul. He moved his hand to his leg, where he rubbed his palm, clearly agitated. "And Zane…he's been more than my brother all these years. He's my best friend. He may be my opposite in a lot of ways, but we are like two halves of a whole. I know how much he has invested in the new company. Not just his time, money and energy, but his passion and heart. If the adventure business fails, where will we—"

She put her hand on his face, and he stopped, his expression bereft. For a moment he gazed at her, silent, as if centering himself.

Finally he whispered, "I've been the irresponsible, reckless twin all my life. I guess I played into that label, because it was a way to be different from Zane, to have my own identity. But with the adventure ranch, I had a chance to be someone else. To be the one who helped hold on to the ranch and preserve the family's heritage. I wanted to use what I did best to save my family. When the zip line fell, once I knew you were safe, all I could think about was how I couldn't fail my family. They are everything to me."

"You did your best. You weren't to blame for the damage the vandal did to the zip line."

"The vandal…" Josh's jaw tightened, his mouth pressing in a taut line, and his face flushed. "*Damn*, but the idea that someone was going after my family in

such damaging ways, that someone could get hurt…"
He shook his head, his gaze distant. "At that point, to
me, giving up on the trip was letting the bastard win.
As good as handing him the keys to the ranch, with
all my family's history and hard work cast aside as
garbage."

He closed his eyes, clearly fighting to bring his emotions under control.

She wrapped her hand around his, the need to support him stronger than her need to protect her fragile
emotions.

"So…" He lifted his gaze from their hands to meet
her gaze. "That's what I couldn't bring myself to say
before now. What I only just figured out for myself. I
dragged you through the trip, cajoled you into going,
against Zane's directive, because I feared failing my
family. And I'm sorry I deceived you about it."

The tears she'd held at bay, suppressed with her
anger, sprang to her eyes. "Forgiven."

He took a deep shuddering breath and smiled, as if
she'd lifted the weight of the world from him.

The thrashing of her heart stilled, and her breath
stuck in her lungs. Hope beat fragile wings inside her.
But then his eyes darkened, and his expression grew
so pained, it frightened her. "There's something else.
The most important reason I came here."

Chapter 18

"Oh?" Kate rasped, and Josh hated the apprehension in her eyes. A look that spoke of how much he'd wounded her, how she'd been betrayed in the past, how fragile her heart was. His gut clenched. He had to get this right. He couldn't stand to let her be hurt any more than she already had. If he messed things up now…

He gritted his back teeth and shoved the negativity down. Even if he left with nothing in return, he would give her his heart and soul. No strings. No reservations.

"When you asked if I loved you—" He paused to swallow hard, and he heard her breath hitch. "I was afraid of how I felt, Kate. There it was again. Fear. And I didn't like it. Not one bit. The sense of helplessness and vulnerability. The unknowns. I mean, what did I know about love? And…I was afraid of failing *you*. Letting you down. Hurting you. I was afraid of going somewhere in our relationship I'd never been before. Going there without a safety harness or net. No belay. So much for 'you only live once,' huh?" He twitched a weak grin.

"Josh—"

He held up a hand to stop her, then forged on. "But after you left, my fear changed. I was afraid of spending my life without you. I was afraid I'd lost the woman I'd been waiting for all my life. The woman I was meant to grow old with."

He moved off the couch to kneel in front of her. "Kate, I came here because you deserved to hear the truth. In person. From the depths of my heart." Her eyes grew damp, and he had to blink when his own vision blurred. "Kate Carrington, I love your courage and your compassion, your wit and your determination. I love that you're not a morning person and the way your eyes get that spark of fire when you kiss. I want to spend the next fifty or sixty years learning all your quirks and secrets and virtues. So while I do like you and care about you, as I so ineptly put it before, I can honestly say, with everything I am, *I love you.*"

She sucked in a sharp breath and let a tear roll onto her cheek.

He wiped it away with his thumb. "I know my future, the future of the Double M, is pretty murky right now. There's no telling what will happen in the coming months. But if you're willing to face the risks with me, I know I can survive anything with you beside me." He swallowed hard and pulled a small diamond solitaire ring from his back pocket. "So what do you say, Kate? Do you want to be a rancher's wife?"

She laughed and wrapped her arms around his neck. "I do. So long as that rancher is you."

Epilogue

"Are you scared?"

"Terrified." Kate sat next to Josh on the end of the bed she'd been sharing with him for the last few weeks. Thanks to technology, she was able to do ninety-five percent of her PR job from the ranch, traveling to Dallas every few weeks for in-person business. Now she gave her fiancé a nod. "And you?"

"I'd be lying if I said no." He laced his fingers with hers and lifted her hand to his lips. "But it's what I want, and we can do this together. Remember that."

She nodded again, buoyed by his reassurances. "Well, then…a December wedding it is."

"You only live once," he replied with a lopsided grin.

They rose as one and stepped over to the wall calendar, where they flipped to December.

"Which weekend? I told Piper I'd watch Connor the first weekend so she and Brady could go into Denver to drive Roy home from the rehab clinic."

Josh cupped a hand against her cheek. "The next two weeks will be busy with sorting the herd and taking them to the sales auction. That leaves the week after Christmas."

She gave a wry chuckle. "I'm planning my wedding around the ranch schedule."

He winced. "I'm sorry."

Kate dragged him close for a kiss and murmured, "Don't be. I wouldn't have it any other way."

Michael checked the hallway and, seeing it was clear, closed his office door and took out his cell phone. When his call was answered, he said, "Hi, it's Michael McCall. I've reconsidered. I don't know where I'll find the money, but…I'm desperate."

He listened for a moment, shaking his head. "No. That won't be necessary." Then, "I'll send the first payment right now. Can I wire you the money? No, not a check or draft. I don't want my wife to know." He sighed wearily. Defeated. "Do you remember what I said about the terms? How I want this handled?"

He listened a moment. Then said, "I'm not sure. I'll make up a reason. Something plausible." His hand tightened on the phone. "No! This is a deal breaker. *No one* can know about this. Don't trust *anyone* until this is over. Do I have your word? If you say *anything* to *anyone*, I'll rip up our agreement." He closed his eyes and nodded, satisfied with the answer he received, even if the whole arrangement made him ill. "All right then. I'll be in touch again when everything is set."

He thumbed the disconnect on his phone and tossed the device on his desk. He hated that the situation had come to this. He hated hiding things from his family, being forced to make the hard choices, because he'd run out of options. His back was to the wall. Time was quickly running out. This was a matter of survival. He would save his ranch…or die trying.

* * * * *

Author's Note

If you've read my books in the past, you know that I include a cat or two somewhere in every story. Oftentimes, the cats belong to readers who have won the opportunity to have their furry friend immortalized in print. Sometimes I include kitties that are especially near and dear to my heart. In the McCall Adventure Ranch series, I introduce you to Zeke, a part–Maine coon, and Sadie, a short-haired black-and-white cat. I've been saving these two for just the right books, because they are just that special. You guessed it, Zeke and Sadie are my cats. They're every bit as goofy, loving, naughty and curious as they are described in the books. Galloping races up and down the halls and fur-flying wrestling matches (all good fun) happen daily with these two. They bring us lots of joy. To honor them, a portion of my proceeds from the sales of the McCall Adventure Ranch series will be donated to help my local Humane Society for Cats to assist in their rescue efforts. Meow!

COMING SOON!

We really hope you enjoyed reading this book. If you're looking for more romance, be sure to head to the shops when new books are available on

Thursday 15th November

To see which titles are coming soon, please visit
millsandboon.co.uk

LET'S TALK
Romance

For exclusive extracts, competitions
and special offers, find us online:

f facebook.com/millsandboon

🐦 @MillsandBoon

📷 @MillsandBoonUK

Get in touch on 01413 063232

For all the latest titles coming soon, visit
millsandboon.co.uk/nextmonth